THE RINGMASTER

CIRQUE DE PLAISIR

ERIKA MASTEN

THE RINGMASTER: CIRQUE DE PLAISIR

Cover design: Robin Ludwig Design
Editor: Jennifer Abel
Book design: A. D. Cooper

This is a work of fiction. Any similarities to actual persons or events are purely coincidental.

Warning: Explicit content. Intended for mature readers only. All characters depicted herein are 18 years or older, and all sexual activities are of a consensual nature.

This is a work of erotic fantasy. In real life, please protect yourself and your lover by always practicing safe sex.

ISBN: 978-1482799415

The Ringmaster

CIRQUE DE PLAISIR

1

GWYNNE'S ITINERARY FOR my last afternoon in London combined, in perfect measure, the most horrendous timing with absurdity bordering on tragic comedy. I slumped in the front seat of her sporty black Mazda—it had taken me the whole month to get used to the left side being the passenger side, and to stop walking up to the driver's door every time we went anywhere. But I'd have to get *un*-used to that presently. Now, past the left-side *passenger* window, I glowered at the dark February day mugging at me for attention from bustling sidewalks and warmly lit shop fronts.

"Enough with the heavy sighs, girl," the redhead insisted in the loud, brash British accent that had made her so popular with our circle at UCLA.

The year and a half I'd spent finishing my college courses

after Gwynne had graduated had paled without the gregarious theater major to goad me into one adventure or other. She'd never succeeded in enlisting me in any real trouble, as I was far too busy with work and school, but that was *entirely* beside the point, love, as Gwynne would have said. I suspected she knew how much her exploits had meant to me, allowing me to live vicariously.

Through the tall English beauty, I had enjoyed the briefest taste of what it was like to skinny dip in the Pacific with not one but two hunky young actors, to drag race a motorcycle cop down Sunset Boulevard at four in the morning and avoid a ticket in exchange for a steamy hot French kiss, and to be the toast of the Los Angeles night club scene—including the most elite BDSM clubs to entertain the Hollywood glitterati. Gwynne was the wild, wicked girl I had the inclination but not the time, finesse, or balls to become.

"Sorry," I muttered back. "I hadn't realized I was doing it." All my powers of concentration were trained on pretending London—all of Britain, really—wasn't the most enticing place I'd ever seen, winter be damned. From the hectic scurry of the Tube to the gleaming Edwardian boutiques of Jermyn Street and the sleek modern facades along South Molton. From prim, rain-washed row houses that comprised what passed for suburbia to the neighborhood pubs with warm amber lights glowing through glazed windows. And the parks. And the out-of-the-way alley lanes with little cafés and galleries. And the rural villages straight out of fairytales. I couldn't have swung my new, oh-so-British Burberry messenger bag without hitting a cottage or a churchyard or even a bloody *lamppost* that had a story and history and *weight* to it.

I tugged my black wool overcoat tighter to my body and

tried to console myself that it was twenty degrees warmer in southern California. "Back to Los Angeles tomorrow."

It really didn't sound that bad, not like I was headed to a hovel in some depressed inner city or a middle of nowhere town, population one hundred and something. Exclusive address, a Mercedes *and* a Porsche in the garage, cleaning and grounds staff. I wanted for nothing, so far as basic material needs went. Just so long as I didn't mind that none of it was mine and all of it came at the cost of—well, everything I had. Time, freedom, identity.

"You're doing it again," my glamour-puss best friend said as she navigated us through the automated gate of a long metal fence. Rust mottled the bars where paint had flaked off. Wheels and pulleys in need of a good oiling squeaked distantly.

I peered past my own reflection in the car window, wondering at how the damn freckles along my upper cheeks and nose could stand out even in such a faded image, and watched a montage of unused warehouses flash past us. As usual, Gwynne sped way too fast along the drive between the great looming rows of the dilapidated industrial hulks. Grass, sprouting up through cracks in the pavement, waved in the flurry of our wake. A wadded take-out wrapper skipped along the dark façades. Not a soul besides us was in sight.

"You said you were taking me to the circus."

Gwynne flipped that long stream of red hair over her shoulder and narrowed her dramatically shadowed brown eyes at me. I didn't think "daytime makeup" was a concept she espoused. "And you sound so happy about it, too."

"Happier than I'd be sightseeing in a warehouse district, I think."

"Think again, Livy." Gwynne was the only person who called me anything but Olivia, and never Olivia, come to think of it.

With her usual flare, she swerved just then around the back of the industrial complex and aimed us at the warehouse tucked into the farthest corner, one with fifteen or twenty rather nice cars parked back at a distance from the partially rolled-up loading door. Closer to the building sat three dark, unmarked semi-trucks, and I thought I could just glimpse several nondescript sedans parked discreetly along the far side of the building. As we approached, I noted a single figure, a man huddled down into the upturned collar of his black leather coat, leaning beside the loading door.

"Pop the glove box," Gwynne told me as she slowed to line her Mazda up with the other cars along their neat row. Very British, so orderly despite the lack of painted stripes for guidance. When I did as she asked, I found two black velvet half-face masks, each with a silk ribbon for tying them around one's head. "One for each of us."

"We're supposed to put these on? Now? In a warehouse car park?"

Turning the key to kill the motor, she shifted in the seat to look squarely at me. "Well, let me see. Have you changed your mind about coming to work with me for Finley?"

I wrinkled my nose. "That's your thing, Gwynne, not mine. It suits you. You're glamorous and bold and a natural drama queen and—"

"And not half the actress you are, if you want to go there. Don't forget I was right beside you in all those classes."

"I only took four of them."

"And still got offered every lead role in every performance, if you'd been *allowed* to accept any of them."

I couldn't keep my gaze from sinking away from hers. "Yeah, some things are more about the name than—"

"Right, so that's a no to working in the most posh, most exclusive BDSM club in London?" I shook my head no. "Not as a hostess?" Another shake. "Not as a waitress?" Another. "Not as a beloved, preening submissive to some of the most handsome and powerful men in Europe?"

This time I burst out in a nervous giggle and rolled my eyes. "Uh, no."

"Because you seemed really very comfortable as a guest those nights you came with me."

"Comfortable slinking around in a cocktail dress and flirting a little, maybe. Comfortable letting someone spank me in front of a crowd, no."

That impish gleam I'd seen so often in Gwynne's eyes practically beamed. "There are private rooms, you know."

"Oh, right. I'm sure I'm ready for that." My face was steaming hot from the flush of just thinking about it.

"You were a great hit with that blond fellow, the one with the stunning green eyes." She nudged me playfully with her shoulder. "Just like yours. He's minor nobility, you know."

And he'd scared the hell out of me, though I couldn't have said why. I had nothing against the BDSM scene or Gwynne for giving up on breaking into television in Hollywood to turn ultra-glam Dominatrix for silly amounts of cash and adoration. But me? I couldn't have let go like that, couldn't have forgotten *me* enough to become something so different—same problem I'd always run into in my acting classes, when the role in question wasn't just my life dressed in different clothing. And the thought of letting a man tie me up, touch me, spank me... while the fantasy got me wet, the reality made my skin crawl, and I'd never even gotten further than observing in the beginners' play room.

I cleared my throat and took a deep breath to keep myself from getting flustered—any more flustered. "Like I said, not my thing."

Gwynne gave me a crooked frown. "And you've not heard back on that last round of résumés to—what was it— *every* PR firm, news agency, magazine, and village gazette in Great Britain?"

"You make me sound desperate." Which I was. "It's hard to impress when…"

"When you can't let people know who you really are or that you've been managing the career of one of the most successful and difficult actresses in Hollywood."

"I don't manage Jade."

Another roll of those expressive eyes of Gwynne's. She really was a born actress, *on* all the time. "No, you're right, nobody can manage Jade, but you are her PA slash nanny slash whipping post. Your CV, and now that communications degree that took you an extra two and a half years to get because you had to trot around behind that bitch, should have earned you your choice of jobs, but her father—"

"Can we please not talk about my uncle right now?" Or I was going to burst into tears. Martin would have been furious if he'd known the ulterior motive for my graduation trip to London to celebrate with Gwynne was to job hunt, to get the hell away from him and his youngest daughter in the one place he hated most in all the world—London. Though, really, I'd have been happy with the smallest, simplest, most anonymous life as a receptionist or a shop girl in the tiniest British village, so long as it was *my* life. They just didn't give out a lot of work visas to foreigners for secretarial work.

"As you say," Gwynne responded with a nod. "If that's a no on all counts, and this is still your last day in my care, I do indeed expect you to put that mask on. Yes, now, in a warehouse car park. And I further expect you to fucking enjoy this."

I regarded her dubiously, even as I tied on the mask and, following her lead, pulled the hood of my coat up over my head. I tucked wayward blond strands back from my face. "Right. Put on mask. Enjoy warehouse. Got it."

We got out of the car and started toward the loading door and the man leaning against the wall beside it. Gwynne checked her watch, then grabbed me by the wrist to hurry me along. The woman could sprint in five-inch stilettos. Not me. I tapped along at a much more cautious gait in my black four-inch heels, elevating me to a positively statuesque five-foot-eight, while I thought that making me wear these shoes to a warehouse was nearly as ridiculous as making me wear them to a circus. What a sight! Tall, fire-headed Gwynne in her bright red coat and her killer McQueen heels, tugging her little blond cohort along at a clipping, clopping, pony pace across a parking lot while we tried to keep the wind from blowing back our hoods and revealing our masked faces.

"Hey there!" Gwynne called as we reached the fellow by the door. "Happy poets' day."

I'd learned that saying soon after arriving in the UK: Piss Off Early, Tomorrow's Saturday.

"Heya," the blond man responded as he turned keen sea green eyes on her and came up from his relaxed pose to stand between us and the door. No reaction to our masks? Despite having half his face hidden by his coat collar, he still gave off the impression of being an exceedingly good-looking man. Perhaps it was the broody arch of his brow, or those stormy eyes or the sharp, high cheekbones. Or all of the above. At his full height, he didn't appear half as casual and non-descript as he had at a distance, and I had to wonder if it was intentional deflection—as intentional as the guardian vibe he was giving off now. "Can I help you, ladies? Are you lost?"

Gwynne laughed with a charming, rich, unabashed mirth she had honed to perfection. Most men went soft-eyed at the sound of it. This one just grinned, I could tell from the corners of his mouth peeking over his collar. "Wandering," she said as she fished a card out of her pocket and presented it to the gatekeeper, "but not lost."

He nodded toward the door. "Almost too late. We're about to close up. In you go."

We had to duck to pass under the loading gate and step into a vast dark space. I hesitated just inside at the sight of the startlingly austere interior, a handful of spotlights trained on a broad area in the center of the warehouse floor. An odd, palpable hush hung from the grim gray walls and ceiling of the cavernous room, like heavy drapes or a long, close embrace. Motes of dust, so delicate, floated in the beams like silvery confetti poised for descent. Like something… something extraordinary and unexpected was about to begin.

All around the bare pool of light sat crates marked with loading instructions—"this side up" and "fragile"—and stamped with the names of numerous countries. More people like us, wearing masks, sat patiently on these boxes. In expensive overcoats and designer suits, and sporting platinum jewelry and two-hundred-quid haircuts, they looked a tad surreal sipping from beer bottles and noshing snacks from red-and-white striped paper bags.

I ignored the sound of the rolling door slamming closed behind us but jumped when a strong hand gently squeezed my elbow. "Take a seat," the doorman urged with a deep mutter into my ear that sent a shiver down my back and… lower. "We're about to set up."

"Set up what?" I hissed to Gwynne as she started into the room, the clack of our heels against the floor an embarrassing affront to the lulling silence. I followed her to a cluster of three crates, the middle being slightly taller and serving as a table. As soon as we'd peeled off our coats and spread them out to sit on, a young woman so slight and quick that I hardly glimpsed her set two bottles and two striped bags down on that middle crate for us. Up close now, I found the beer was actually small green bottles of very good champagne, with gold French script scrolled across the tasteful pale pink label. A sniff at the peanut-and-popcorn bag yielded the scent of garlic, saffron, and an undercurrent of white truffle. "That's a new take. What kind of circus is this supposed to be?" With champagne and gourmet popcorn but no tent, no ring, no…nothing.

"The kind you've never seen before," Gwynne promised, just before an ear-spitting bang drew our attention to a man on the far side of the spotlighted area and the heavy duffle he had just dropped on the concrete floor.

My adrenaline level surged with a shot of nervous heat through my core, with an electrical bristle of shivers over my skin at the first sight of him—of them, the performers who suddenly melted out of the darkness all around us and pranced and tumbled into the light with a clamor of laughter and cries and husky commands. They dressed like escaped characters from an Oliver Twist meets *The Story of O* mash-up novel, in old-fashioned hats and newsboy caps, in black and chocolate brown and chambray work shirts hanging open to reveal leather and metal bondage harnesses stretched over their perfectly toned and defined athletes' bodies. Tool belts jangled around rippled torsos and slim hips with an assortment of hammers, screwdrivers, handcuffs and floggers. Cargo pants and scruffy jeans and denim cutoffs hugged shapely legs—thighs so muscular they bordered on lewd, and high, round, taut asses.

Gwynne leaned my way without taking her eyes off the men and women tossing tools and heavy, lengthy pieces of metal back and forth as they began to construct a round platform. "You warmed up quick, didn't you, Livy?"

"Quiet, you," I muttered with *somewhat* feigned annoyance. "I'm watching this."

Watching the shouting, cavorting, preening performers in their grease paint, thick streaks across their eyes—their version of masks—and the odd black smear at chin or cheek or flexing forearm. Watching the positively enormous fellow, at way *way* over six feet, heft up a long metal pole laid against the muscles banding his upper back and neck, petite women hanging from either end of the steely bar and using it to swing and twirl as the strongman pretended anger with them. Watching the playful way this woman or that man wiggled their butts for a smack from the black flogger carried by the suspiciously familiar blond foreman supervising them.

Watching…him.

He stood at the edge of the performance space, almost directly across from me, and I could have sworn for a moment that I caught those topaz blue eyes trained steady on mine. A flare of heat at the suggestion of his attention, a flutter of wildfire lust, sparked deep inside my sex, under the slim black pencil skirt and between my legs as I pressed them hard together. This new performer stepped into the light, all six-feet-plus of him. No hat covering the luxurious waves of his short black hair… Grease paint striping his eyes and the bridge of his flawless patrician nose but leaving unmarred that granite chin and rock-solid jawline… No bondage harness visible through the loose V of his unbuttoned black poets shirt, just smooth skin and rounded pecs and Michelangelo-grade abs… At his hip coiled a black whip with an alarmingly large handle that had me making unwarranted sexual inferences about what he had inside those snug black trousers. Well, maybe not entirely unwarranted, from the way the contrast of light and shadow played along the thick bulge running just to the left of his zipper, almost as high as his waistband.

Again without turning, Gwynne reached out to offer me her champagne bottle. "Dry mouth, Livy?" Not just to teach her a lesson, I snatched the bottle from her and took a lengthy drag, then glared when she stole my bottle from the crate between us.

I had to concentrate on swallowing as the black-haired man sauntered unhurriedly into the midst of the stage-building activity and assumed a commanding pose, with his broad shoulders squared and large, gloved hands clasped at his back. As he pivoted slowly, little by little, to survey the full scene, I caught myself staring at his corded thighs in those skimming black pants and the curve of his muscular ass. And those hands, encased in black leather. My imagination kicked in so strongly that I could hear the soft creak of the material, smell that lingering musk of animal, feel the chill of a single finger tracing my cheek. My nipples peaked painfully hard through my lacy bra and black cashmere sweater in response.

Was it a blessing or a curse when eight swathes of scarlet silk, spaced evenly in a circle around this dark fantasy man, unfurled abruptly from ceiling to floor and broke my shamefully vivid reverie? One blocked my view of him, and I nearly slid off my crate leaning to see what he was doing. Only the white-knuckle grip I just then realized I had on the edge of my seat kept me from tumbling to the concrete.

They slid down the glossy material with such precise timing that I heard only a single swish—eight lithe women clad in considerably racier gear, from thigh-high stockings to leather-and-chain harnesses, complete with matching collars and cuffs. Their long, willowy limbs wound with strength, grace, and consummate skill along the unexpectedly stretchy material as they slowed their reckless plummet and suspended themselves in a variety of acrobatic poses mere inches from the floor. One had seemingly braided the silk around her upper thighs and waist so that she could hang upside down with her arms folded behind her. Another hung in a severe backward arch with her curled toes touching the top of her head. A third had let the silk encircle each slender ankle and pull her legs into a perfectly straight, vertical set of splits, her hands grasping the lower foot and her long ponytail coiling beneath her.

The workmen-performers all dropped to their knees, busying themselves with tying leads and tightening bolts, probably to keep from blocking the audience's view as the acrobats stopped swaying on the silk lines and hung suspended so still. No one among the spectators made a sound. None of us fidgeted. I didn't even want to blink.

I might have actually gasped when the dark man rested his hand on the handle of his whip and, as though obeying his very will, it unwound from his hip. Gwynne's smirk certainly suggested I'd emitted some sort of exclamation; I just hoped it hadn't been audible to anyone else—the other spectators…or a black-haired man who just that moment was the center of attention. The center of the universe, as far as I was concerned. My pulse, throbbing from my temples to my pussy, seconded that sentiment.

The hush still dominated the room as the commanding figure grasped his whip and, with the barest flick of his wrist, sent a rippling wave through the leather thong. It cracked lightly, threateningly, *promisingly* along the hard, cold floor. As though in response to a whispered order, the eight acrobats tumbled from their perches and assumed identical poses—bent double on their knees, bowing to the man in black. And for the first time, a hint of understanding stirred inside me—in the back of my head, in the pit of my stomach, at the juncture of my tensed thighs. I could imagine why a submissive would want to prostrate herself before a man, a Dom like him. I could have. Maybe. For a night, at least.

Then he raised his arm, drawing his whip in a fierce circle around his body before snapping the lash with a fury against the concrete. The crack rang as loud as a gunshot. Workman-performers froze in place and gaped, feigning shock and alarm while the eight costumed acrobats leapt back and scurried to hide behind their brethren. As their Master snapped his whip again—and again and again, louder and harder each time—the workers began to dance and wrestle with the acrobats to toss and shove them back toward the dark man in their midst. The blond foreman chased them with his flogger.

I should have been taken aback, repulsed by the sudden

show of force. The few times at the club here in London when someone had gotten forceful with me, I had balked and run to Gwynne for the key to her flat. I should have wanted to leave right then, even if it meant driving me straight to the airport and back into dear Uncle Martin's clutches. Instead, I was wringing the hem of my skirt and tugging the collar of my black turtleneck, imagining myself kneeling for the approval and ministrations of the black-haired stranger.

One by one, the women threw themselves at his feet, only to cuddle and claw at his legs and torso and hug him fiercely. Only when all eight clung to him and to one another did the Dom lower his lash and raise his gaze. It found mine again, as I perched rigid and breathless on my crate. I wasn't the only one who saw him focus on me. From the corner of my eye, I saw Gwynne glance back and forth between us.

"Positions," he growled in a low voice that carried as well as any theatrical bellow I'd ever heard—and I'd heard plenty.

All eight women flung themselves to the outer edge of the spotlight, in a variety of submissive, suggestive, sexual poses. One knelt with her cheek to the floor and her ass pushed up in offering, hands clasped at the small of her back. A second fell hard to her knees and bent backwards with her mouth open wide for—I didn't want to let myself imagine. Another put her weight on her shoulders and the balls of her feet, bent her spread knees, and held her hips thrust upward.

And while the workers converged on the center of the spotlight in a furious effort to construct a raised dais, the Master of the performance went round to each of the posed submissives. He used the handle of his whip to correct their posture, to make this one arch harder, that one bend deeper. The poses stretched and strained to near contortions, exact and unforgiving and beautiful. Behind him, the workmen bustled, rushed, panted, grunted. They slammed metal braces into place and pounded at thick bolts with sledgehammers, setting a pulsing rhythm with voice and tool and thumping boot heel, with brute strength applied to wood and steel.

At its crescendo, as the Dom of the circle was correcting the last of his acrobat slaves, the workmen drove home the final nail and collapsed into panting heaps of sweaty muscle all around the finished stage just in time for the black-haired man to turn and stride up onto it, into the center of attention again.

"Ladies and gentlemen," he called out in a smooth, subtle English accent, "this concludes the public portion of our set-up routine. Please do join us this evening. You will find the Cirque de Plaisir has so much more to offer…*after dark*."

Everyone came up off their crates to applaud, including me, though it took me a moment to steady myself after I found my knees trembling unreliably. As both the audience and the performers scattered, my gaze followed only the movements of the dark man as he stepped off the dais and made his way straight across the warehouse floor to a set of metal stairs along the far wall. When he disappeared behind the first of an array of office doors, my chest seized with smothering disappointment.

"Right then," Gwynne said in her much stronger, northern-tinged accent, "jaw up off the floor, Livy."

Even after I turned to face Gwynne where she stood beside me, it took me a second to really focus on my friend. I'd never experienced that kind of lust at first sight before, and I had the most irrational urge to plop myself down and cry until the black-haired man reappeared—no matter how long the wait. Of course, it was just that I was tired from all the activity of my stay in London, upset at the thought of flying out the next day. And that I hadn't had anything resembling a steady boyfriend in… far *far* too long.

"The Cirque de Plaisir?" I asked before finding my mouth and throat parched, and pausing to take a very long draught off the nearest champagne bottle. The light fluid tickled the inside of my mouth and warmed my chest. "What *is* that?"

The redhead smirked at me. "You took French."

"Yes, okay, fine. Circus of Pleasure. But what is it? I've never seen anything like it. I've never even heard of anything like it."

Gwynne took me by the arm and gathered me up close, starting to walk with me as she chided, "You would have if you worked for Finley. All the most elite clubs bring their best clients here when the circus is in town." I vaguely realized she was urging me deeper into the warehouse while the rest of the crowd headed the other direction, but I didn't want to interrupt as she continued, "And not just anyone. Politicians, footballers, pop stars, captains of industry, foreign royalty. That's why we all wear masks, even the performers. Admission is by invitation only, of course."

We were at the foot of those stairs before I realized it and before Gwynne stopped to hand me my forgotten coat and brush my long dark blond hair back from my shoulders. She removed her mask, then mine, as I stared at her quizzically. "Now take a deep breath." I did. "And stop those knees

16

from trembling, if you can." How had she known? "Are you ready?"

Panic flared like a stomach-turning sugar rush right to my bloodstream. "Ready for what? Honestly, Gwynne, I'm not sure I have the energy for any more surprises after that. I mean, did you see that? Did you see them, with the harnesses and all that sleek, sweaty muscle? And him? Oh my god, the man with the black hair? Do you know who he is? Do you know his name?"

"Calm down, Livy. Get a grip. I need you to focus."

"On what?" I sighed. "Why?"

"Because it took me a fuck lot of talking to get you this audition."

2

FROM WHAT I could see, Gwynne Cadogan had a peculiar sense of humor. A casual but perhaps ill-advised mention to Finley—when I'd called the club owner about our impending arrival in London—that my assistant had left the troupe after our final performance in Lisbon had resulted in a barrage of phone calls from the most mouthy and persistent of his Dommes. It was a good thing for her I liked mouthy and persistent and redheaded, especially when the redhead in question worked for somebody else. But after all that begging for an audition, for all her insistence that she had the perfect submissive for me, what did Gwynne bring me?

Fine, dark blond hair and light green eyes the size of saucers. Prim black turtleneck and modest pencil skirt. And a petite little body that trembled and jumped so visibly at the slightest sound, she'd have shuddered herself into a faint before the end of her debut performance. That was what I was looking at right then, behind me in the mirror as I wiped off the grease paint from our little warm-up exhibition.

While a good fifteen or twenty of my troupe crowded around mirrors propped up on crates (the most practical travel version of dressing tables) to remove their makeup, or darted about the room peeling off bits and bobs of their costumes, Gwynne brought in her little blond kitten, still wide-eyed and stiff-backed. Without the glare of the spotlights in my eyes, though, and without the shadows to hide her, Kitten was… a little curvier than I'd gathered from that first impression. With a sensuous red mouth to offset the pale skin and little-girl freckles. And enticing telltale points pressing out from the front of her sweater where it stretched over the swell of her breasts. That right there, the fact that I had noticed as much and the unexpected tightening in the crotch of my pants, was reason enough to call off the audition.

"Donovan Haigh." Gwynne sighed in that pushy Leeds accent she put to such good use, and folded her arms. "Stop pretending you're not watching everything in that mirror. Give us a hug, then."

My best effort tamed my smile down to a sardonic smirk as I stood up and turned to face my guests. I'd only met Gwynne during our last stay in London, right after she'd started working for Finley, but she was hard to dislike, harder to deny, and impossible to forget. She met me with a bright red kiss on the cheek, and I playfully winced.

"Don't whinge," she said, and grabbed the cloth out of my hand to wipe away the lip prints. "You were taking off your stage makeup anyway."

Though I tolerated her attentions until she was done, I snapped the rag back out of her hand immediately afterward and shook my head at her.

She widened her eyes theatrically. "Oh, sorry, you're being dignified. Trying to impress anyone I know?" With her glance, she directed my focus to the blonde watching us with her face turned slightly downward, green eyes peaking up through veiling lashes. Kitten stood waiting so proper, hands clasped in front of her with her coat thrown over her arm, heels together. What exactly was it about the innocent miss that made me want to lift that skirt and see if she kept her soft, snowy white mons and delicate lips dutifully shaved?

The thought slapped me in the face so abruptly, I was shaking my head. "Gwynne, I don't think—."

"Livy, this is Donovan. He's the owner, manager, and Ringmaster of the Cirque de Plaisir. Donovan, this is Livy. Olivia. She's the ideal replacement for your assistant."

"Assistant?" the blonde echoed, and I wasn't sure if I was struck more by the American accent—Californian by the sound if it, light and tending to end on a slight up note—or the fact that she sounded as though she didn't know why she was here.

"Well, not the typing and filing sort, no," Gwynne said as she left my side to stand between her friend and me. They muttered to one another, but I caught on quickly enough from snippets of the conversation that the redhead was pressuring Kitten into the audition. "Really, Livy, trust me. Do this for me, as your friend."

I leaned back on the edge of the makeshift dressing table with a half-suppressed sigh. Now I felt sorry for the blonde, as browbeaten into this situation as I had been, our fondness for Gwynne wielded against us like a bludgeon. But I didn't anticipate what I saw then. After the barest suggestion of a frown passed over this Olivia's face, momentarily wrinkling her brow, she straightened her shoulders and took a deep, steady breath. She shoved her overcoat into Gwynne's arms and stepped around the tall redhead to march right up to me. Even in heels, she had to be a good fifteen centimeters shorter than I was—easier to loom over, which would have looked good on stage, and just the right height to bend her over a chair and… That idea hit me somewhat lower than the face and again warned me this wasn't the kind of girl I was looking for as my assistant, if I was already having unprofessional urges toward her.

Still, I couldn't help staring at her and thinking her remarkably, unconventionally beautiful as she said, "Mr. Haigh, I'm ready to audition for you. I don't have anything prepared, but if you'll tell me what you want…"

Tell her what I wanted? Another terrible idea. But there she stood, and I had to admire the way she steeled herself despite her obvious nerves after Gwynne had sprung this little surprise on her.

Instead of letting the poor girl down easy, as I should have, I peered hard into that smooth young face. She probably wasn't more than twenty-four or twenty-five, about eight years and a world of experience younger than I was. I could have broken this girl if I was the least bit careless—another reason I knew already this wasn't going to work. And yet I couldn't take my eyes off her without conscious effort.

Ah, Donovan, such a bad idea, this.

"When we're in costume, no one calls me Mr. Haigh." I glanced sidelong and caught sight of raven-haired Naomi stripping off her kit without the slightest embarrassment in front of our guests. Though still masked, she was down to harness and shorts when I said, "Naomi, who am I?"

After a moment's pause, the leggy acrobat shrugged. "You're the Ringmaster, sir." She went back to getting naked when I nodded.

"Ringmaster," I repeated to Olivia, then cleared my throat to regain her attention as she stared after the utterly unselfconscious Naomi. "You may call me Ringmaster."

The blonde swallowed with obvious effort and nodded in acknowledgement, flushing disarmingly across the apples of her cheeks and the bridge of her nose. "I'm ready to audition, Ringmaster."

"That I highly doubt," I muttered under my breath as I motioned for my guests to follow me and led them back down to the warehouse floor, where the real work of the set-up for tonight was taking place now that the audience had cleared out. "Have a seat," I told Gwynne as I pointed to one of the crates that hadn't been moved yet, then to Olivia I said, "Up, onto the stage."

She did as commanded and without hesitation, I noted with approval, but she turned with a concerned look, bending her tawny brow. "I'm going to audition here? In front of everyone?"

I glanced about the vast, open room. Rafe, still dressed as the foreman from the performance, was marking out directions on the concrete floor for what stages and equipment went where. Slighter, sandy-headed Thom was passing around small bottles of sports drinks and cautioning everyone to mind their electrolytes like the mother hen he was, combination admin manager/chef/physical therapist, keeping my athletes in top shape. Griffin and his pixie-faced partner, Piper, were working with the crew installing the

Chinese pole, making sure it was secure enough for their performance.

"No one is paying attention to us, Kitten," I said before I thought better of it.

I avoided looking down again into that delicate, angular face, not wanting to see her reaction to the spontaneous endearment, and took the whip from my hip. From the corner of my eye, I saw her hand clench into a sudden anxious fist at her side. A most curious reaction, like I was going to use the lash on her, and further proof this was a futile exercise. If she was this skittish now…

Still, she persisted. "All right. What do you want me to do?"

So many things. In part to give myself time to consider my response, I stepped up onto the stage and made a slow circuit around waiting Kitten, made a show of studying every line and curve of that petite body. As I noted the firm, smooth musculature along the back of her calves and the front of her thighs, along that delightfully heart-shaped buttocks, I asked, "Are you trained in dance?"

"No," she began, shaking her head and sending shimmery waves of movement through the sleek curtain of her hair. I was actively resisting the urge to run my hands through those strands when she corrected herself, "Well, sort of. A little. It was someone else actually taking the lessons, but I was her partner for practice." I stopped and narrowed my eyes at her. Was every interaction this awkward and difficult for her? As though she read my expression, she hissed her breath out hard through her nose and her clenched teeth. "It's complicated. Ballet and modern dance, to answer your question." Finally.

I resumed my circuit. "I can tell; you have a dancer's

legs." From the confusion clouding those pretty green eyes, she looked like she wondered if that was a good thing. My hardening cock certainly thought so. The parts of my brain not currently occupied with inappropriate considerations of all the ways I could stroke this kitten wholeheartedly disagreed.

The narrowness of her waist made her hips seem larger than they were, lending an alluring sensuality to a body that was actually quite lean upon close examination. The full round swells of her breasts were a perfect counterpoint to the curve of her ass. In a harness, with a tight leather cincher around her waist, she would have looked stunning—in an Old Hollywood, vintage erotica way.

When the impulse to thread my fingers through her hair overtook me again, and I reached a gloved hand out for her, Kitten—Olivia—caught the movement from the corner of her eye and flinched away so slightly. And I caught my breath, though I wasn't entirely certain why. Perhaps because, though I was of the cooler and more aloof variety of Doms, I was unaccustomed to women wincing away from me. Or perhaps because her apprehension made me wonder if she just expected rough treatment, if someone had misused her in the past. I took the touch of nausea in my gut for the sickness I'd have felt at the thought of any little innocent being mishandled and abused.

"Easy there," I muttered as I removed my right glove before tangling my fingers in the silky strands just above the nape of her neck. It was unexpected, both my urge to soothe her—I was not the fawning Daddy Dom sort, even outside the performance ring—and the cool softness of her hair, like cream flowing along the back of my hand. "It's good that your hair is so long and straight," I continued to encourage her despite being at a loss still as to why I would. She smiled nervously. "Though it could be a bit longer." And at this she frowned, leaving me with the smallest hint of guilt.

I peered at her again, feeling my own lips pressing into a subtle frown—at myself. This Olivia was so unlike Evelyn, my last assistant, and not what I'd have expected of any of my performers. When I'd auditioned Evi, the busty brunette had thrown back her shoulders and cocked one hip provocatively, exuding sex appeal and a larger-than-life personality that made her a natural for the stage. She was a brat submissive par excellence. Every facial expression, every sigh, every tiny gesture had always been a choreographed reaction playing for maximum effect.

Olivia? She was an open book, a bundle of live-wire nerves without the least protection. What she felt down to the bone was the reaction that rose to the surface, unfiltered and unadorned, so vulnerable and honest. The stage was going to break this girl's heart, assuming I didn't do it first.

At that thought, I snatched my hand away and stuffed it back into my black leather glove. Time to stop playing, stop indulging the false hope that Kitten was going to be my new assistant. Standing directly in front of Olivia, a mere half-step from her faintly trembling frame, I ordered, "Take off your clothes."

"W-what…? Excuse me, I… What?"

Yes, I was trying to scare her when I crooked one corner of my mouth in a subtle leer. "Take off your clothes," I repeated with painstaking enunciation, my gaze drawn to those lush red lips as they parted to gasp a panicked breath. "The sweater and the skirt will be enough, for now."

"Take off…?"

"Yes, the sweater and the skirt." I glared over my shoulder, commenting to Gwynne, "I don't think she's ready for this."

"I am," I heard Kitten say in a surprisingly forceful voice then, and by the time I turned my face back toward hers she had whipped her turtleneck over her head and cast it to the dais. My turn to catch my breath, at the smoothness of that fair, peaches-and-cream skin kissed with tiny freckles along the top of her shoulders and under her collarbone... at the rigid points of her nipples begging to be pinched and sucked even through her thin black bra... at the erratic pulse playing havoc at her throat...

Swallowing a knot of hesitation and feeling an abrupt flush along my own cheeks and straight through my groin, from twitching cock to swelling balls, I reminded her in a husky voice, "And the skirt."

She complied smoothly and obediently, her gaze fixed over my shoulder at a point in the distance as she visibly calmed herself and stilled her quavering. Fuck if she wasn't actually going to do this, going to go through with the audition. And why did I find the thought so dismaying?

Careful, I heard myself cautioning in my head. *Too rough and you'll break her.* But a voice further distant added, *too gentle and you lose her, the willing innocence, all that delicious vulnerability laid out just for you.* Damned if just then I wasn't feeling like two entirely different people.

"Right, then," I said as I finally allowed the whip in my left hand to uncoil and refrained from commenting on the way Kitten tensed as the lash clacked against the hardwood stage. "I'm going to teach you six sub positions. You assume the first position, and when I crack my whip, you'll move smoothly to the next and the next."

Standing beside Olivia, I dipped my head just slightly,

almost as though to whisper to her. Her scent accosted me like a flurry buffeting the high-wire. She smelled like…too many things to keep straight…sweet fruit, licorice and lily, vanilla and caramel, and… *and cotton candy*. She smelled like the first time a child walked into a circus, that moment of excitement beyond expectation or expression. It felt like my stomach dropped, as my erection rose with a fury. And I drew back, fighting obvious and utter dismay.

In a flat, guarded monotone, I instructed, "Keep it fluid. Breathe with it. Feel it. Can you do that?"

"Y-yes," she responded, her gaze still distant. I was surprised at how irritating I found that, the fact that she was not entirely there within my grasp, absolutely invested in my service. In my pleasure. While I stood there with my head spinning from the mere *scent* of her, for fuck's sake.

Despite feeling out of sorts—unbalanced—I forced myself *cautiously* to bring my lips to the curl of her ear. "Yes, Ringmaster," I reminded her.

"Yes, Ringmaster," she repeated in a breathless murmur. Exactly the reaction I wanted from her. That and a deep breath settled me, if only by a few degrees.

"Good. First position, then. Legs spread and arms folded behind your back. If you can, I want you to use each hand to grasp the opposite elbow." It was a difficult position for a newcomer, and I knew that. It forced Kitten's spine into a hard stretch, an unforgiving arch, even when she could only touch her elbows with her fingertips.

Again with my lips at her ear, I warned, "I'm going to correct you. Breathe into the stretch. Let it burn, but stay with it. Do you understand?"

She nodded almost imperceptibly, then remembered herself. "Yes, Ringmaster."

"Very good," I commended but immediately cursed myself for it. This wasn't going to work, I didn't *want* it to work, so why was I encouraging her?

Taking care not to allow my frustration to vent itself in my handling of her, I let my hand rest between her shoulder blades—on her warm, silky skin—and laid the firm handle of the whip along her collarbone to correct her posture, draw her shoulders back, deepen the arc to her spine and the delicious upward thrust of those rounded breasts. I stepped behind her and used my feet to nudge hers farther apart, silently biting down on the inside of my cheeks when this brought the curve of her ass up against the swell of the member straining in my pants. The crevice of her buttocks, soft and inviting and perfectly fitted to me, cradled the demanding ridge. She said nothing at the sensation, but I'd have sworn she leaned just a millimeter, just a breath, harder into me.

I stepped back abruptly when I felt my cock twitch and realized how easily I could've broken my first *and second* rules with this one. Never a member of my troupe, and never ever my assistant-submissive.

"For the second position, put your right foot behind your left and pivot to face me while you bring your feet together."

The heels were a bit much for her, though in her defense, they had no straps to hold them in place. She lost her footing and shuffled, just a bit, just enough to make me sigh—in embarrassment for her, and in frustration at my urge to reach out, steady her, encourage and console her not to be so nervous. It was an urge I stubbornly refused to satisfy.

Instead, after circling behind her, I indulged in a light

caress low along her hip, straying to the back of her thigh, not quite as high as her ass. "Keep it crisp, Olivia. Tense your legs, and lock your knees. It's okay; you'll only be in this position for a few moments." I dared another whiff of whatever her perfume was as I nuzzled my face into her hair to mutter, "Shoulders back a little more, yes. And tighten your buttocks."

Her breath squeaked out of her in the tiniest of mews as she complied, wrestling her anxiety every step of the way, if the harrowed look pursing those rose-petal lips into a tight little frown was any indication. Looming over Kitten as I was, I could see her nipples were still stiff and ready, her body reacting like a submissive's even if her mind wouldn't settle into "sub-space."

"All right, that will have to do," I said, knowing she'd think me a demanding asshole. It was better than revealing that this awkward, nervous little girl had my groin throbbing and my mouth watering. "I want you to throw yourself forward to curl over your knees as you crouch. Stay on your feet, and put your hands to the floor if you need it for balance. Otherwise, extend your arms back and slightly outward as though you're taking a bow."

This third position was better—surprisingly so. Though I feared she'd stumble, Olivia flipped her hair smoothly down over her bent face and whipped herself forward to sit on her heels. It was a distinctly passionate movement that belied her dance training. After using her hands to steady herself for only a couple of seconds, she extended her arms for a flawless bow.

Kitten didn't need correction this time, which both impressed me and fueled my exasperation. As I made my inspection circuit, I dragged the cool leather thong of my whip along the back of her neck to get a rise from her, to remind her she was too skittish a bird for this. The shiver along her spine and the subtle shift of her hips suggested a level of physical excitement that made me instantly regret the ploy.

"Fine," I sighed roughly, "that'll do. Next position. Use your hands to catch your weight as you fall back to lie on the floor. Keep your knees bent. Then, as you spread your legs, lift your hips as high as you can and hold them there."

Offer your pussy to me, was what I was really saying. That was what the audience would see—*would have seen* were I inclined to offer Kitten the job as the Ringmaster's slave assistant. Which I wasn't. It was, yes, probably very intentional that I hadn't made my directions more specific, so I had something to find fault with this time. So I could stand over her, between her splayed legs so slim and taut, and use my feet again to make her spread herself. "Wider, Olivia," I demanded. Then I swung my whip gently but quickly under her to curl around the small of her back. Holding both ends of the lash, I jerked upward on it to make her thrust those hips higher. "Push harder. Tighten that arse, Kitten."

I didn't care if she'd heard what I called her this time. My tone made it clear I wasn't fawning. It was a pet name in the strictest sense—she was, for the current purpose, my pet, my plaything. So why, I groaned inwardly in renewed frustration, was the expression on Olivia's faced one of soft, flushed languor? Lips slightly parted, eyes gleaming, the tip of her tongue just visible tracing the edge of her upper teeth.

My face burning with pronounced heat, I stepped hesitantly back from Kitten, my gaze still riveted to hers as I trailed the lash of my whip around her hip and over the silky crotch of her lacy black panties.

Goddamnit, Gwynne, what have you done?

Wiping the lightest sheen of perspiration from my stubble-roughened upper lip with the side of one finger, I muttered, "Roll over to press your shoulders and cheek to the stage, arse up. And keep those knees bent and spread."

Beg me with your body to take your ass.

"Stretch your arms out above your head, palms down, like you're trying to push back harder with your hands. Reach for it, Olivia." *Strain to please me.*

Her breath escaped her in a low sigh that I saw in the sudden contraction of her chest more than heard. Those light green eyes sank closed in a moment of…desire? Pleasure? Release, as the position inflicted physical tension while relieving its sexual counterpart? Were those my observations or my fantasies flaring?

"Final position, Olivia. Straighten up on your knees, dragging your fingertips along the floor. Bend back and come to rest as flat to the wood as you can. Then lay your hands palms up at your sides and arch your back to thrust up your chest."

When she had complied, when Olivia laid bent back for me, with her breasts jutting upward and chest pumping out her thickened breath, I could hardly look at her. In the back of my head, I ran through the mobile numbers of the three or four women I had occasion to play with here in London when the sexual tension of running an erotic circus got to me. Obviously time for a visit, if a simple audition with a jittery little girl was affecting me this badly.

"Up, Kitten," I ordered without looking at her. "First position. Remember to listen to the whip for your timing." I hurried through the instructions, supremely eager now to be done with this charade of an audition and get my mind back on preparations for that night's performance.

The first crack of my whip was hard and sudden and unsubtle, without regard for Olivia's nervous disposition, which meant she jumped and hesitated before moving to second position. Thrown off her timing from the start, she shuffled and teetered on her stiletto heels, and the tension in her posture was weaker than before I'd corrected her. After the next crack, she stumbled over the forward crouch she had earlier executed perfectly. The shaking in her shoulders was becoming painfully pronounced. I'd have wagered that at any moment she was going to dart offstage and seek shelter from me in Gwynne's arms.

Which would have brought this audition to its inevitable end. All for the better. And yet… and yet I couldn't do it to her, couldn't degrade and embarrass her and send her off thinking herself so completely inadequate, even knowing her so little. She wasn't a performance whore like so many others who had cycled through my service, not preening and posing and playing for attention. Not thick-skinned and mercenary in her bid for praise and adoration. Not Kitten.

I crouched carefully to lay my whip down upon the wooden stage, and caught Olivia peering at me through strands of her hair. She was waiting for the next crack, the next command, and the distraction of my private thoughts stilling my hand had left her uncertain, without direction.

When I stood, I motioned with a careful gesture for Olivia to follow me. "Up, Kitten. You're too anxious." Rising, sweeping all that blond hair back from her face with delicate hands, she regarded me warily. "Come on. First position. We're going to go through this together." With my arms wrapped around her waist with unwise familiarity, and my body pressed to her back with dangerous intimacy.

I breathed in all that promise of raspberry vanilla cotton candy and murmured into her ear, "You have to picture the scene we're setting for the audience. You're my submissive, and your movements are like a love letter to me, the private supplications of a slave begging for her Master's touch." I dragged one hand up her smooth body to grip her shoulder and harden the arch of her posture. "Every muscle is tensed." My other hand slid down to toy with the lace at the waist of her panties. "But inside she is weak with hunger."

So unexpectedly, Olivia leaned back into me, finally able to just barely curl her fingers around her elbows, so close to perfecting the position. It bent her spine so hard that she could rest her head back on my chest. Without thinking about it, I let my lips graze her temple.

It was an indulgence I couldn't allow myself, not for more than a moment. I stepped away, reluctantly withdrawing my touch. "But her lover denies her," I whispered, hunching just slightly forward to breathe against Kitten's ear. "He moves away from her. She can't feel him. But she can't be without him, so she turns."

With flawless timing, flawless instinct, Olivia pivoted into second position so smoothly, so fluidly. Her eyelids had sunken down to narrow slits over her eyes, red lips just slack enough to suggest the greatest depths of lust and to invite her lover's kiss. It made my mouth go dry, suddenly empty and ravenous.

"Yes, Kitten, that's it. She wants him to know she'll do anything for him. So she bows to him." And she did, flipping her hair forward in a pale wave again, folding herself down into a deep, plaintive bow that almost took my breath away with its unspoken emotion.

"She can no longer restrain herself, Olivia. Her lover

must know how much she wants him, so she throws herself to the floor and spreads herself for him. She thrusts her sex up for him, begging him to see her need." I leaned over her as she reenacted this pose, unable to keep my hands from exploring her hips and the flat of her stomach. "She's begging for satisfaction, Olivia."

Without prompting, Kitten flipped herself over to offer her ass as she stretched, so like a little cat in heat. She had me following her movements, her timing, at the very moment she flung herself backward, bending over my arm as I hooked her at the small of her back.

And it was done, the full circuit. That should have been enough, too much. Instead, I said, "Again. First position."

Whip forgotten, and with the whole purpose of this audition aside, I moved behind Olivia and with her as she snapped into her pose with the sharp click of her heels and the soft hiss of her sigh. I didn't so much step away as stumble back in a haze of lust, as she spun to second position. In third position, the deepest bow of all, I ran one hand down her spine while the other tousled and pulled that sheet of silken hair. I practically threw her into fourth position, so I could kneel between her legs and jerk her by the hips against the bulge of my erection as we both heaved for breath and grunted with the effort burning in our muscles. Fifth position had Kitten straining back like she wanted nothing more than a hard ass-fucking, her sweat-slicked palms squeaking against the polished grains of hardwood beneath her as she stretched and struggled for better leverage to grind against me.

But sixth position, that was all me. I gripped her by the hair and twisted toward her to fold her backward over the other arm. And in this final pose, this perfect climax, I sealed my lips over hers and drove my tongue deep into her warm, sweet mouth.

3

THERE WASN'T ROOM for anything in the world but Donovan Haigh. The firm but velvety plumpness of his lips—edged in rough stubble that cast a rakish shadow around his mouth and along that strong chin—made me want to suck at them, nip at them, plead against them. His breath swirling steamy over my skin raised goose bumps from the nape of my neck to the insides of my trembling thighs. Short waves of his mink-soft hair crested down over his forehead to tease my cheek. And the scent of orange, cinnamon, and smoky wood all mixed with the musky dew of sweat we'd worked up making our way to sixth position, to this heaven that was the suggestion of tart-sweet flesh... His demanding tongue laving the inside of my cheeks and the roof of my mouth until I moaned into his kiss....

Each probing swirl of his tongue sent a ripple through

the slicked walls of my sex. Each little jerk on my hair, as Haigh held my head for the onslaught from his lips, renewed the feverish shivers down my spine until my arms lay stretched out limp on the hardwood beneath me, my body splayed like a willing sacrifice. It was all I could do not to squirm my hips in an obvious plea that he fill my pussy with the rampant erection I'd felt rubbing against me so often, but all too briefly, as he had guided me bodily through the positions of submission.

Was the kiss part of the act? An improvisation born of the moment? Who knew? Only one thing was clear, with my senses filled as they were with the man who made me call him Ringmaster: an audition with Donovan Haigh was better than any sex I'd ever had.

It seemed like we kissed for fifteen or twenty minutes, though that was an absurd idea. Surely someone—Gwynne—would have stopped us, cleared their throats, snickered even. No, it was just that a few moments at the mercy of Donovan Haigh's mouth were worth an hour with anyone else. When he lifted his face from mine, I should have been too shy to look him in those impossibly bright eyes, or at that vaguely dimpled smile only hinted at along the corners of his sensual lips. But I wanted to see… Was his skin as flushed as mine felt? Was his breath this hard, this thick? And the growl I'd heard in the back of his throat—was that all for show, or had he worked himself up as badly as he'd done to me?

What I saw was a soft blue-sky gaze blinking almost tenderly down at me for only a moment before the hard glint returned to the Ringmaster's eyes. Haigh helped me to my feet with patience and care before retrieving his whip from the floor and stepping back a pronounced distance from me.

He had only just opened his mouth to speak when a chorus of wolf whistles and the low patter of applause pulled him up short.

Flushed with the embarrassment of realizing it had only *felt* as though the world had shrunk down to the two of us, I turned my head to find everyone in the room staring at us, at me. My hand pressed flat to my stomach—my bare stomach, I recalled abruptly—was a meager defense against the need to be just a little sick. "Well done," called one voice from the crowd. "She's a keeper," insisted another. But from far back in the gloom, a third warned, "Not after that show. He won't go there." And I blushed furiously at the thought that I'd just made a horrid spectacle of myself.

It was Gwynne in those killer heels tromping up onto the stage beside me and declaring, "Bravo," that helped me tear my gaze from the strangers' beautiful faces, only now one by one turning back to their tasks. "Stunning," Gwynne insisted. "The way you two moved together... it was amazing." Then she winked at me and growled. "And so sexy."

"You're easily impressed, Cadogan." Haigh's voice—that smooth, understated accent—sounded oddly flat and disapproving. "It was..." I finally found the nerve to glance sidelong into that chiseled face. As soon as my gaze found his, he focused on Gwynne instead. "It was adequate."

Adequate. One of the better descriptions frequently applied to me in my life as professional wallflower, perpetual second fiddle, eternal bit-player.

I felt my chest fall, felt myself crumbling from the inside at the folly of giving myself to this moment of spontaneous, irrational hope. A couple of hours ago, I hadn't even heard of the Cirque de Plaisir and had no warning of the impending audition. Thirty minutes ago, I certainly hadn't thought

I might actually have considered a job with a masked erotic circus. But even ten minutes ago, I hadn't been pinned to the floor while Donovan Haigh plundered my mouth with his tongue. And now I had to deal with losing something I had only just realized I wanted. The impending sense of defeat that had been closing in on me over the last several days, the soul-sucking disappointment of going back to being a footnote in someone else's glamorous life, left me so suddenly and so completely exhausted that I could've fallen to my knees right there…again.

Fighting off one of those heavy sighs that had plagued the drive to the warehouse, I snatched up my sweater and skirt and trudged off the stage to the crate where Gwynne had left my coat. This was the very definition of awkward, getting dressed with the feeling of a few dozen strangers watching.

"I'm sorry I wasn't what you were looking for. Thank you for the opportunity to audition for you, Mr. Haigh," I said without turning, struggling to keep my voice firm despite a swell of bitter regret trying to tear its way through my throat.

As I stuffed my arms fitfully into my overcoat, I whirled to face Gwynne and instead found Donovan standing directly behind me. God, but he was tall. And wide-shouldered. Had the smoothest, most perfectly defined chest. And smelled like pure, uncut sensuality from a full foot away.

"Ringmaster," he said in a voice not nearly so cold. A little sad, in fact. Disappointed, maybe, that I hadn't lived up to the hype Gwynne no doubt had fed him about me?

"Excuse me?"

"When we're in costume—"

"No one calls you Mr. Haigh," I repeated once I'd

caught on. With my throat and chest still burning with bile, I choked out, "Thank you, Ringmaster."

"Thank *you*, Olivia," he said graciously, in that same practiced tone he'd used to conclude the exhibition performance, before stepping back and grazing both Gwynne and I with a quick glance. "I assume I'll be seeing both of you tonight at the performance, as my special guests, if you'd like."

Gwynne came down off the stage to shake Donovan's hand. "You will, and we would," she told him. "But for now, we'll leave you to get ready." Then she walked me out of the warehouse, one arm around my shoulders, comforting me like I was a pathetic child. Which was exactly how I felt as we emerged into the late afternoon under a sky that threatened a stormy night.

The redhead waited until we got into her car before she confronted me. "Don't be so defeatist, Livy. I thought that audition was bloody fantastic, and he never actually said he didn't like you for the job."

I sank into the seat, slumping hard, moping despite my best efforts. "If he'd wanted me, he'd have said so." Cripes, that was saying something, on several levels.

Which got a dismissing tsk from the Domme as she started the engine. "What, you never saw Ilsa or Jade get a role on callback?"

Gwynne didn't know my cousins very well.

"Ilsa doesn't really audition for parts anymore. I think that's what she likes about indie films; they call her when they know they already want her. Plus she likes the mystique of all that critical acclaim for being so anti-commercial. And Jade... No, nobody does callbacks with Jade. She knows she's got to get the role before she leaves the room, or all that force of personality will fade and they'll realize that she has no range. But if she can get them to commit then and there, and if they change their minds later, the vague allusion to the publicity nightmare of offending the Hollywood dynasty that is the Keane family usually saves her." I rolled my eyes. "God knows I've seen that enough times."

"Ever thought of trying that yourself?" Gwynne asked.

"What? No. Martin would never let me act, let alone threaten to…" I mocked the deep baritone he used when he wanted to sound Shakespearean. "To bring down the wrath of a four-time Tony award winner, the man who has graced more Broadway stages than any other living human being." In a smaller voice, I added, "Janitorial staff excepted," to which Gwynne predictably guffawed.

The redhead reminded me, "But no Academy Award for his film work, remember. And no BAFTAs, either. Heavens no!"

An observation which, yes, actually got a snicker out of my gloomy little self. The British Academy Awards in particular were a taboo subject in the Keane household. "Christ, don't *ever* say that around him. It makes him seethe. That's the biggest reason he hates London—passed over for the BAFTAs all six times he's been up for one." I mocked him again. "And four times in favor of that drunken Irish bastard Quillan Teague. Britain hates me, and I hate Britain right back."

Swinging her Mazda through the rolling gate and back out onto the street with a brief screech of rubber on pavement, Gwynne reached over to squeeze my leg. "But we love you, Livy. We won't let you go; you'll see."

The only thing I wanted to see after getting all hot and bothered, rolling around panting and sweaty on the floor with a certain Mr. Haigh, was a glass of wine and a steaming bath—served together, preferably. My hostess obliged me back at her flat. I sank into the soapy water to the top of my chin and let my head loll back onto a handy little cushion balanced on the edge of the tub and made just for the purpose.

With the heat of the water soaking the mounting stiffness from my overextended muscles and the warmth of the wine burning slow and easy along my throat and all through my chest, I could almost make myself believe one last night in London was going to make everything all right. Especially if it was a night at the Cirque de Plaisir. Rested and renewed, I'd be able to face Los Angeles again. I could rise to any challenge Jade threw at me. I could shrug off the casual slights of being the Keane who didn't act, who made the dinner reservations and returned the calls and toted the tiny dogs around in designer carriers when my cousin got tired of them. I could disavow the very memory that I'd ever tried to run away to a nine-to-five office job as a publicist's assistant or a garden page journalist, or secretly tried on a British accent when alone in Gwynne's guest room.

Forgetting today and Donovan Haigh would have been a real trick, though. I had never thought I'd enjoy being talked to like that, directed, guided movement by movement to bow and kneel and beg with my body. I'd have never believed a man could smell that good, even in cologne. Never thought I'd ever fantasize about being called Kitten while being stroked like a precious little pet and taken like a complete harlot, a shameless libertine, a... a willing slave. Even now, I shivered so hard at the notion that I sloshed wine into the bathwater.

I mentally replayed every moment of the audition, and not so I could fault my performance, for a change. No, I was conjuring the memory of oranges and cinnamon filling my nostrils and the intoxication of pure desire surging through my bloodstream at the sound of that British accent as it coaxed me through the submissive's lustful supplication of her Dom. Strange for me, to be so attracted to a man I didn't know at all. I had to wonder....

How much of my sudden infatuation had to do with Donovan Haigh being exactly the opposite of what I would have expected from such a man? He walked around with a leather whip on his hip, for chrissake. People didn't call him Donovan or Mr. Haigh; it was Ringmaster. Yes, Ringmaster. No, Ringmaster. Please kiss the hell out of me again, Ringmaster.

When Haigh had raised his hand to touch me, when he had first cracked that lash against the hardwood to command me, I had gone lightheaded and queasy. And I recognized that feeling, from being a child growing up part-time in Uncle Martin's Beverly Hills estate, part-time in a luxury apartment overlooking Central Park, from hearing the front door slam and realizing he was home. Even as an adult, my stomach still got nauseated at precisely seven in the evening, the time Martin would call us all into his study to report our day to him—his daughters, Ilsa and Jade, and me. Assuming he wasn't away performing or filming on location. Those times were actually tolerable.

But with the man they called Ringmaster...the hand he raised to me had tangled and tugged my hair with a steady, sensual pressure instead of grabbing me by the lobe of my ear to make me whimper or by my ponytail to pull me this way or that. The crack of Haigh's whip rang far more softly than a cutting word from Martin's lips. And when I'd stumbled, flubbed my steps, Donovan had caught me, started over with me, drawn me tight to his warm body to walk me through what he wanted from me.

My sigh blew little bubbles in the bathwater. It might have been nice to work under the direction of a man like that, assuming I could have gotten my runaway libido under control around him. Not much value, though, to an exercise of might-have-been. But the memory of that audition was going to sustain my private fantasies for a long time to come. A few of them might even have included being the Ringmaster's submissive *offstage*.

No, I thought and smiled to myself; in the end, despite how it had all turned out, I couldn't really regret auditioning for Donovan Haigh. Even if I had made a bit of a fool of myself.

The tap on the bathroom door from Gwynne reminded me that it was time to get ready for the evening, my last night of freedom, a last hurrah. It would've been a shame to waste it with cursing and tears, so I finished off my last half-glass of wine in one go and left a watery trail down the hallway to the guest room. The sexiest of the little black dresses at my disposal closely resembled a stretchy, body-hugging slip. Silly of me, I knew, but I squirmed into the vintage-looking garment wondering what Donovan Haigh would think of it, the way it showed off my shoulders and pushed up and presented my breasts. And the vaguely shimmery black stockings. Would he like those? The black Mary Janes I chose had heels a little thicker and a little shorter than the stilettos that had me tottering through my audition, but they still did wonders for the line and shape of my legs. Again, would the Ringmaster appreciate it? Assuming I actually got to speak to him again. Who knew what being his special guests really meant? Maybe nothing.

I complemented the noire look with tiny diamond earrings, understated makeup except for the dramatic black mascara and the crimson red gloss, and my hair pulled up into a high ponytail. Gwynne, all in red again, stood behind me and smirked as I hung my overcoat over my shoulders and examined my reflection in the mirror above her dresser. Draping the coat like that left a broad white expanse of my chest exposed, a single pendant dangling at a suggestive but not crass proximity to my cleavage.

"You're going to freeze to death like that, you know?" Gwynne said, the unexpected voice of practicality.

"Only until we're inside. After that, I'm sure I'll warm up."

The purpose of snickering behind her hand was, of course, to emphasize her laughter. "No doubt, Livy. No doubt." Then she entrusted me with my black velvet mask again, and we were off.

Through damp streets as a heavy mist moved in over the British capital in prelude to rain... beside sidewalks streaming with smiling, well-dressed Londoners out to enjoy their Friday night... past brightly lit restaurants and clubs and pubs, theaters and bustling transit stations....

I couldn't help giggling when we stopped at a traffic signal and I caught sight of a huge advert for the upcoming British Academy Awards on a bus stop. Among the featured nominees was tall, dark, handsome, *Irish* Quillan Teague. Back in L.A., that had to have had Martin fuming.

The thought of my uncle slowly worked at my mood, but only until I caught sight of the line of cars cued up at the gate to the industrial park. Two figures in full-length black coats, hoods drawn, checked each vehicle before waving them down the long drive through the rows of empty warehouses. Between the heavy mist, the car lights and my unreasonable expectations, the night was already glittering with promise and excitement. And there was light—yes, colored light—beaming over the far rooftops, from the back of the lot. Again, I pressed my hands to my stomach, feeling a deep flutter that was a cross between nausea and sexual tension. A glance at the digital display on the dash told me it was just after seven, but this wasn't my usual anxiety.

"Masks on," Gwynne muttered as we spent a moment idling in line. This time, knowing what I was doing, tying on the velvet mask felt so much more decadent, thrilling, almost dangerous—feeding a night of fantasy that would either haunt or sustain me for some time to come. I was finally having my adventure with my British femme fatale best friend, just like the stories she used to tell me.

I blew my breath out hard. No pressure, Olivia.

As we neared the gate, cars splitting off into two rows, Gwynne pulled the Mazda to the left and depressed the button that rolled down my window. Too nervous to focus, I let my gaze skim the linen cardstock invitation, noting only one detail amid the elegant red script.

"Show begins at eight?" I asked." What do we do for an hour?" Besides skulk around backstage staring after the Ringmaster, if I was lucky.

A broad, suggestive smile spread over Gwynne's face. "We see what we see, little Livy. I promise you won't be bored." And this time, how could I doubt her?

The procession down the drive between the dark, unused industrial buildings dominating the business park was a good deal slower than it had been earlier in the day. And this time we didn't get around the corner before more black-coated figures waved us to a parking spot to one side of the driveway. More vehicles lined the narrow alleyways between buildings, and the small parking lots I glanced now and again set back from the drive looked full.

"My god, Gwynne, how big is this going to be? How many people are here?"

Still sitting in the car, the redhead joined me in craning this way and that to survey the crowd of vehicles and smartly dressed, masked spectators making their way toward what could only be described as a barricade of crates. Festooned with banners and posters, it rose precisely where we would have turned the corner to approach that far warehouse.

"Four or five hundred a night," Gwynne estimated as she urged me out of the car and linked arms with me to join the stream of foot traffic toward that barricade. "The circus will do two or three weeks here, probably, at five shows a week. A good portion of the attendees will return to see the show multiple times, though, so I'm going to guess only two or three thousand people total have warranted an invitation."

I cocked one brow. "Expensive to get in?"

"Oh, yes, but it takes more than money to find your way to the circus. Charm, fame, influence with the right connections." She nudged me as we walked, throwing me a half-step off balance. "And a wicked disposition."

I'd have fished out a witty retort for that comment had we not just then reached the makeshift gate, where more hooded figures examined our invitation. My stomach lurched inside me, halfway up my throat by the feel of it, as my ears caught the first strain of distant music bobbing amid the low clamor of laughter and many voices. We stepped into what that morning had been a bare car park, and it was as though someone had drawn back a curtain to reveal a hedonist's paradise.

We entered through a gauntlet of scantily clad, gold-costumed jugglers throwing luminous neon spheres back and forth above our heads, and dancers gyrating inside the orbit of swirling LED-lit hula hoops. Of course, the bondage edge was clear in the lattice of leather straps and delicate chains stretched over bulging arms and crisscrossing lean torsos. I giggled when I realized one Adonis of a performer—adorned in swirling gold body paint and little else—was juggling small red ball gags. I gaped as I moved on to find three strongmen juggling—tossing—three delicate women back and forth between them as the ladies squealed with delight.

"My god, Gwynne," I exclaimed again as I whirled to try to take everything in.

She nodded emphatically. "I know."

The crowd of spectators all around us was as much a part of the show as the performers. Some were obviously Doms, usually dressed in all black, whether that meant an Armani suit with platinum cufflinks and a silk tie or a tailored linen shirt over leather pants. The Dommes wore floor-length Gucci or body-skimming Prada or high-drama McQueen. This one carried a whip, that one a flogger. Frequently, it was simply their posture and demeanor that marked them. That, and the two or three elaborately costumed submissives following in their wake. Even being utterly heterosexual, I could appreciate the surreal sensuality of voluptuous women dressed in high ruffled collars and long fishtail skirts, conservatively tailored but made entirely of skintight latex in black or crimson or midnight purple. Even being a little on the submissive side, apparent from my reactions this afternoon, I lusted after the male subs with nipple rings gleaming subtly inside partially unbuttoned silk shirts, trouser flies cut away to reveal constrictive leather G-strings over already en-gorged erections.

Despite the February cold, my skin flushed warm from the sensual glamour, the concentrated sexual energy surrounding me. More than one ardent stare from fellow spectators accentuated the sense that I was having a very good dream, laden with the subconscious desires I dared not entertain in waking life. The evening mist diffused the glow of lights strung between posts and freestanding heat lamps spaced throughout the lot, leaving a fine mesh of color hovering over the throng of beautiful masked revelers and performers alike. Near the loading door, up on the con-crete platform, an eight-piece orchestra in elegant fetish gear played a cross between classical and playful circus music that bobbed and swirled above our heads almost visibly, tangibly as we mulled around displays and concessions.

I was staring at a scarlet-painted carousel featuring not wooden horses, but pony girls and pony boys being stroked and ridden and even cropped by patrons. A long line of ticketholders waited for the pleasure while a masked circus Dom in riding clothes cut pieces from a candied apple so spectators could feed them to the statuesque pony girl stand-ing beside him in severe but elegant tack. To one side of me, I heard the most surreal exchange of a woman ordering a hot dog from a concession at a place like this—and a male voice responding that would be a hundred quid. Gwynne and I glanced at one another at the same time.

Leaning in close to her, I asked, "What kind of hot dog is worth a hundred pounds?"

From beside me, opposite Gwynne, a devilishly hand-some young man carrying two fluffy bundles of dark pink cotton candy provided the response, "All Kobe beef, hand-made and cooked in olive and truffle oil, served with mustard made from the best cognac available in London." The lean but athletic, sandy-haired man flashed a boyish smile beneath his gold mask and shrugged, sending suggestive ripples through the muscles high on his arms, left bare by the gold and black satin vest he wore. "Hell, knowing what a hot dog is really made of is probably worth a hundred quid."

I blinked repeatedly at him, not only at his answer but at his charmingly boyish manner edged in barely contained sexuality—in the tautness of his body under that thin layer of satin, in the gleam of his light eyes, in the aggressively apparent bulge in the front of his tight black pants. "How do you know that?"

"Because I'm the one who came up with it." He bowed shallowly. "*Master* Chef to the Cirque de Plaisir, at your service. If you'd rather…" He motioned toward another concession. "The snow cones there are made with a champagne and strawberry reduction. The cherry brandy and plum wine ice creams are also excellent."

I could tell Gwynne fancied him when she put on her special laugh. "And here you stand with cotton candy?"

"Ah, that." He handed one to each of us. "Made from a special recipe ordered just today by the Ringmaster himself in honor of his special guests. Raspberry vanilla cotton candy. My new favorite flavor, I think." And he winked at me.

"You know who we are?" I asked, feeling my skin prickling with the hot-and-cold shivers of anxiety.

He feigned bashfulness with the bow of his head and the shuffle of his feet. "I never forget a beautiful woman I've seen in her underwear." Then he leaned in just a tad. "Well done at the audition today, miss." I had to wonder if he could see my blush even in the glare of colored lights.

Long after he excused himself, my cheeks still glowed hot at the idea that he had recognized me, that even this mask afforded no protection, that he considered me beautiful and even worthy of a compliment after that embarrassing performance. I had told Gwynne I could warm up once I got here, and I certainly had. By the time we settled on the bleachers set up along the inner walls of the warehouse, I was almost feverish—and strongly aroused.

"You all right, love?" Gwynne asked me as I sat beside her, feeling and apparently looking rather dazed.

I nodded dumbly. "Why?"

With her eyes, my friend motioned to all the wonders surrounding me unnoticed. I gasped when I realized we sat beneath what appeared to be an enormous red-and-white striped tent attached to the warehouse ceiling. On the floor, three daises sat evenly spaced, the center one raised but the outer two made of embankments filled with shimmery champagne-gold sand. There the BDSM version of clowns, brightly dressed submissives buzzing about and exasperating and preening for three Doms, occupied the gathering audience in anticipation of the start of the show.

Gwynne tore off a bit of the cotton candy I held and put it to my lips. "Don't forget your treat, either," she teased. "Made in your honor."

Strong, tangy raspberry with an immediate aftertaste of caramel, followed by a lingering but mellow note of vanilla. And all sugar—just what my little overwrought nervous system needed. But made for me by the Ringmaster's order. The idea, along with the confection, fed a tickle of persistent excitement in the bit of my stomach. Was I going to see him again tonight, I asked myself over and over, right up to the moment the lights went down and the audience quieted to an expectant hush.

For the next two hours I doubted that I even blinked… or stopped trembling from my shoulders to the core of my sex to my tightly curled toes. The eight acrobats from the exhibition were back, plus more, coiling and swirling and swinging along bright lengths of silk. Carefully paired Dom/ sub couples executed physically demanding and sublimely suggestive balancing routines that hoisted the submissives' exquisitely contorted bodies into midair. A lion tamer cracked his whip to direct three animal-skin-clad submissives through a series of sometimes elegant and sometimes comical tricks, all while they bared their nails and hissed and swiped at him. The Chinese pole, with acrobats swinging from it like rippling flags in a hard wind, was breathtaking. The German wheel, containing the writhing bodies of lovers enacting a tumultuous power exchange even as the metal cylinder rolled around the rings, was astounding. The naked trapeze act…both distressing and thrilling.

Yet every other breath, every other moment of my attention, was reserved for the man who occupied that center dais. Donovan Haigh, the Ringmaster, presided over these athletic feats and sexual wonders with such confidence and skill, it was almost unfair to the audience whom he played and directed and manipulated so easily. His current costume was quite different from the simple black shirt and snug pants I'd seen him in that afternoon. He now wore a rather short but jaunty top hat, all black but with a feathered band that included an unruly red or gold plume nestled in here and there. The poet's shirt had been replaced with something akin to a traditional red ringmaster's jacket, with tails but cut in front so the edges didn't close. Behind the fabric straps that buttoned across his chest lay glimpses of lightly tanned skin and deeply etched muscle. The trousers that hugged his thick thighs and the perfect high half-moon curve of his ass glinted with metal detailing—rivets along the seams, loops of chain along his hips—before disappearing into shiny black riding boots.

More than anything else, though, it was the Ringmaster's face that kept drawing my stare. A black and gold mask obscured the right side of his face from temple to jaw, but the left side… With silver and black grease paint, he'd painted his left eye and drawn sensual swirls along his cheek. His lips shimmered fleshy pink with a hint of bronze. Small diamond studs in the lobes of his ears winked in the spotlight. The overall effect was that of an upscale, brooding emo sex god—hungry and ready, wicked, half-mad, all hedonist.

After the final parade of performers and two encores, the "clowns" began to usher the crowd back through the loading doors. Gwynne didn't move, so I sat fidgeting and shifting beside her.

"Do we get to go backstage?" I finally blurted. When she smirked knowingly at me, I took a moment to regain my composure, then chuckled at myself right along with her. "Well, he did say we'd be his special guests. I assume that means more than my own flavor of cotton candy."

"It might," the mischievous ginger hinted unhelpfully before rising and leading me through a split in the tent walls, toward those metal stairs that had taken us to the dressing room the first time we'd been here.

My steps clacked along hurried and clumsy as I tripped up the stairs behind Gwynne. At the upper landing, I made myself take a halting breath and reminded myself to *glide glide glide* on my black high heels. But I shuffled awkwardly again when the redhead didn't stop to lead me through that dressing room door.

"Gwynne?" I asked, as I hesitated at the door I remembered from that afternoon. She smirked at me again from over her shoulder and crooked her finger to beckon me to keep following. Past several more doors, to the very last, Gwynne lured me, until we came face to face with a stunningly well-built man blocking our path. Those firm, sculpted shoulders clad in fitted black satin—with metal rivets and a zipper he'd left open to just below his hard pecs—were wildly distracting, to be sure. But the burnished blond waves of hair and the green eyes visible past his black mask were easily recognizable from the loading door where he'd first greeted us and the persona of the exhibition foreman.

"We're special guests of the Ringmaster," Gwynne told him, and this time I got to see the full, pale curve of his lips curl into the bright grin his coat collar had hidden.

"I know," he replied in a rougher, more playful British accent than Haigh's. It suited him.

Gwynne cocked one hip and one brow at him. "Can we go in?"

The blond tilted his head flirtatiously and affected a disappointed sigh. "If you're sure you wouldn't rather keep me company here."

This got an appreciative snort of amusement from me. "Can we have a rain check?"

"Oh, no, love. Not for you," he said as he rested his hand on the door handle, about to pass us through the heavy metal access. "My boss wouldn't stand for any of us trying to *play* with Kitten."

The sound of that endearment brought back all the anxiety and excitement of the audition, with a flutter of nerves just under my skin and a gush of sudden wetness between my legs. That abruptly, my mouth was awash in saliva, the sweetness of raspberry and vanilla, and a touch of sour bile from the distant acknowledgment that this was just flirtatious banter. It had to be. There was no way one audition, especially that audition with me having to go through the routine so many times to get it even half right, had impressed Donovan Haigh enough that he'd really have a special flavor of cotton candy made for me. Or that he'd suddenly become possessive enough to tell his troupe they weren't to play with me, whatever that meant. But the idea still had the walls of my pussy trembling, starting to burn with need that hadn't been answered in too long. The weakness in my knees spread up the back of my legs, up my spine, until my shoulders shivered and went slack.

As though that had been some sort of trigger, the blond performer opened the door and admitted us into the furthermost reaches of the warehouse's upper floor. Into a… a sort of after party, I guess I would have said. Into a beautiful, dark, decadent movement of sexual energy, with swirls of half-naked performers circulating around a cluster of guests here, and eddies of exquisitely vulnerable and attractive submissives displaying themselves there. The Dominants were the stones in the river of desire, everything washing around and past them as they remained unmoving, letting the delights of the Cirque de Plaisir come to them.

The eight-piece orchestra was back, serenading the crowd with the most enthralling and sensual classical music I'd ever heard, from *Carmen Suite No. 1* to a deceptively subtle rendition of *Bolero*. Candles, hundreds of them, in wall sconces and in standing candelabras, on long shelves and tables, glistened like the mist outside past the broad warehouse windows, carefully frosted so as not to reveal the secret delights contained within the room. Yet the very size of the expansive hall ensured that an alluring, concealing darkness still hung above us, encircled us, embraced us.

Gwynne had just grabbed two glasses of champagne from a passing tray and started to hand one to me when Donovan Haigh, still in full regalia, stepped in front of us and collected both glasses—along with my full attention.

"Please, Cadogan," the Ringmaster sighed as he placed the glasses on the next tray to pass through his personal space. His smooth showman's voice perked my ears, my tender nipples, even the fine hairs on the back of my neck. "You think *that's* what I give to my special guests?"

I squinted over at the table along the side wall, where somewhat more conservatively costumed sommeliers tended to multiple cases of expensive French champagne in distinctive green, black, or gold bottles. Not exactly supermarket swill. What *did* Donovan Haigh give his guests?

Appearing as if on cue, the lean young chef who had presented me with the cotton candy emerged from the mulling crowd with two champagne flutes in hand. "Veuve Clicquot, of course," he muttered as he handed me one glass of the light, bubbly fluid with a wink. Then, before I could thank him, he turned to Gwynne, who looked only too glad to come eye-to-eye with him again. She was pulling out all her finest tools, from the lash flutter to the half-smile that coyly curled one corner of her crimson lips. "Why don't I get you one of those hot dogs to go with this? Yes? Come with me, little girl."

She cast a quick glance at the Ringmaster as she coiled her arm around the one offered by the dark blond master chef. I had to wonder how that would have worked, if the title *master* was an inclination more than an effect. Gwynne was a professional Domme, after all. "Hot dogs and champagne," she said with a chuckle. "Only you'd think of that, Haigh."

Straightening his back and his cuffs, Donovan regarded her with a subtle shake of his head. "Rein it in, Gwynne. Thom plays for the same team you do, and very well."

As she blinked at the handsome chef, Gwynne's spirits sank visibly with the angle of her shoulders, until Thom frowned at Haigh and grumbled, "Was that strictly necessary, Ringmaster, *sir*? I enjoy the company of a beautiful woman as much as anyone else. Don't cockblock; it's beneath you." Then he led Gwynne away as he muttered something about Haigh taking his frustrations out on everyone else today.

Standing there alone with the Ringmaster, or at least feeling awkwardly isolated in his presence despite the throngs of people drinking and laughing and seducing one another all around us, I had to wonder if he'd arranged for Thom to get Gwynne out of the way… to get me alone. Wishful thinking on my part, no doubt. Haigh hadn't been able to get rid of me fast enough after the audition. But still, I was aware I'd had some kind of physical effect on him. The memory of his erection pressing against my ass as he'd walked me through the precise positions he'd… wanted me in… intruded into the forefront of my thoughts and made my skin tighten and tingle, made my head swim with a rush of vertigo-inducing anticipation. Now I lingered in the discomfiting moment of silence between us as we both watched Thom and Gwynne walk away, before I gave myself to the temptation to glance into the Ringmaster's face.

Donovan Haigh really was just too damned handsome to look at for very long, with eyes so clear and smooth a blue they almost glowed, and a gaze that made me understand the description "penetrating" far better than I ever had before. With faint dimples that deepened whenever he even *thought* of smiling, when the vaguest hint of amusement lit those eyes. I was certain that if I stared at him for more than a moment at a time, he'd be able to read my mind, all the embarrassing, hungry thoughts that were making it hard to breathe just then.

He turned and stepped toward me abruptly. His gaze narrowed and focused hard on my face, shifting from my own eyes to my suddenly dry lips and back again. Up close, the stage makeup did nothing to disguise the visage of the man who had me tripping over myself during the audition. When his attention wandered down to my tight slip dress, as I'd hoped it would, excruciatingly sensitive goose bumps rose up to cover the bared skin of my arms and chest. The man's expression was intense but otherwise unreadable when his eyes shifted upward again.

"Champagne doesn't get any better than Veuve Clicquot, Olivia," he said with something almost chiding about his tone, and I realized I hadn't taken so much as a single sip from the flute in my hand. It was a relief I wasn't visibly shaking as I brought the glass briefly to my lips to taste the light gold liquid, and I smiled at the slightly sweet, rather dry flavor. Donovan nodded. "Good." It didn't seem a comment on my appreciation so much as my obedience to his inferred command that I at least sample this latest offering *for special guests only*. I broke my gaze from his with pronounced effort and pretended intense interest in the tiny bubbles coursing through the champagne.

Consequently, I didn't see it coming when the Ringmaster took me by the wrist of my free hand, his own warm and dry and strong as it locked around me. Just that quickly, I was protecting that glass of champagne as Haigh pulled me along beside him, weaving through the thick of the crowd and nodding and smiling graciously at the praise cast out to him as we passed appreciative guests.

"What are you…?" I tried to ask, finding myself breathless, my throat aching, constricting. "Where are we…?"

"We have matters to discuss, Kitten," Haigh responded, only half-turning his face to speak to me over the broad expanse of his shoulder.

So I was Kitten again, thrilling almost painfully at the suggestion of endearment and… and possession. Like he had the right to call me something other than Olivia, as Gwynne called me Livy. But the redhead had known me for years. Shouldn't I have been offended at the presumption? Or was it just that I knew this fantasy was momentary and fragile, too delicate for the disapproval of such real world concerns over propriety and gender equality? The power exchange of BDSM knew no gender, Gwynne had long ago explained to me; there was the desire to dominate or submit, physically and emotionally, sometimes sexually, leaving room for nothing else.

So I let Donovan Haigh lead me from the after party, through a door in the rear of the room, down a short hallway and into a large office. Here the merriment and music faded to a dull, rhythmic throbbing that coursed along the floors and beat suggestively at the soles of my shoes. But if anything, the unbearable tension of seduction only intensified. Yes, one half of the room contained a writing desk and wooden chair, laptop, piles of paperwork. The other half, though, harbored a bed made of a thick, dark red futon laid out on the bare wooden floor. A small crate acting as nightstand supported unopened wine bottles, leather-bound books, and several small pots of metallic face paint. Some-one had tacked gauzy red material to the ceiling around the mattress, creating a makeshift canopy with curtains to shield the bed from direct view from the door if so desired. He liked a lot of big, soft pillows, I noted, assuming… assuming this was Haigh's bed. The racks and open trunks of clothing certainly suggested the Ringmaster's style. Meaning I was alone with Donovan Haigh *in his room*.

When the Ringmaster finally released my hand, it was to gather a thin, neat stack of papers from that battered, black, turned-leg writing desk. He held them out to me.

"What is it?" I asked without reaching for them, my confusion leaving me wary, my giddy desire making my voice quaver.

"An employment contract." When I tilted my head, holding my breath, Donovan sighed lightly. "Take it, Ol-ivia." Startled that I still hadn't accepted the paperwork held out to me, I shook my head slightly to rouse myself and obeyed.

"Employment contract," I repeated in a murmur, almost to myself. "You…?" I had to do it, had to look again into Donovan Haigh's face despite my dread at that torturously magnetic attraction I felt to him. "You're offering me a job?"

"Not just *a* job, Olivia, *the* job. My assistant, the Ring-master's submissive." My eyes must have flared at this, be-cause Haigh stepped back, removing his top hat to reveal the shiny waves of tousled black hair. He tossed the hat onto the desk before leaning back against the edge and folding his arms over the gently bulging curves of his chest. "It's purely for show, for the performance. Our arrangement would be *strictly* platonic, if that's your concern." And he was adamant in his pronunciation of "strictly." Not just clear—insistent.

"But I thought…" I swallowed hard to suppress a near sob of confusion, surprise, and nagging disappointment. "I thought my audition was adequate at best."

There it was again, that steady stare I could feel as it homed in on me. "Adequate, yes," he sighed, his voice unexpectedly husky and low. "But you have a raw talent I can work with."

One step up from *merely* adequate, I thought with an edge of bitterness. I spent what felt like long, drawn-out minutes staring at the black characters lined up in uniform rows across the top page, my mind whirling without purchase in a storm of conflicting thoughts. After spending the last several days acclimating myself to the harsh truth that I was going back to L.A., the possibility Haigh now laid out before me was terrifying.

Of course, he had no way of knowing what this meant to me, what it saved me from, what it would cost me over the next ten years. I had to ask myself now how sincere I was about my professed willingness to give up everything that came with the Keane name and my life on the fringes of fame. And there was more… the promise of tremendous freedom and self-possession if I could tolerate Uncle Martin's hold on me a few years more…. Even thinking that, though—a few *years* more—made me feel like I was going to be sick all over the floor. But if I defied Martin now, with my future still firmly under his control, it meant providing for myself without all the advantages and connections and protections that came with being Hollywood royalty, minor celluloid nobility though I was in relation to the rest of the Keanes.

So romantic, I sighed to myself as I stood there blinking

blindly at the paperwork in my hand, this idea of running away to an anonymous life of adventure living out of crates and sleeping on pillow-covered futons, like a cross between camping and a tale out of Arabian Nights. But how glamorous would it really be, behind the grease paint and the colored lights and the scent of raspberry and vanilla, saffron and white truffle? And as the submissive to the Ringmaster, an agonizingly sexy man who couldn't disavow a sexual interest in me fast enough or in stronger terms?

Perfect, though, wasn't it—that last part? Wasn't that the reason I refused to work with Gwynne for Finley? Because I knew I'd balk at the thought of being touched in an even vaguely sexual manner as a house submissive at the club? Now Haigh was offering me immunity from that kind of discomfort. We'd be playing to the crowd and nothing more. Routines like the one he'd taught me today would become the rote movement of a mundane exercise, nothing to be nervous about, nothing as intimate as it had felt today.

So why the mass of disappointment weighing heavy in the pit of my stomach?

"I don't require an answer this moment, Olivia," Donovan said, and I jumped to find him standing over me. I hurried to gather a deep breath—yes, I wanted to smell him again, spicy orange and cinnamon. "But I do need to know by morning. Show up with the signed contract by eight tomorrow, or I'll assume the terms were not acceptable. Have Gwynne go over it with you tonight, especially the stipulations on page three."

It required all of my self-control not to flip immediately through the contract to the referenced page. Instead, I nodded, unable to trust my voice enough for a verbal response. I didn't speak to Donovan as he led me back to the party and helped me find Gwynne, where she huddled happily between Thom and the blond we kept running into standing guard over doorways. With great effort, I gathered myself enough to say thank you to Haigh, only to find him gone, lost amid the sea of masked faces and dramatic costumes.

Gwynne, to her credit, stepped away from her admirers to huddle close and ask, "Are you all right, Livy?"

I let out a breath that I didn't realize I'd been holding, hugged the sheaf of paper to my chest, and nodded. "I think I'm running away with the circus."

4

I TRULY DIDN'T think she'd take me up on the offer, and now it looked like I'd underestimated Olivia again, just as I had when I'd bet she couldn't go through with the audition yesterday. In the gloom of the warehouse, just inside the loading door, I stood with arms folded tight over my chest and watched a black Mazda with a familiar redhead behind the wheel dropping off the petite blonde and her overabundance of suitcases in the rain-slicked parking lot. Thom and Rafe had rushed out into the damp morning air to help Olivia with her bags without my direction, and that left me strangely disquieted.

A little girl on her first day of school, uncertain and lost. But excited, too? And already making friends, apparently. It bothered me that I wondered what was going on in Olivia's head, even though it was a perfectly legitimate concern, something any good Dom would want to know. It would affect how she bonded with me, how she held up to the stress of performance.

She was wearing her hair in a high, sleek ponytail again, just like last night. I didn't like it any better today. The style was too... I couldn't have said. Chic? Sophisticated? Outright sexy? Like the dress she'd chosen to display herself in at the after party. A little black slip of nothing begging to be hiked up over her hips, jerked down her shoulders, ripped to shreds. She didn't seem to realize the dark desires she invited in these circles.

Clearing my throat and unfolding my arms, I readjusted the uncomfortable swelling of my cock in my trousers before she'd drawn close enough to the warehouse to see me. When she did, when Olivia's gaze wandered from Thom's face after one of his reassuring compliments and caught my eyes, she came up short just inside the loading door and didn't take another step for several erratic heartbeats—mine. All smiles for Thom but big round eyes for me. All the better if I made her nervous, kept her off balance, I supposed. Better for the performance.

"Good morning, Olivia," I told her, gentling my voice.

"Morning," she whispered back. Then her shoulders stiffened. "Ringm—" She stopped herself. I wasn't in costume, just jeans and a white t-shirt suitable for rehearsals and working in a warehouse we were still cleaning up little by little.

Rafe swayed toward Olivia and murmured, "Donovan," into her ear, and I frowned at him.

"Give us a minute," I told my men as I held my hand out for Olivia. She looked for a moment like it was a snake ready to bite her, but she set down the one bag she carried and grasped my fingers with hers, so little in comparison to mine. Again I felt a terrible premonition that she was too delicate for this—this life, this role—and I was going to be responsible for breaking this woman to pieces. I wasn't prepared for a different thought to intrude. *Then I'd better make sure she gets stronger.* My job offer, my submissive, my responsibility.

Inside my office, I closed Olivia in with me and, just walking toward her, backed her into the desk. Still so bloody skittish….

"If you're here," I said, stuffing my hands into my pockets to show Olivia I wasn't about to grab her, "it means you've signed the contract, and that must mean you've read and understand page three."

Staring unblinkingly at me with those big green don't-eat-me-Big-Bad-Wolf eyes, she quoted, "Oral to oral penetration may be required."

And I nodded. "Yes, during a performance or a rehearsal I may kiss you." I wasn't sure which description made it sound dirtier or more enticing.

"As well as digit to oral penetration," she continued.

"And you understand that one?" I asked, feeling my own face heat as I watched her go red.

"I think so." The flush upon Kitten's skin washed down her neck and chest, and I couldn't tear my gaze away from the progress of the rosy glow. Through her thin white pullover, her nipples stiffened and protruded. Under different circumstances, I would have taken that as an invitation.

My hands sank even deeper into my pockets as I said, "Let's put that in context, Olivia. Get down on your knees for me." And damn my own voice, but even issuing the command sent a hard twitch up the shaft of my dully aching member to the engorged head flirting with the waistband of my briefs.

Of course, Olivia's obedience made the sensation worse. She didn't just drop ungracefully to the floor. Instead, she grasped the edge of the desk behind her and sank down slowly to rest first on her heels, black skirt inching its way up her toned thighs. Her gaze flitted from the hardwood floor to my face, back and forth, so demurely. I focused on the girlish freckles on her cheeks, reminding me of her innocence and making me feel like a pervert for being tempted to tell her to spread her knees. Finally, she rested her weight on the floor, palms folded in her lap, as she gazed up at me.

"During…" I paused to clear my throat and slowly, carefully remove one hand from my pocket to toy with her ponytail, to drape the silky stream of tarnished gold over one shoulder. Such soft hair… "During the performance, I might simulate oral sex with you." Was it me or did her eyes subtly flare? Was Kitten holding her breath? "I might expect you—force you—to rub your face against my groin."

Another pronounced twitch in my pants, followed by a painful throb. What the hell was I thinking hiring this girl? Ah, right, that she'd be a novelty with her unpracticed manner and brutally raw reactions. That it would be refreshing to work with a talented novice instead of a calculating professional for a change. That I could surely control the urge to dominate her and fuck her within an inch of our sanity. And so I would. I was the goddamn Ringmaster. She was just a kitten awaiting obedience training.

Less gently, I pressed down on Olivia's delicate chin and slid my thumb between her lips. "Digit to oral penetration," I said instructively. "The audience's dirty minds will, of course, picture something slightly different as you—" I gasped under my breath when I felt Olivia begin to suck and snatched my hand away as though I was the one who'd been bitten.

She drew back in surprise, catching her lower lip in her teeth as she jostled the narrow writing desk behind her. "Sorry."

"Don't be," I insisted. "That's exactly what you're supposed to do." Exactly what a submissive was supposed to do. *What she was meant to do for me.* I helped Olivia to her feet before stuffing my hand back into my pocket. Quickly, firmly, I added, "But there will never be real genital to oral contact and *never* vaginal or anal penetration of any kind. We will never have sexual intercourse, onstage or otherwise."

Head so slightly bowed, as though I were chastising her, Kitten nodded. "Yes, sir."

"Say that again, Olivia."

"Yes, sir?"

My tightened shoulders relaxed. I liked hearing that form of address from her. "Very good. I know Rafe told you to call me Donovan, but I have other ideas, and sir is perfect for those." I hesitated for an instant, pondering how to spring this on my new assistant without sending her fleeing. "Gwynne said you were both trained actresses. You are familiar with method acting and total immersion techniques?" When she nodded, I stepped forward, so much less careful, and took hold of her chin again to make sure she looked at me. Silky skin against my fingertips... "Good. I'm going to have you learn your role by experiencing it. At least for the first few weeks, you're going to live as my submissive, offstage as well as onstage. Can you do that, Olivia?"

"I thought you said..." she choked out haltingly, "no sexual contact, completely platonic."

"Mm-hm, and so it will be. You will serve me my meals, groom me, dress me." I watched Olivia's reaction—and my own—closely as I added, "Sleep with me. *Just* sleep. All part of the immersion into the life of a submissive, experience you will carry with you into your performance. Again, can you do that, Olivia?" Should I have pushed the idea upon her so soon? Was I going to lose my assistant as quickly as I'd hired her? And... and wouldn't it have been better if I did—got it over with already?

But I'd seen that reaction before, when Gwynne had pressed her into going through with the surprise audition. Olivia squared her shoulders and breathed out slow and steady through her nose. "Yes," she said. "Yes, sir."

It didn't matter to me that I could see her body shaking and the edge of panic in her eyes. How could I not admire her will, her commitment to her choice, whatever it was motivating her to do this? After all, I knew better than anyone that a place among my troupe, a home with the Cirque de Plaisir, wasn't a job. Waitressing and building houses were jobs. There were thousands of easier ways to make money. Building fantasies for an eager audience, understanding and playing to them, *playing them*, and raising it to a level of performance art... That was what we did here, and everyone had their special reasons for it. Just now, I told myself I didn't need to know—at least not yet—what Olivia's reasons were.

"Good," I said again, then mentally cautioned myself to stop praising her so much just because she was anxious. It wasn't my style, and the worst thing I could do as a Dom or as the Ringmaster was coddle one of my performers, my own stage submissive most of all. "Then let's get started with your training."

Without missing a beat, she asked, "Should I change?"

My instinctive response...*not at all.* But I stepped back from Olivia and crossed the cluttered room to hold the door open for her. "No need, I'll just have you strip down the way you did for the audition."

I suppressed a smile at the way she wiggled and pulled her skirt back into place almost compulsively as she walked toward me. "Are you sure? I mean, I have workout clothes in one of my bags. Yoga gear, maybe?"

"You won't be wearing yoga clothes in the center ring, Olivia. Far from it. You have thought about that, right?"

As she came to a stop beside me in the doorway, I loomed over her, picturing her in a bondage harness, lean limbs bound in leather and laced with chains. Or a pair of tight *tiny* black latex shorts over thigh-high boots. No, for Kitten it needed to be old school erotic—stockings and corsets and thick ribbon binding her wrists instead of harsh metal cuffs.

"If there's an exhibitionist in you, young lady, we're going to find it."

And I underscored my point by walking her down to the performance floor, where several members of my troupe were cleaning up from last night. Others performed routine safety checks on the equipment while a few more stretched and warmed up for rehearsal. As Olivia and I stepped up onto the center stage, I whistled for attention. "Rafe, Griffin, Naomi, give me a hand over here." And to Olivia, I said again, "Take off your clothes."

I liked the little blonde's habit of flushing and shivering and demurely averting her gaze as she peeled off her sweater and skirt again and tossed them to one side. The anxious tremor along her bare inner thighs caught my eye and interrupted my train of thought until my three best performers were all lined up beside me. It was Rafe who cleared his throat pointedly. Cheeky bastard.

With a sweeping glance, I included all of them before turning to introduce them to my new assistant. "You all know who this is," I told them. "Olivia is going to be my submissive." A sidelong glare at Rafe kept the man from voicing whatever was causing that grin on his face. "Olivia, the blond with the perpetual smirk is Rafe. He's an adagio performer. That's the two-person balancing act. He acts as the base, and the lighter performer with him would be the flier, the one who ends up in the air as they execute their poses."

Standing with feet spread and hands clasped in front of him, casually flexing the muscles in his bare arms below the sleeves of his blue t-shirt, Rafe piped up with, "Base *and Dom*. But no flier for me right now, so I'm filling in on the Chinese pole when needed or with the general gymnastic floor routines. You've got a great frame for flier, I've got to say."

"Thank you, Rafe," I said with a distinctly nonplussed tone that did nothing to erase that bloody grin. "I believe Olivia already has a position, as I might have just mentioned." Which got me a good-natured shrug that didn't display half the deference I'd have liked. Too many Doms in one room sometimes….

The chestnut in the group gave a little nod of his head, his shoulder-length hair falling forward to frame his strong features, as he interrupted the impromptu pissing contest with his own introduction. "I'm Griffin. My partner, Piper, and I are usually on the pole, as we Americans like to say."

Then, bouncing on her heels like the hyperactive minx

she was, black-haired Naomi waved to Olivia. "I'm one of the acrobats in the lion tamer act, the tiger from last night. You can call me Naomi or Mimi." I cocked one brow at this. Half the troupe hadn't been afforded the right to call Naomi by that nickname, and Kitten got the privilege right off? Just by virtue of being Kitten?

Rafe's grin caught my attention again, and we exchanged glances. I was beginning to understand his amusement. Not enjoy it, mind, but comprehend it. Olivia was just nodding and taking everything in, about to comment on one introduction when the next one rushed at her.

"Right," I said, frowning and folding my arms again as I began to pace a circle around the stage. "Now that we're all friends, I want to see Olivia build rapport with each of you." Then to Kitten, I said, "Do you understand what I mean by that? Improvise with them. Sync yourself to their energy and style. Give them what they want from you."

Rafe stepped forward first, without being invited. We were going to have a talk later, the adagio Dom and I. "Let's see you fly, Olivia," he said an instant before gripping my submissive by the back of her bare thighs and hoisting her up into his arms as she gasped, her legs instinctively circling his hips. Then he used her own weight to bend her backwards over one arm he'd wrapped around her waist, without prelude or warning, making her yelp. And giggle.

"Cute," I commented, frowning. "But I see no sexual tension between you two. Build it. Can you make Rafe believe that you want him, Olivia? Can you make an audience hold their breath waiting for the two of you to lose yourselves to one another?" Could she make me believe it when I had no particular inclination…or desire?

Rafe lifted Olivia back up with a swirl of that long ponytail, and they stilled for a long moment breathing hard and staring at one another as their laughter subsided. I was about to intervene, to coach her through the exercise, when the Dom ran one hand smoothly up Olivia's spine and she responded by running her palm down the center of his chest, lightly scratching his skin with her fingernails. Eyes still locked, green on green. His fingertips teased the nape of her neck, then gripped her hard until she let her head roll against one of her shoulders and around to the other, before she leaned back into a more fluid arch over Rafe's arm. When he pressed his cheek to her stomach, she let her arms sink down and fall open, like spreading wings. It wasn't perfect. It wasn't mesmerizing. But it was artful and alluring and a damn sight better than I'd actually expected of this exercise the first time around.

"You can put her down now, Rafe," I intoned flatly. When he did, I noted the adagio master was sporting an obvious ridge in the front of his jeans. Then Griffin stepped forward. "No," I told him. "She's got the idea. You three can go."

"Really nice job—" Naomi started to say to Olivia.

"Go," I ordered and found myself the target of the stink eye from our tiger girl. She whipped her own full black ponytail over her shoulder and turned her back to me with a flourish before following Rafe and Griffin away.

Olivia stood silently awaiting my instruction, fingers fidgeting slightly as her arms hung at her sides, one leg bent and pushed a few centimeters forward, like a pose I'd expect from classical Greek sculpture. And she certainly had the skin for it, the form, the quiet grace. I stopped just behind her, not touching her, craning enough to catch her profile.

"Do you know what you just did, Olivia?" The crease

of her brow told me she didn't. "There are ways of communicating, verbally and nonverbally, that influence a person's reaction. That make them more favorable toward you. One of those techniques is mirroring posture. I fold my hands in front of me, and you fold your hands. I lean forward, and you lean forward. Little by little, I begin to feel you are in sync with me, on all levels—mental and emotional—just because you are physically synced with me. Then…" I circled Olivia to stand in front of her, keeping my hands clasped behind me, knowing that made my chest seem broader and my posture more imposing. It wasn't intended to make her feel comfortable. "Then, once you have me, you change that balance of power and shift the natural order. You cross your legs and watch me respond by crossing mine. You rest your chin in your hand, and I mirror your body language. That's when you have me, following your lead."

"But just now with Rafe…I didn't…"

I shook my head no. "Precise mirroring wouldn't have worked in those circumstances, so you responded with equal but opposite reactions. His hand moves up your spine while yours trails down his chest. His grip tightens on your neck, so you loosen your posture and toss your head. He curls in toward you while you lean away, but while arching your lower body to him. If I'd let you two continue, I'm guessing in three or four more movements you'd have flipped the dynamic on him and had him responding to your lead."

"Why didn't you let us?"

A good question.

"The primary rapport you need to build is with me, so the audience can sense our connection." And there was definitely a connection, an electrical tension that arched between us as soon as we entered one another's proximity. A difficulty to be addressed cautiously, I knew. "Next in importance is your connection to the audience, which is a bit trickier since you can't possibly interact with each of them individually. That's more a matter of… persona, projecting an image that will be as pleasing as possible to as many of them as possible. And we'll have to find that persona for you." Olivia blew her breath out, stirring loose strands of hair hovering around her face. I smiled. "Don't worry, Kitten, we'll get you ready." And then I frowned. So much for not coddling my submissive, not praising every little achievement, not coaching her over every little bump in the lane.

"What? Why do you look…?" she asked, then apparently thought better of it and trailed off, and only then did I realize she was studying my expression, gauging my thoughts as they passed over my face.

"You'll also learn about power," I told her, perhaps too bluntly, too honestly. I normally wouldn't have armed an inexperienced submissive with such information. Or any submissive, really. They grasped it themselves soon enough, if they remained in the lifestyle, and heaven help their Doms once they did.

"Power exchange?"

"The subtleties of it, yes. The aspects that are lost on the less insightful players." I watched those green eyes carefully as I continued. "I don't know what brought you here, Olivia, or what you're leaving behind, but it's obvious you've been living under someone's thumb." Her sandy brow dipped, and the minute lines around her eyes deepened. "It's the way you tense and jump when I reach for you, the way you hold yourself, with your head bowed and your shoulders stiff. And you're always watching, aren't you? Trying to anticipate what I want. That's going to serve you now instead of the other way around."

And this…*this* lit her eyes and shifted her focus from my lips to my steady gaze.

I dipped my head and lowered my voice. "It's true. There is strength in submission, and you've been building a reservoir for a very long time, I think. You can turn that around to woo your masters and make them serve you, turn their whole purpose in life into caring for and pleasing you—even as they keep you on the end of a golden chain. Do that on stage, Kitten, and we'll bring the house to their feet every night."

Those glossy lips of hers parted as my persuasion took hold, as the possibilities flashed almost visibility through her mind just behind her eyes. An unexpected wave of excitement churned in my gut at the idea that I might spend the next few months watching Kitten grow into her role as my assistant, mature as a submissive. So much possibility.

The rustle of paperwork and the thump of steps approaching me from behind broke this moment of daydream, an abrupt irritation leaving a jagged scratch along the back of my mind. As Thom walked across the stage toward me, I glared so hard over my shoulder at him that when he finally looked up from his notebook and saw my face, he shuffled to a hurried stop. Our resident jack of all trades half-turned as though he meant to flee.

"I'm interrupting," he muttered, taking a backward step.

"Yes, but the damage is done. What do you need?"

"You wanted me to let you know when I'd gotten hold of anyone with Ties That Bind."

I stared blankly after him for a moment. "Oh, right, the custom fetish wear designers I wanted to invite into the concessions."

"That's them," Thom affirmed. "They can't make it before late next week, but I have a line on two more possibilities that might even be better. I just wanted to see if you had your mind set on TTB or if we could take a look at the new vendors."

Holding my hand out for his notebook, I asked, "You have samples of their work?"

The admin manager handed me the pad, with color printouts paperclipped to the top page. "Yes, from their web sites."

I grimaced. "Web sites?"

"Private, password access only. You know me better than that, Donovan. This isn't prêt-à-porter vinyl and Velcro bullshit."

At that, I finally chuckled. "Fair enough, Thom. I'll take a look and make some calls."

The man tilted his sandy head at me. "You're…" He glanced at Olivia and smiled at her. Everyone was forever smiling at Kitten. "You're busy with training. I can handle this."

But I shook my head. "There's a huge commission to be made if we find the right vendors for this, not to mention the cachet. I'll take care of it personally."

Under his breath, while rolling his eyes, Thom muttered, "While curing cancer and scrubbing all the loos to boot."

"Excuse me?"

"Oh, sorry," Thom popped off, the soul of insincerity. "I just thought it would be nice if you occasionally let your admin manager, you know, manage things."

"You exaggerate, Thom."

"Not by much."

"By enough," I assured him before turning my head to gaze down at Olivia again—big green eyes taking everything in moment by moment, breath by breath. After a split second's consideration, I told Thom, "Take her to Naomi to start working up a stage persona."

"Oh, my," he said, all too quickly grabbing Olivia's hand and pressing a brief kiss to the back of her fingers. "Entrusting me with his submissive."

"Do bring her back unmolested, please," I called after them as Thom drew my new assistant away from me.

"No promises, mate."

I shouldn't have trusted him or Naomi. So said a gnawing apprehension that followed me up the stairs to my office. My mind wandered as I reviewed the online images of custom fetish couture on the sites Thom had noted down for me. A couple of times I caught myself sitting idle for several minutes at the thought of what Olivia would look like in a crystal-studded corset or a white leather dress laced so tight down the back that it couldn't help lewdly exaggerating the curve of her hips as it nearly hobbled her with a mermaid skirt. When my hand strayed to the bulge tenting the front of my jeans, it was time to power down the laptop and make the bloody vendor calls. By the time I'd finished, I had to scour the warehouse to find where my admin manager and lead acrobat had absconded with my assistant.

They were all three huddled around a mirror in one of the ground floor offices tucked into the gloomy back recesses of the building, where we hadn't finished cleaning. A dusty film still shaded the huge windows and cast the room in a conspiratorial shadow, but they'd pried open one large pane so that what sunlight there was for the day threw a spotlight on the chair where they had Olivia sitting. They'd obviously gotten right down to work, by the looks of the costumes strewn everywhere.

When Naomi caught sight of me as I strode through the long gray room toward them, she pursed that little china doll mouth of hers to suppress an enthusiastic grin. I read her lips as she whispered to Olivia, "He's coming. Are you ready?"

And when Olivia stood and pivoted carefully toward me, flanked by a beaming Thom and Naomi, I choked on a ragged breath and came to a halt with the hard rap of my shoe heels on the concrete floor. How long had I been gone, up in my office staring at the screen and entertaining useless daydreams? Far longer than I should have been, apparently.

They'd had time to streak Olivia's hair with champagne blond highlights and chestnut red lowlights before twisting it atop her head in a vintage updo baring her pale neck and bound with a red-and-cream striped ribbon. The thick, shiny strip of silk matched the tight red merry widow they'd laced her into, complete with ruffled cream ribbon details along the legs and the top of the bodice and more striped ribbon binding the whole thing closed along her slight torso and now straining breasts. The cream-colored stockings, attached to old-fashioned garter straps, shimmered faintly as they hugged her legs from the upper curve of her thighs to the slender joint of her ankles where they met red Louis the Fourteenth-style heels, modernized to two or three times the traditional height. She looked like a World War Two bondage pin-up begging to be petted in all the most private places.

"So is this what you had in mind?" Naomi asked, hands clasped excitedly before her. "We tried a black leather vamp look and a harlequin theme, but they just didn't *pop* like this. Isn't it perfect?" Thom nodded as his cohort gushed, and even my normally anxious new submissive betrayed a hint of a giddy smile at the corners of her dramatically red lips.

But I shook my head. "No," I lied. "Not at all what I wanted." Truthfully, it was what I'd wanted, but not like this. The whole persona... the way the costume cinched in Olivia's waist and pushed out her breasts... the way the sheen of the material and the line of the seams directed my gaze down to her satin-covered mons, inviting a firm caress... the soft sophisticate effect... was far more overt and glamorous than I thought it would turn out. How was I going to sell the crowd on my submissive being a breathless, untried novice if she looked like a blond Betty Page made-to-order wet dream?

The look on Olivia's face, of course, the doe eyes and the lush lips parted in surprise, fired the immediate urge to smooth over her distress at my reaction. This time I refused to let myself act on it. My submissive was going to have to get used to this demeanor from me and the fact that I wasn't always going to be cooing over her—unlike key members of my troupe, apparently.

Glaring doubtfully at me, Naomi offered, "Well, there are still a few hours before we need to start getting ready for tonight. I guess we can find something else."

"Tonight?" Olivia asked, face paling. "You don't mean you're planning on putting me in the show already?"

"Don't bother for now," I told Naomi as I collected myself and strode forward again to stand over Olivia. I was vaguely aware I was still frowning at Kitten's costume. "We'll make do with what you've done so far."

Then to Olivia, I said, "You remember those six positions I taught you?"

"Of course," she breathed out defensively, nostrils flaring slightly, and I noted her fists were clenched at her sides. The little flare of temper almost made me smile coming from Kitten, when it should have made me cross. She corrected herself to say, "Yes, sir."

Useful, I thought. That edge of outrage was going to get her through her first night jitters.

I responded with a terse, "Good. Follow my lead for the performance. I'll start you out slow." Lips clamped tight now and glaring up at me almost petulantly, Olivia nodded.

To Naomi and Thom, I said, "Brief her on the general structure and timing of the acts while I make some calls and get ready."

Olivia piped up with, "I thought I was supposed to help with that, sir," which earned me odd looks from my troupe. In fact, every time she called me sir, Thom's gaze speared me, though his obvious questions remained unspoken.

"You've had enough to deal with for one day," I told Olivia, then bit the inside of my cheeks in frustration. I was coddling her again, but I couldn't take it back now.

I hurried from the room with Thom on my heels. "Implementing a new training regimen, Donovan?"

"My prerogative."

"True," the manager agreed as he followed me out to the main floor and back up the metal stairs almost at a run to keep up with my long, aggressive strides. "I've just never seen you deviate from your standard rules before. We're all used to you being predictably anal about everything around here. It's a comforting constant."

"Really? Yet you complain about it incessantly," I threw back at him over my shoulder, as I pushed on through the flurry of pre-show activity toward my office.

"We're British, Donovan. It's the national hobby and completely beside the point."

"You have a point?" I growled.

The rhythm of Thom's footsteps behind me dropped silent as he abruptly left off following me. "Be careful with her," he said, not overly loudly nor with particular vehemence, but it carried and struck me with a tingle along my spine. Enough so that I stopped and turned back toward him.

"I'm not going to eat her up, Thom," I insisted, then regretted my choice of words, as that was exactly what the basest part of me wanted to do. "I have better control than that, and you know it." Even if I was putting my powers of self-restraint to the test with the *unusual* stipulations I was making for her training.

Thom regarded me calmly, steadily, as he shook his head. Ignoring the other members of the troupe bustling around us, he said, "You're not getting me, Donovan. She's not the one I'm concerned for."

Ridiculous. Concern for me? After she'd been here only a few hours? It was so absurd a thought that by the time I'd fully grasped it, Thom had spun on his heels and left me standing there dumbstruck and indignant. The offense stuck with me like a thorn in a shoe while I made calls and reviewed revenue figures from our opening night, while I washed and dressed for the next performance, even as I made my way down the stairs to find Olivia waiting for me with Thom at her side.

As I'd ordered, Kitten still wore the red and cream costume, playing so well off her pale peachy skin. Now there was a red velvet mask to match. I felt the unreasonable urge to march up to her, take her by one hip and that silky hair, and thrust my tongue into her mouth for a kiss that would leave her as weak and pliant as she had been yesterday with me on stage, at the end of her audition. To prove to Thom that I was still the one in charge. To show Olivia the kind of Dom she would be serving when we were in character. And to settle this damned nagging dissatisfaction whispering behind every thought. But she was nervous enough, wasn't she? About to face her first real audience as the Ringmaster's slave…

Then the stage managers were pulling the edges of the tent back to usher us through, the Ringmaster and his personal submissive, to the center stage. The center of attention. The center of the glittering flurry of sound and color, desire and temptation, that was the Cirque de Plaisir. And in an instant, the tension of the day and of Olivia's training and of butting heads with Rafe and Thom and Naomi dropped away from me like a heavy coat falling from my shoulders. From the center ring, I waved my hand, and the crimson aerial silks unfurled. I inclined my head, and submissives throughout the tent fell to their knees for their Doms. I motioned to my left, and our lion and tiger and panther submissives staged an escape that had them vaulting over their cages, swinging on the hoops they had been jumping through, circling the trainer who then seduced and dominated and brought each of them to heel again. I motioned to my right, and fire dancers writhed and twirled while wielding batons that flamed at both ends, melting suspended wax pillars that dripped with strategic timing onto the bodies of "captive" slaves prostrating themselves to beg for mercy and then for satisfaction.

Olivia fell easily into her role as my attendant. No one

mounted the center stage except the two of us. When I removed my top hat, she passed it to an acrobat just offstage to spirit it away. When the animal performers broke from their trainer and rampaged through the tent, it was Kitten who read the unspoken command of my hand on her shoulder and clung in fear to my thigh. She improvised like a consummate professional, moving to kneel before me, between me and Naomi when the tiger made to stalk me—the slave protecting her master. And when it was time for us to perform, it was Olivia who had to walk so carefully in those red high heels to the trunk at one edge of the ring and bring me two heavy black leather floggers. I could just imagine the anxiety, even fear, coursing through her as she hefted up the heavy lashes and knelt to present them to me, knowing I was certainly going to use them on her. I could imagine it so perfectly, in fact, that I had the hardest erection of my life before I'd even taken the floggers from her hands. Her fear and hope and excitement were the strongest aphrodisiacs I'd ever encountered.

"First position," I muttered under my breath as I rotated my wrists subtly to loosen them up before wielding the massive floggers. Even this moment and a hard, deep breath couldn't banish the anticipation I felt at what was about to happen.

Trembling so visibly that I was genuinely worried she'd faint, my kitten obeyed, and damn it if I didn't grow harder at the sight. The orchestra music faded by degrees until it was a suggestion of color playing against the emotional tension of the hushed audience. I let it hang there for a good long while, the elongated notes of string and horn, the impatient murmurs fluttering through the crowd, the burning tightness in the muscles and the coppery taste of anticipation in the mouths of everyone here, including myself.

The first two strikes of the floggers, one following immediately after the other, issued dull *thwacks* against Olivia's smooth back. Some among the crowd gasped sharply in surprise with Kitten, as she started and jumped but held her position. Her shaking had to be visible to most of the audience by now, but I was more concerned with the gorgeous pink flush that immediately rose to the surface of her skin. I hadn't struck her hard; one didn't need to do so to impress with the sound and weight of the thick straps or to sensitize soft, unprotected skin. A few more strikes, in constant, careful rhythm, taught Olivia that the size of the lash was not indicative of the pain it inflicted. No, this beating was more like a massage, stirring circulation while lulling her mind and body.

"Second position," I ordered, and she executed it smoothly as I exchanged the two heaviest floggers for two more in the mid-range. This time the slightly sharper bite on her flanks even through the lingerie and on the outside of her bare thighs, curling around her hips to nip at the invitingly round cheeks of her ass, made her gasp her breath open-mouthed. As her hips grew restless and shifted to meet my strikes, an aching need set in at the base of my cock, in the swelling of my heavy balls.

I felt pre-cum slicking the head of my member in my pants as I snapped, "Position Three." Without switching to a smaller flogger this time, I spun the lashes in each hand in a continual fan of leather thongs cutting the air, and let just the tips graze Kitten's already tender pink spine. These snaps were louder, higher, sharper. Though bent forward in her hard bow, her body danced for me, wincing away, arching for more, wiggling and shuddering, her hands clawing at the wooden platform as she finally gave up struggling for balance and used them to steady herself.

I didn't issue Olivia an order to assume the fourth position, but grasped her by the hair and jerked her into it. Because she knew what I expected of her, it was a controlled roll that looked rougher and more dramatic than it actually was, but then… Then I left her there like that, legs spread, hips thrust up in offering and longing. Embarrassingly wanton and panting. Every muscle taut and quivering. I selected the smallest of my floggers, and only one of them, and calmed my breathing before returning to stand over her.

There were adagio acts in progress all around center stage. The animal performers still used the metal bars of their cage to support acrobatic feats. A half-dozen submissives swung from the suspended rings and wrapped themselves into exquisitely severe restraint with the aerial silks. But I felt every eye from that audience on Olivia and me as I brought that painfully thin flogger down across her satin-covered torso.

The strikes were light at first, then harder, then faster. Then the lash was biting at the smooth mounds of her breasts where they swelled above the corset, at the inside of her thighs as she subtly pumped her hips and tossed her head, tousling that perfect updo into a sensual mess. The music rose with Kitten's distress as I worked the thongs up her inner thighs and finally, *finally* brought the leather lash down on her mons. Olivia cried out in an incoherent plea with equal chance of expressing pain or pleasure, anguish or rapture. But the upstroke… It was the upstroke that curled the leather along the cleft of her sex beneath the satin, and lower along the crevice of her ass. The whistles and appreciative calls from the audience receded behind the sound of my throbbing pulse as I applied the lash to Olivia's pussy twice… three times.

"Fifth position," I demanded when I could no longer take the sight of her sex offered up to me while she mewed and panted through the torturous teasing of my lash. And I took my frustration out on the smooth, pale globes of Olivia's ass, heating them to a bright red with hard, continual strokes.

Sixth position was Kitten's declaration that she could take no more. Without direction, she whipped herself back to arch for me, her hands thrown up at first in a plea for mercy before she let her arms fall limp to the floor in surrender. The motion tore her hair loose from its ribbon to spread the wild curtain of gold strands into a fan at my feet.

I knelt then at Olivia's head and grabbed her hair to wrap it around my fist. Breathing into her open mouth, I *felt* her gasp as I trailed the flogger slowly between her legs, up over one hip. Then I lifted my face from hers and dragged the thin leather thongs along her lips. The sight of Kitten's little pink tongue darting out to trail against the lashes was my undoing. My mouth was on hers, lips sealed to lips, my tongue driving deep into her warmth. With her tongue swirling against and around mine in a show of submission I shared with no one else.

As promised, we brought the house to their feet.

And I knew in that moment, with utter certainly, that I had to fire Olivia immediately, that very night, and get her the hell away from me. It was worth paying her a year's wages. It was worth putting up with the attitudes I'd catch from my troupe. Worth it to keep the discipline and detachment I needed to run the Cirque de Plaisir. Worth it to never let anyone have this kind of influence on me ever again. There were some vows a man made to himself that he just could not break.

After the show, I worked through the glad-handing I needed to do with important clients as quickly as possible, ushering them up the stairs toward the usual after party for the most exclusive guests among an elite clientele. Still on the ground floor, I turned to look for Olivia, who had disappeared from my side without me realizing. My gaze connected with Rafe's as he praised one of the Dommes in attendance on the impressive retinue of submissives she'd brought with her that evening.

"Where is she?" I mouthed to him, and his gaze indicated the direction of the stairway.

"After party with Gwynne."

Cadogan. Trouble with red hair, I thought as I started through the crowd, but then wondered if it might have been better to have Gwynne here tonight for this. After I settled matters with Olivia, she'd have her friend there to take her home and soothe any hurt feelings from being let go so soon.

Concentrating on just how to phrase Olivia's dismissal, and striding through the doorway to the after party, I nearly barreled into a burly red-haired client I would have tagged as a Parliamentarian from the sum of his physique, carriage, and the somewhat conservative cut of his expensive gray suit. It was Thom who put out an arm to slow me down and deflect the collision.

Roused from my thoughts, I blinked hard at the men. "My apologies, gentlemen. A few last-minute business matters require my attention, but please have a glass of champagne. I won't be long."

My ruddy guest grabbed my hand to shake it. "I'll only take a moment of your time, Monsieur Ringmaster," he assured me in the gruff accent of a self-made man. "I understand you can make arrangements for private performances—command performances—with certain of your performers. I would be very interested in securing such an appointment with your lovely assistant."

Part of me recognized immediately that I was gaping, even if negligibly, at the man, at the idea. Olivia's very first performance had earned her an admirer, already? My inclination was to dress the man down for suggesting I would provide him private access to such an inexperienced submissive, even if he understood that "command performance" was not a euphemism for prostitution. And I wasn't at all sure he did understand that, from the eager glint in his eye and the flush of his cheeks. I settled for sighing out a chuckle, shaking my head, beginning to formulate a polite denial.

That was when Thom leaned close to mutter into my ear, conveying a figure that was more than three times— British pound sterling—what we'd normally ask for a private performance with Naomi or Piper as submissives or Rafe and Griffin as Doms.

Left gaping, twice in one night. Not the best showing for the Cirque de Plaisir's Ringmaster. "It sounds as though you are a great admirer of my assistant, sir," I told my dark ginger guest. "Let us discuss this at our leisure after you've enjoyed some refreshments and I've laid to rest a few pesky details of business."

He'd hardly had time to agree before I was pressing past him again, even more determined now to find Olivia. I caught sight of her across the room and shuffled to a stop, studying her. While Cadogan, dressed in her trademark scarlet, allowed other patrons to distract her, a number of guests had surrounded Kitten. The blonde maintained her demure demeanor, with coy glances and a nervous hesitance to let anyone too near, but she was also... also preening, even posing subtly, subconsciously maybe. And the Doms around her were eating it up. For a moment, it was like Evi was back, playing the crowd like a virtuoso in a village pub. Only I never wanted to shove a guest against the wall for pinching Evi on the bum.

"She's a hit," Thom said from right beside me.

Too busy watching my self-conscious little assistant flirt with three dangerously intent Doms, I didn't turn my gaze to him. "Obviously."

"That fellow we just spoke to was the fifth offer on her so far tonight."

And that earned my stare. "The show let out less than thirty minutes ago."

My manager nodded. "If it keeps up at this rate, you'll have to schedule her for three or four appointments a day until we leave London to even accommodate the requests from our favored clients."

"Forget it. She's not ready." And I was firing her. Tonight.

"The offers are exceptionally generous, Ringmaster. We even have requests for additional tickets for the next four nights. Not that I would lay that solely at her feet, but..." His shrug said that was exactly what he was doing. "She was pretty damn impressive with that willing innocent routine."

It wasn't a routine, I wanted to protest, but I suspected Thom knew that better than I did and just wanted to prod me with the knowledge.

"Before you say no out of hand, you should look at the names and figures associated with these offers, Ringmaster, sir. You owe it to the crew."

A point I couldn't argue with a clear conscience. The

Cirque de Plaisir was a profit-sharing endeavor. Every performer got a share of the revenues after costs. The funds from a command performance went half to the performers who took the assignment, half to the kitty for general distribution. And even a handful of private performances at the rates being bandied about for Olivia would have made for a lot of black ink.

"You know what I want to say," I told my admin manager blandly, resentment tightening the back of my neck and the muscles across my shoulders.

Thom nodded. "And I know you'll take the rest of us into consideration just the same, so I'm not really worried… about us, anyway."

Again with the insistence that I was somehow imperiled. I shook my head and glanced back in Olivia's direction… to find I'd lost her again. "Where did she go?" I asked myself more than Thom. Then I demanded of Gwynne, inserting myself between the Domme and her admirers, "Where is your friend?"

Cadogan glanced toward the space I'd last seen Olivia. "Is there a problem?" Gwynne asked, her voice lowered and dead serious.

"Other than a nervous daddy? Probably not," Thom assured us with a calming wave of his hands. "Let's just find her."

We wasted a half hour searching the after party and the main floor of the warehouse, and even the parking lot, before I checked in on the costume room where Naomi and Thom had prepared Olivia's persona that afternoon. She was standing in the middle of a pool of moonlight streaming in from the forgotten window with a thin, brown-haired man who held her arm entwined tightly with his. She motioned to the various racks and trunks, makeup and props, small tools and assorted bondage accoutrements as she spoke with him.

"Fascinating," he was saying in a smooth, overly calm voice that struck me as slick, conniving, and insincere. "So how many performers are there with the troupe? Are you all trained athletes and dancers?"

In an enthusiastic tone I'd never heard from her, Kitten was rattling off praise for all the people she'd met so far, though she had the presence of mind not to name names. When our mystery guest started to inquire about our client list, I stormed the room with Thom and Gwynne a half-step behind me.

"I'm afraid that information is confidential," I declared as I pried the man from my submissive and advanced hard on him. He retreated three steps. Shifty, nervous eyes. A compulsive clearing of the throat. An anxious gesture of straightening his unwrinkled suit jacket. I plucked the fountain pen from his breast pocket and dropped it unceremoniously on the floor as I used the eight or ten centimeters of height and the stone and a half of muscle weight I had on him to cow the man into standing still for it. When I'd ripped the silver watch from his wrist and tossed it to the concrete with the pen, I stomped them both to bits. "As are the details of the conversation you were recording and the images you were catching with that cheap watch camera." He was stammering his protest as I fished inside his jacket for his wallet. "So which is it, mate? The *Sun*? The *Mirror*?"

Even with me looming over him and Gwynne and Thom flanking him, he still stiffened that narrow chin and lifted it. "The *Guardian*."

This clod, a journalist with the *Guardian*? "Not likely."

A freelancer maybe, trying to open the right doors with a scandalous exposé piece on Tories and footballers mingling with glamorous submissives in a circus-themed orgy.

I flipped through an assortment of credit and business cards from his wallet until I found identification. "Philip Walker. I bet that's not the name you used on the waiver we make all first-time guests sign." At least the ones with less than utterly impeccable references from the most trusted clients. "I still think it will hold up with our solicitors. No recording of any kind, Mr. Walker. You acknowledged with your signature that we have the right to confiscate and destroy any surveillance equipment we find on the premises or on your person." I emphasized my point by grinding my heel into the shards of metal and plastic under my foot.

"You think I need some grainy photos and fuzzy recordings to break this story?" he asked in challenge. "I've seen three pop stars, two footballers, and one of the highest-ranking clergymen in England here tonight drooling over your assortment of corset-clad whores. The tabloids could paper London for a year with that kind of scandal."

Advancing another step, I lowered my voice and snarled, "So says a man who lures a young woman new to the job into a back room alone with him."

The reporter's spine went rigid as he caught my meaning. "I never touched her, not that way at least." Then he snickered. "Don't worry; I'm sure you can still get top dollar for her."

It was Gwynne who slapped him in the side of the head. "And I'm sure there aren't enough doctors in the whole NHS to put you back together if you make one more crack like that."

Thom, much stronger than his lean frame would have

suggested, gripped Walker by the arm. "Let's show you out, then, before we have to carry you out." My man took Cadogan to help him, leaving me alone with Olivia, who hadn't made a peep all this time.

When I turned, seeing her with the cool moonlight haloing that fall of mussed hair, I couldn't quite make out her expression, but I could tell she had one hand pressed over her mouth.

With sudden concern, I stood over her and took her by the shoulders. "Did he hurt you?" But even before Olivia could answer me, my anger and irritation took over. "I can't believe you'd let a stranger talk you into giving him a fucking private guided tour. You're part of an erotic revue, Olivia, and the patrons are naturally going to get ideas."

"God," she choked, finally moving her hand from her mouth to her forehead. "I'm an idiot. He was just so polite and mild-mannered, and I was only going to walk him around the rings, but we ended up…"

Christ, was that all it took to turn my cautious, nervous assistant into a naïve teenager? A little bit of positive attention? As irate as I was with Olivia, I couldn't help feeling a stab of sympathy and protectiveness over what kind of neglect and censure had left her so vulnerable to the lure of any man with a smile and a word of praise. That gave me a whole new reason not to cosset and fuss over her. I didn't need her forming that sort of infatuated attachment to me based on the fact that I might have afforded her the very basic human kindness.

"I said too much," she sighed raggedly, panic fraying her voice. "Not anything specific about anyone, but things I wouldn't have said if I'd been thinking." Even in the gloom, I saw the wet gleam when she turned that gaze of hers on me. "I'm sorry, Donovan. Sir. Ringmaster. Oh god, I know

I fucked up, and I do know it's serious. I would never… I'm sure this is grounds to fire me."

And a shiver bristled along the back of my head as Olivia offered me the perfect excuse to do what I already knew needed to be done.

"Please don't," she whispered, still and breathless, heartbreakingly fragile. "Please don't fire me. I'll never do something this stupid again."

The sound of Olivia begging reached out and gripped me by the solar plexus, by my insides. There was a deadness to her tone as she spoke, a hopelessness that made me wonder, made me want to ask things about her I had no business knowing. She didn't cry. She just stood there, shoulders sagging, arms hanging limp, as she bowed her head and regarded me with a quiet bleakness about her. Like she knew I was about to send her away and she was just waiting to accept her fate.

As my breath sighed out of my dully aching chest, my hands closed on the cool skin of her face. My senses filled once again with the faint scent of vanilla and caramel and cotton candy, promising pleasures not intended for a man as jaded as I was. "I'm not going to fire you, Olivia," I promised while asking myself what the hell I was saying. I didn't think she realized she'd stepped closer, almost cuddling against me, little hands gripping and twisting my jacket.

"Thank you, Donovan. Sir."

"Ringmaster," I corrected her in a sigh mixing frustration and amusement in equal measure.

"Ringmaster," she breathed, and it sounded like a relief, like a vow of loyalty, like an endearment.

This was no good. She was going to fall for me. And I was going to break her heart.

5

PERHAPS I HADN'T made the worst mistake of my life after all.

That was my first thought as I opened my eyes in the stillness of a quiet morning, in Donovan Haigh's bed, in Donovan Haigh's arms. With his bare, muscular arm tucked around my waist and one heavy thigh pinning my legs to the pillow-covered futon. With the soft hiss of his breath against my ear, sending warm shivers down my neck, as he slept beside me. I could almost forget the exasperation of the man running hot and cold with me all through the previous day and night. One minute he seemed to approve, when I'd gone through the rehearsal exercise with Rafe, and the next he couldn't have disapproved more obviously—at my make-over into the Ringmaster's submissive, for instance. Foolish of me to think he'd find me alluring in the tight red merry widow, after all his insistence that he kept his involvement with his performers completely platonic. And yet there had been that moment in the costume room after that damned reporter had lured me from the after party, when Donovan had seemed so concerned and protective and even tender with me, as he'd leaned so near and held my face.

Wishful thinking again, I supposed, based on how wildly attractive I found him. I couldn't help wondering what kind of woman appealed to Haigh. A femme fatale like Jade? A glamorous acrobat like Naomi? The kind of seductress who could make a whole crowd hold its breath at the very sight of her, glittering and poised, like his previous assistant? Not me, that was certain.

What time was it? Whatever the hour, it would have been eight hours earlier in Los Angeles. My flight from London Heathrow to LAX had left without me yesterday. The thought made me nauseated with worry and excitement that burned in my stomach. Had the plane landed already? Had our driver reported to my uncle that I hadn't arrived? I made the mental note that I needed to email my family today, not Martin or Jade but my oldest cousin, Ilsa, to let her know I'd found a job in the UK and wasn't coming back to work for her sister anymore.

The die was cast. I had walked away from my uncle's control of my trust fund and of me. There'd be no more Keane money to support me until I turned thirty-five and gained control of my inheritance. No more limo chauffeurs and jaunts to Cannes for the film festival. No more half-empty champagne flutes hurled at my head because critics panned Jade's latest performance or interruptions to my anemic dating life with a phone call demanding I come back to clean Pomeranian vomit off her powder pink carpet. No more caustic criticism and glares and interrogations from Martin.

Now this *had* to work, this job, this arrangement, this new role I had assumed as a performer and submissive. No going back. I would prove my skill and dedication to the Cirque de Plaisir and to the Ringmaster, no matter how much he doubted me, how much he exasperated me, how much he unnerved me with the overwhelming lust I felt whenever he was within sight, let alone close proximity.

And with that, Haigh shifted beside me on his bed of apple-red and crimson-red and watercolor-red pillows, embroidered and tasseled and fringed and overstuffed—a sensual, sink-down embrace of softness. I could hardly believe he expected me to endure this kind of intimacy without sex or emotion. It wasn't training so much as torture, but there were moments already when I relished it. Like now, lying next to him in one of his silky cotton t-shirts, his body curled over and around mine while he wore nothing but a pair of snug sweatpants. Baby-smooth but rock-hard chest. So warm. And the firm ridge of his cock pressed to my hip. If that was what he felt like at rest, I envied any woman who got to be on the receiving end of his desire. He was… impressive.

Then Donovan took a rousing breath and released me as he rolled onto his back. I'd never seen anyone wake up so completely so fast. Within a couple of seconds, he had opened those clear blue eyes, spent just a moment staring up at the makeshift canopy suspended from the ceiling, and sat up in a mouth-watering display of flexing muscles along his naked back.

He turned his head smoothly toward me, without even an instant of forgetfulness or confusion at finding a virtual stranger in his bed. "Good morning, Olivia."

"Good morning, sir," I rasped, my mouth and throat dry from the inappropriate thoughts I'd been entertaining before he awoke. I swallowed with difficulty and tried again. "Good morning." Combing my fingers self-consciously through my messy hair, I sat up beside him, unable to resist hiding behind my bent knees beneath the quilt.

Almost gently, he said, "Time to get your Master set for the day. You ready for that?"

Ready to act the part of his servant and submissive, to pretend an intimacy with him that every fiber of my body ached to realize despite the clear indication it never would? "Yes, sir." I was such a liar.

"Okay, so how are you going to go about that?"

Stunned, I regarded him silently, my brain seizing up with the worst case of stage fright I'd ever felt. "Wh-what do you want me to do?"

Donovan shook his head, tousled black waves falling over his forehead and adding a dreamy look to his vivid eyes. "If I told you what I expected of you, you'd just do it. I want you to *be* it, Olivia. Be my submissive."

Fuck, I hated improvisation. It required a level of abandon I'd never achieved, always too much myself to fully give in to assuming a character's identity. "I… I could get you dressed for the day," I suggested.

"Then do so."

Trying not to imagine that I could feel Donovan's gaze on my ass and bare legs as I ambled out of his bed and crossed the room, I padded barefoot along the cool grainy floor over to the travel trunk filled with street clothes. Looking over my shoulder at him, I asked, "What do you want to wear?" *Stop staring at his chest, Livy*, I heard in my head in Gwynne's voice.

"No more questions," Haigh insisted.

This was worse than my toughest acting class, worse than Martin watching while I helped Jade with her ballet lessons, even worse than all the auditions and premieres with all those pitying looks as people wondered why Eric Keane's daughter was just a personal assistant instead of an actress like her cousins. I could hardly see through the blur of panic as I randomly fished a t-shirt and pants out of the trunk, realized they didn't match, and had to force myself to pay attention.

When I returned to Haigh's bed with a bundle of clothing, he rose to his full height over me. "Ready," I sighed.

He pursed his lips, but I couldn't tell if it was a sign of impatience or amusement. "Dressing me in those is going to require undressing me first."

"Undressing?" Oh my. "Um, okay. Yeah, of course." My hands shook as I stacked the pile of clean clothes on the futon and straightened up to face Donovan again. How exactly did one undress a man she hardly knew? I started to reach for the waistband of his sweats, the only article of clothing he wore, but I hesitated, hands frozen in mid-air. This was unbearably familiar, impossibly awkward.

Goddammit, just do it. And I did. I ignored the flexing of Haigh's delectable abs as I gently dug my fingers into the waist of his pants and dragged them down his tight, muscular hips and over his thick, powerful thighs as I lowered myself to a crouch before him. Predictably, this put me eye-level with his crotch, and I immediately discovered that he wasn't wearing briefs, or boxers, or anything. That he kept himself shaved. That his testicles hung round and large and heavy…so smooth and masculine…below a broad, veined cock that stood out from his groin at a hard angle. His skin—everywhere—was lightly tanned and perfect and temptingly, well, lickable.

Page three, I reminded myself.

Donovan said nothing as I fumbled with the elastic to pull the pants over his feet, or when I kept getting in my own way as I tried to dress him. We were like mismatched dance partners moving in opposite directions, bumping into one another, stepping on toes.

"Olivia, look at me," he finally sighed with obvious frustration. When I did, he stared into my eyes for a long moment without speaking.

"What do you want?" I asked when I couldn't stand the suspense any longer.

"Watch my breathing and match it." Simple enough but it took a surprising amount of effort, especially when I was distracted with worries over Haigh's growing impatience and by the rise and fall of that sculpted chest. By the blue *blue* eyes. By the lush cushion of his lower lip. "Try again," he coaxed me. "Anticipate my movements when you can. React quickly to them when you can't."

And it was better, yes, a little. I finished dressing him without us bumping heads, without any ripped seams or unsightly scratches from my nails. When we were done, I wanted his praise, the way he'd occasionally doled it out to me yesterday. I wanted his hands on my face. His tongue in my mouth.

Instead, he said simply, "Get yourself dressed. I have a busy day in mind for you." At least he didn't watch while I changed, not so far as I could tell from periodic glances over my shoulder as I hurried to stuff myself into black yoga clothes that ensured comfort and flexibility for whatever training lay ahead of me.

We split up at the gender-specific bathrooms to take care of brushing our hair and teeth and met up again in the hallway, before Donovan led me down to the ground floor room that acted as a mess hall for the troupe. A long table supported a heaping buffet of oatmeal, ground turkey patties, whole grain toast with the optional traditional British pairing of beans, fresh fruits, bran muffins with honey, and a variety of juices. An athlete's meal rather than decadent gourmet circus fare, and all Thom's doing, I suspected as I watched him pacing behind the table directing members of the troupe to eat a little more of this, a little less of that. Seeing the manager's smile at our arrival was the relief I needed after an already trying morning.

Grabbing an apple for himself, Donovan motioned toward me and told Thom, "Set her up with breakfast, then get started on her visa paperwork before you start to familiarize her with your admin duties."

This perked Thom's well-groomed brow. "I get an assistant out of this, too?"

Haigh shrugged. "Might as well. I have business to attend to, and I need something to keep her out of trouble." No reaction to my instinctive glare, not from Donovan anyway. Thom almost managed to suppress his snicker.

"Now we're *both* flattered by your concern," Thom assured the Ringmaster before Donovan strode away without so much as a goodbye.

I turned from staring after Haigh to find Thom carrying two plates toward the crates that acted as tables and chairs. "Come on, Olivia. If you let his morning demeanor spoil your appetite, you'll starve around here." He winked at me as I perched beside him and tentatively nibbled on a muffin, worried about my nervous stomach. "Same with lunch and dinner. He's like that pretty much all the time. You'll get used to it."

Doubtful, but I could hope.

"He will occasionally surprise you, though," Thom said as he spooned beans onto his toast, then eyed the clutter of condiments on the table. I handed him the pepper that was hidden behind the bottle of brown sauce. "Ah, that's what I wanted, thanks. What was I saying? Oh, yes. Surprises, like this morning. I guess he had some morning exercises he wanted to work on with you?" There wasn't even a hint of suggestiveness in Thom's voice, telling me everyone knew Donovan had zero sexual interest in me. A great compliment, I fumed. Couldn't even arouse a man when I was crouched down in front of his naked morning erection.

"For once, I actually got to reconcile and record last night's revenue."

"Hm?" I grunted through a bite of fruit, realizing with embarrassment that I hadn't really been listening to Thom. He hadn't seemed to notice my inattention, as his gaze scanned the table again. I handed him a napkin.

"And thanks again. I mean, I'm an admin manager who hardly ever gets to manage any admin, which is why I have time to be the resident chef and physical therapist on top of that. To say Donovan has trouble delegating would be like predicting the sun will rise in the east tomorrow and he'll be his usual somber, anal self. It's a given."

As Thom finished his last bite, I collected our plates and handed them off to the crew members on cleaning duty before I followed the manager into his makeshift office for paperwork. If only I could have anticipated Donovan's needs as easily as I did Thom's, handing him stapler and pen and highlighter as needed. Really, why couldn't I? Why was Haigh so impenetrable to me?

Unable to contain my irritation and doubt, I abruptly asked Thom, "Why is Donovan having me help you with this? I mean, is he trying to shunt me away?" Like my family did? Was I going to be the wallflower here, too?

The handsome Brit set his paperwork carefully aside and settled back a little in his chair. "Donovan's a control freak. I think I've mentioned that, right? But I suspect he's not sure what to do with you." I knit my brow at the way Thom phrased that. "Not sure how to handle you, if that makes sense?"

It didn't. I was still pondering the odd suggestion when Naomi showed up to collect me from Thom, one babysitter handing me off to another. "Donovan has some new costume ideas for you," the statuesque acrobat told me as we tugged our overcoats on, "so I'm taking you to see one of the custom fetish wear vendors we've been thinking about adding to our vendor list to see what they can come up with. You're their audition."

Trailing Naomi out to a plain, dark sedan, I wondered at her wide-hipped, leggy physique with a touch of jealousy. I'd always assumed acrobats needed to be petite and small-framed, like female gymnasts. Yet Naomi was tall for a woman, maybe 5'10", with a body that managed somehow to look both athletic and voluptuous. And the way she balanced and swung on her cage and the rings when she was playing tiger and even the Chinese pole when she was horsing around with Rafe and Griffin... she had no problem maintaining precise control of every muscle and movement.

"Naomi, would you work with me on my gymnastics?" I asked as we settled into the car.

Instead of wondering why I'd make such a request, she broke into a broad grin that plumped her high, full cheeks and responded with an enthusiastic, "Of course."

Which made me feel a little more relaxed as we zipped through the damp London streets to a secluded lane where an elegantly gothic shop girl greeted us at the black-lacquered door of an Edwardian boutique that bore no visible name. Inside the dim but sumptuous parlor atmosphere of the shop, which smelled of musky incense and a sweet touch of anise that made me think of absinthe, the girl measured me and conferred with Naomi before bringing out a tiny white leather bustier with snowy fur trim and matching boy shorts. Together they zipped me into white leather boots before finishing me off with pink and white cat ears on a crystal-studded mask, plus a little harness that went around my waist and thighs to secure a long white tail to my backside.

I blinked at Naomi. "What the…?"

Her giggle was earthy and open and good-natured. "Don't be self-conscious. It's cute, and it's only the first look we're trying. Donovan has an idea for a routine with you as his kitten, so he wants you outfitted and tutored on appropriately feline behavior."

I thought I was already on the verge of acting like a cat in heat every time he was near. How much more feline could I get?

While the shop girl was out of the room looking for white leather gloves, I confided to the acrobat, "I'm not sure how seriously I can take myself like this."

Naomi tilted her head, the full black fan of her ponytail swaying with the gesture. "I'm not sure you have to be completely serious about this, but really, think about it. There's tremendous value in role play and fantasy. After all, don't you learn something about yourself whenever you assume a new character as an actress?"

"Theoretically," I murmured, unwilling to reveal my inability to embrace that aspect of acting. I peered at the image in the full-length mirrors facing me, unable to recognize myself in the exotic surroundings of dark Victorian couches, antique candlesticks on polished tabletops, and Persian rugs interspersed with racks of ornate clothing detailed with leather and straps and fine strands of chain. Unsurprising that I hardly knew myself, wasn't it, after all the strange, impetuous choices I'd made over the last couple of days? Now I looked as foreign as I felt.

"There are a lot of reasons for running away to the circus, Olivia," Naomi told me, her little smile quirking conspiratorially at one corner of her mouth. "Adventure and romance and the chance to design a whole new you. Maybe you're a seductive pin-up."

"Donovan didn't think so," I grumbled under my breath.

Naomi ignored my sour response and continued, "Perhaps you're a playful harlequin darting away from ardent suitors until one of them catches you." She circled around to stand behind me and grip my shoulders supportively, peeping around one side of my head with our cheeks touching as she addressed my reflection. "And maybe you *are* a kitten. You get to decide if you're the kind with claws or with the heartwarming little mew that even has all the neighborhood dogs rushing to protect you. Have some fun, Olivia. Try the possibilities on for size."

It was something to think about. A lot to think about, actually. "It would help if I understood what Donovan wanted me to be."

My new raven-haired friend pursed her lips. "He'll have

to figure that out before he can tell you."

"Meaning?"

"He's really not behaving like himself these last couple of days. I've rarely seen him turn down so many requests for command performances."

I shook my head. "I don't know what those are."

With her dark eyes widening, Naomi cursed under her breath. "If he didn't tell you, he probably didn't want me to say anything, either. You… well, you got a lot of offers for private performances, and for substantial fees, too."

"Private performances?"

"Yes, like by-appointment-only exhibitions. A client pays an extra fee for a sub or a Dom to come to their home, escorted of course, for a personal play session. Sometimes they just want to watch someone like Donovan or Rafe discipline the client's own submissives, or maybe they want to have the chance to dominate one of the circus submissives or have one of our Doms impose specific forms of discipline. Nothing involving intercourse. They're not paying for sex, though… though voluntarily liaisons are not unheard of. That's what happened to Donovan's last assistant. Every time we went to Lisbon, the same wealthy businessman booked her for as many command performances as he could, and she started dismissing her escort to be alone with him. He proposed to her on our last trip, so she left us to marry her perfect Dom."

I shook my head in disbelief. "And someone asked for a command performance from me, after seeing just last night's performance?"

"Sweetie, you got *dozens* of offers. So far, Donovan hasn't accepted any of them."

Dozens of offers. Disbelieving, I made Naomi repeat

herself twice more. The only reason I didn't keep hound-
ing her was that I didn't want to appear falsely modest or
let on what a terrible creeping delight I felt at the thought
that someone… *a few dozen* someones… found me attractive even if Donovan didn't. What was it that would make
them do such a thing? What had they seen in me? Was it
that amazing red costume Naomi and Thom had put together for me, to Donovan's dismay? Was it the passionate
routine that Haigh had drilled into me during the audition?
Or could they sense how much I wanted to give myself to
the Ringmaster when he had dragged that flogger over my
body, between my lips? Should I have been embarrassed instead of flattered?

By the time Naomi and I got back to the warehouse
to get ready for the Sunday evening performance, I had
worked myself into a warm haze of fantasy, so wet that I felt
the moisture gathering along the juncture of my thighs. I
couldn't stop imagining what the men—maybe even some
of the women—in the audience the night before had been
thinking as they'd watched me. I was unusually brave as I
dressed Donovan in preparation for the show, letting the
back of my hand brush against his groin as I fastened his
jacket, glancing up at him coyly. I posed and bent suggestively before him as I helped him slide into his shiny black
boots. My breasts, my stiffened nipples standing out hard
against the red satin of my costume, grazed his chest as I
reached up to place his top hat at a stylish angle over those
luxurious waves of black hair. If he noticed my coquettish
attempts at seduction, he ignored them, and all I got for my
trouble was a frown and a mounting sense of sexual frustration that I took with me into the center ring when the lights
went up that night on the Cirque de Plaisir.

For the spotlight performance, Haigh gave me no warning, leaving me to comply awkwardly as he stood behind me and strapped me to a huge wooden X facing the audience. I became the canvas for a demonstration of the Ringmaster's prowess with his whip. The first crack didn't hurt, but it was loud enough that I jumped and cried out in surprise and distress. I quickly learned that, like the flogger the night before, the whip was not the implement of torture I'd expected it to be. In Donovan's hand, it was fanfare and flash, gently grazing my back like the caress of his fingernails. And how I wished that was what it was—his hand, his touch. How the fantasies of the afternoon rushed upon me, leaving me feverish and lightheaded with want.

The light scrape and teasing bite of Donovan's lash only made the ache deep in my pussy a hundred times worse. My skin tingled with want of a harder stroke, and I arched for it as best I could while bound by wrists and ankles to the cross frame. I envisioned those few moments this morning when Haigh had made me look him in the eye and match his breathing, syncing myself to the rhythms of his body, though I hadn't quite been able to accomplish it. My eyelids sank half-closed as I conjured up the image of Donovan's blue eyes, plump lips, smooth model-perfect angles to cheek and jaw.

It felt like the inside of my head was a churning whirlpool of half-formed thoughts, as the buzz of Donovan's spinning whip and its rhythmic nipping at my back and shoulders lulled me. When he occasionally caught the side of my breasts or my hip with the tip of the lash, it bit at me just hard enough to rouse me from my heated languor, just often enough to keep me writhing and straining for more.

Then it happened, quite unintentionally. As I rested

my head against my shoulder, gnawing my lip to keep from moaning, my gaze scanned the audience until it locked with the blue eyes of a dark-haired man in the front row of the audience. Beneath his black wolf mask, his face was broad and strong and suggested a classically handsome man, just a hint of gray showing at his temples. It was too easy to imagine him as a slightly older Donovan, but a version who was watching me with rapt attention instead of mild disinterest. I pictured that look, the one the stranger wore—with parted lips and cheeks vaguely hallowed in hunger, in captivation—on Haigh's face. And I struggled against the hold of my thick leather restraints, squirming in the embrace of my fantasy, breath now falling in time with this stranger in the audience. While Donovan nipped and harrowed my inner thighs with the quick, sharp tip of his whip….

The stranger's breathing quickened with mine, by slow but steady degrees, his tongue darting briefly along his lips. Though he was feet away, I felt as if I could have leaned out and kissed him, my surrogate Donovan. "Yes," I saw him mouth subtly as my squirming mounted, as the real Ringmaster assailed the vulnerable flesh of my inner thighs and tightened buttocks. When Haigh's lash snapped at my flushed pussy through the satin of my costume, not once or twice but over and over, I had no warning and no defense. And a hard, intolerable tickle buried deep at my core blossomed and burst into a sudden orgasm that I wouldn't have believed possible until it shuddered through me like a force of nature erupting from inside me. My keening cry was unmistakable.

And all I could think was how much I wished I was looking into Donovan's eyes, pinned beneath him. That and page three. Over and over. *Remember page three*. Haigh was going to be furious with me, I just knew, even as pleasure rippled through me and tensed my body from my toes clear up to the back of my neck. God, was I going to end every performance in fear for my job?

Then the house was on its feet again, applauding... what? The Ringmaster's technique? His submissive's moment of abandon? I could hope they'd believe it was part of the act, that I hadn't simply lost control in a moment of impulsive fantasy.

I avoided Donovan's gaze the rest of the performance, then made the questionable decision of downing two quick glasses of champagne at the after party waiting for the Ringmaster to appear and scold me within an inch of my life for my embarrassing display. I couldn't bring myself to entertain even the smallest hope that he'd think I improvised a fake climax for the show. No, Donovan Haigh surely knew what had happened, how I'd let my professionalism slip so soon after he'd forgiven me for the indiscretion of letting a reporter roam around with me behind the scenes just last night. Quite the track record I was earning myself.

"If I might interrupt the lady's private thoughts..."

The deep rumble of a warm British accent made me turn with a start, and I was suddenly facing a black wolf—the man from the front row. My stomach tightened. Up close, his eyes weren't really Donovan blue so much as a sky-tinged gray, and his wavy hair shone dark chocolate brown instead of true black. But his smile and the intensity of his gaze remained unchanged, and I felt myself blushing and hoping he wouldn't comment on, well, the quite literal climax of the performance.

"I just had to congratulate you on such a passionate enactment on the St. Andrew's Cross."

So that was what it was called. Haigh hadn't bothered to tell me or warn me or prepare me in any way. A moment of resentment swelled in my chest, fueled by Donovan's rejection of my earlier advances. Unreasonable of me, I knew, as I'd clearly known the ground rules when I'd accepted the job. Unreasonable yet real, nonetheless. But now this handsome stranger's attention was something of a salve on my wounded pride. I thanked him for his compliment, though cautiously, wary after the problem with the reporter.

"I'm guessing you were classically trained in dance and theater," he said, continuing to smile gently in complement to his praise.

It was refreshing to have someone notice. "It runs in the family," I commented offhandedly, without meaning to, and made a mental note not to let any more details like that slip, even casually. I didn't know who I was talking to, other than a good-looking man who was generous and open with his admiration—unlike Haigh.

"Really?" he persisted. "You come from a theater family? A background in theatrical circus, maybe? That would make for some entertaining stories." He chuckled, and it was a low, warm, disarming sound that could have relaxed my shoulders and spine had I let it. "Trapeze artists parents and tightrope-walking siblings roaming Europe like romantic, upscale gypsies."

He earned my sincere laughter with this. "Nothing so colorful, I'm afraid. We were a good deal more conventional than that." If one could consider anything about Hollywood film and New York stage life conventional. Compared to the Cirque de Plaisir, though, it was positively mundane.

"That's an American accent, isn't it?" my stranger asked. "Such an alluring lilt to it."

"We don't have the accents," I insisted flirtatiously, willing myself to enjoy this moment of frivolity. "You do."

"Ear of the beholder, I guess. I shouldn't monopolize you, but I wanted—"

The arrival of an oversized bouquet of flowers, the kind I was used to seeing presented to the leading actress in one of Martin's Broadway plays on opening or closing night, interrupted the stranger's comments. It was Thom who shoved the impressive bundle of red roses into my arms with a grin.

"There are two more of these waiting for you, love," the manager informed me, "but I thought you'd enjoy this one the most. It's the biggest."

"Flowers?" I asked dumbly, even while delighting in the overpowering scent rising from the broad, unmarred blossoms I cradled in my arms.

"And an assortment of small packages. A certain feline friend of yours is shaking and sniffing at them now. I'm sure she'll give you a full report on what she thinks they are."

I felt my brow crease as I stared at Thom. "Gifts for me? Are you sure?"

The sable-haired stranger inclined his dark head just a touch. "It looks as though I'm not your only admirer, and I'm not surprised. I was going to inquire about—what is the term?—a private appointment, but…"

"A command performance?" Thom suggested.

"Yes, that's it."

"Let me take your information, then," the manager insisted, "and I'll pass it along to our Ringmaster."

I had just a second to wonder if that meant Haigh was considering the offers he'd already received for me. What an odd thought to occur to me… *the offers he'd received for me*, like I was a work of art or a prize mare or….

A hard grip on my elbow, jerking me back from Thom and the handsome wolf of a stranger, interrupted this train of thought. I whirled to find myself facing the glare of Donovan Haigh. My stomach dropped, and my chest seized. Time for a dressing down.

Too professional to lay into me in the middle of the after party, Haigh dragged me out the rear door and down the corridor to his room. I didn't argue or resist, knowing I'd earned the reprimand. No matter how callous it was of Donovan to treat me as inconsistently and coolly as he had, it was my responsibility to maintain control and professionalism. Instead, I'd acted like a hormonal teenager, flirting and cooing and… and embarrassing myself.

Shut away behind closed doors, Haigh squared off at me, fire in his eyes. There was a moment of distraction as he focused on that bouquet of roses, before he grabbed them from me and tossed them on the narrow black writing desk.

When he spun back to rear at me, he demanded, "What are you thinking, Olivia?"

"I… I mean it wasn't…," I stammered, folding my arms defensively, tight under my breasts. I was acutely aware how close I was to spilling out of the top of the corset, and I felt my skin flush.

Haigh stepped up a breath from me, looming, towering, imposing, claiming my personal space as his territory. The scent of citrus and spice had my mouth watering despite the bristle of tension and irritation creeping along the back of my neck and scalp. "You go from teasing me shamelessly before the show to writhing and begging like that during the performance. What am I supposed to think?"

"I didn't think you'd noticed," I snapped before I could stop myself, then gritted my teeth at my own folly. Way to make it worse, Olivia.

"Noticed?" he repeated with a note of incredulity in his tone. He ripped away his mask so I could see the angry arch of his black brow. Then his hands shot out to lock around my wrists, pulling my arms apart as he advanced on me. He didn't stop until I gasped at the chill of the textured plaster wall behind me, and even then he took a half-step more, pressing all that heated muscle against my body until my mouth fell open in an obvious gape. His erection fitted itself into the juncture of my thighs and made the sensitive sheath of my sex pulsate with sudden need. "Does it feel like I noticed, Kitten?"

It felt like an impossibly firm, thick demand at my aching entrance. Like a hard, lewd wet dream that could never happen in real life. Certainly not to me, the lesser Keane.

"Donovan, what are you—?"

"Ringmaster, Kitten, Ringmaster," he corrected, then enunciated again, "*Does it feel like I noticed*?"

"Yes," I gasped again, just before Haigh pinned my arms to the cold, bare wall above my head and robbed me of breath.

"Then what did you do, Olivia?" he growled, tension sharpening his jaw, deepening his voice.

At a loss, I shook my head, too overwhelmed at his sudden force to put together a coherent explanation, let alone a defense. I had been asking for this, but it hadn't turned out to be what I expected—sudden and terrifying and overwrought with too many sensations to fully grasp. I'd never felt such a muscular, sculpted body against mine or heard a man use that tone of voice on me. Never been pinned and pressed and *handled* at the mercy of such thinly restrained desire.

"Why would you let go like that in front of five hundred people? It would have served you right if I'd fucked you in front of all of them," he said, his forehead pressed to mine. I felt his words steamy and rushed against my face.

My thoughts skewed and twisted at the suggestion—not even truly the realization, just the suggestion—that while I had been fantasizing about Donovan staring at me like the handsome stranger in the front row had, Haigh actually had been watching my body wiggle and arch for him. And his body had responded not with disinterest but with this, with violent hunger and undeniable demand. With vehemence I'd never encountered or felt, until now.

"And then," Haigh said slowly, carefully, "you let yourself come right in front of me, in front of everyone." He ground his hips in a hard circle, and the lips of my sex blossomed for him, cradling his cock through our clothing. The pressure on the tender pearl of my clitoris was beyond maddening. There was the very real danger of an encore performance of my earlier behavior, and I couldn't stand to imagine or hope what Donovan's reaction would be. "What did you think that would do to me, Olivia?"

I shook my head so slightly, speechless.

In an instant, Donovan hefted me against him and spun me to face the wall, arms once again pinned above my head. Now my body was spread the same way it had been on the X-shaped wooden cross. Only this time, the Ringmaster wasn't a figure lurking somewhere behind me, distant and untouchable. He was pressed flush to me, his torso bared by his open jacket, his naked chest and abs laid hot against my shoulders and back as I shuddered and went limp in his grasp.

"Do you know how seriously I take this?" he rasped into

my ear. "That I have never broken my rules about sexual involvement with my troupe, especially my assistants? That I have never violated that contract? But I look in those bloody doe eyes and hear you sigh when I touch you, and for fuck sake… the way you smell, Kitten."

Before I could respond, before I could even wonder how I would answer him, Haigh reached between my legs and deftly plucked at the hooks at the crotch of the merry widow. That quickly, that simply, I was bared and wet and open for him. When he withdrew his hand, and I felt his weight shift against me, I rested my feverish cheek against the wall. Knowing what was coming, what he was doing. Or at least hoping, something I hadn't let myself do in so long. The sound of his zipper was a whisper of a hiss in the still room, under the thick rush of heavy breath.

There was nothing else in the world that felt like the velvety firmness of a lover's cock taking me, and there was no thrill or primal fear to match the knowledge that the warm member now nudging the smooth lips of my sex was Donovan Haigh's. With the broad head of his cock pressing slowly into me, he rested his smooth cheek on my bare shoulder, his weight bearing down on me with an intensity that tempted me to panic and struggle, but also with a closeness and possessiveness that left me feeling so very safe. It was hard to breathe trapped and hard-pressed like that. I didn't care. The sensation of smooth skin on smooth skin, of the Ringmaster… *my Master* shifting and flexing and tensing as he prepared to enter me, paralyzed me with disbelief and terror at the thought that this was only a dream after too little sleep and too much to drink. This man was fantasy incarnate, the personification of sex and desire driven by the will to possess. The kind of lover who claimed in a heartbeat what mere mortal men had to earn over weeks and months—the soul-deep adoration of a woman.

Pain was a welcome relief from the dread, an intrusion of cruel reality that brought with it a bittersweet reassurance. I hadn't had many boyfriends, and the last had been some time ago. As soon as Donovan's cock pierced the tight ring of my entrance, I bit my lip to stifle a whimper. No doubt, he was larger than average, thicker and longer than any man I'd been with before. And I was tighter than he had any reason to expect. The small grunt in the back of his throat and his sudden stillness as my sex grasped his cock told me as much.

"Kitten," he rasped, satiny lips brushing the curl of my ear. For several long heartbeats, he didn't advance, and I refused to breathe, willing him not to change his mind about this, no matter how much it would hurt at first. No pain compared to the ache of wanting Donovan Haigh and not having him.

I could've cried when I felt his hips shift against me again, pushing his member just an inch deeper, stretching me just a bit wider. The pain-pleasure that gripped me was like the satisfaction of working a sore muscle. I pressed my forehead to the wall and filled my lungs to brace myself, then so slowly and deliberately shifted to push myself back on him.

One of Donovan's hands reached down to grab my hip, fingertips digging into satin and skin. "Stop," he groaned, the word almost lost in the husky growl of his voice. "Stop, Olivia." He took a moment, panting hot against my neck, which made me shudder and shift again involuntarily. "Fuck, slow down. I'm… I'm trying not to hurt you, baby."

I turned my head to gain the briefest sidelong glimpse

of the haze of lust softening his painted face. Nuzzling his cheek with mine, smearing my skin as well, I whined, "Hurt me, sir. Ringmaster."

"You don't mean that," he insisted, but his body took the invitation to sink another inch deeper. Aching inner muscles throbbed and convulsed around his veined shaft as we both gasped.

"It hurts not having you inside me," I breathed, turning my face back toward the wall to hide my embarrassment at the confession. "Please, all the way. It will be better." Like ripping a bandage off quickly, jumping all at once into a cold pool, downing a bitter tequila shot to get to that moment of warmth burning its way down my throat.

The hand at my hip slid around my waist, and I knew he was ready. Was I? I had to be. We both groaned, finally in sync, as Donovan pushed his groin forward while pulling me back along the length of his cock. Even as slicked as I was by hours of arousal, days of unanswered attraction, his progress was agonizingly slow as he made my body fit him. The hand still on my wrist above my head slid upward to lace his splayed fingers with mine, and I buried my face against his sleeve, muffling my cries.

After three anguished strokes, sweat breaking out along the curves of our faces and shoulders, we had taken as much of each other as physically possible. I couldn't take Donovan an inch deeper. He couldn't open me any wider. The pain of accommodating his body inside mine faded in favor of a stinging, throbbing ache that demanded more—more movement, more friction, more heat.

Experimentally, Haigh held his breath and dragged his cock half out of me, only to vibrate my whole body with the moan that escaped him with his renewed advance. "Is that what you want, Kitten? Is that what you need from your Master?" he groaned into my tangled hair.

"Yes, god, yes. Take what's yours," I said in a flurry of breath and foolish candor. "Take me, please." *Want to take me. Want to claim me, own me.*

"Close your eyes," he commanded, but gently. "Feel yourself on that cross again and think about how much I wanted to jerk this costume off you and make you ride the cock you made so hard." His voice, wild and dirty, sent quivers through my flesh deep beneath the skin. And another thrust, harder, underscored the image he conjured in my willing mind. "Picture the masked faces in the crowd, baby, with their eyes gleaming in lust and anticipation. They want to watch me use my soft little slave." Two driving jabs drove him so deep that I felt and heard his smooth balls slap my bare ass. "That would bring them to their feet, wouldn't it, Kitten?" he chuckled haltingly, beginning to pant with effort. "The Ringmaster binding my innocent, teasing little assistant to the cross so I can use your body, so I can spend the need I've never unleashed on anyone else. All on you. While they watch and envy me every fucking blissful stroke."

Every. Fucking. Blissful. Stroke. Each word was a new plunge into my core, reaching a new depth inside me, until Donovan's cock kissed my cervix at the apex of each thrust. The brief, repeated discomfort roused me from the dreamy rapture of the rhythm set by our writhing bodies.

I could hear the taut cry of the orchestra violin again holding a long, agonizing note of expectation and the flute keening like the moment before an overdue orgasm. I saw the crowd. I felt the hot, tight grip of the leather restraints on my wrists and ankles. But this time, they were the fantasy, and Donovan's body at my back and his cock inside me were real.

As Haigh gave himself to the mounting pace of his member sliding in and out of his slave's eager sex—my eager sex—I sank into a haze of half-imagined colors, faces, sounds and half-realized dreams of this man's perfect body fusing itself to mine. Fingers laced with my fingers. Slick skin on slick skin. Thrust meeting thrust.

"Can you come for me, Kitten?" he asked in a husky whisper, as two fingertips slid into the trimmed cleft of my pussy and found my clitoris. "Let me feel you lose control sunk all the way down on my cock. Will you do that for your Master?"

Strangling on my haggard breath, I nodded languidly, feeling as though I hesitated on the brink of dream, delusion, hallucination…ecstasy in the truest sense.

"No," Haigh insisted, his voice growing more forceful with this thrusts and the pressure of his fingertips. "Say it, Olivia."

"Yes, Ri-Ringmaster."

"Say it," he insisted again, bouncing me back on his unyielding cock.

I fought for enough breath to obey. "Yes, Ringmaster."

"Again," he snarled, doubling his effort, his pace and his force.

The walls of my sex, forced wide, twitching and throbbing, tightened…and tightened…and tightened around him. The tickling pleasure of Haigh strumming my clitoris grew sharp and bordered on pain. "Yes, Ringmaster," I cried in distress, my fingernails scraping the aged plaster of the wall.

Louder, riding me furiously, he huffed, "Tell me you're coming on my cock, Olivia. Say my name. Come with me inside you, and say my name. Say. It. Kitten."

"I'm coming," I said, less because he commanded it than as a statement of surprise, shock that he could order me to climax and my body would obey. My core fluttered and pulsed and seized for a second, then again, longer. "Oh, fuck, yes, I'm coming...coming on your cock. Donovan..."

My body clamped tight around Donovan Haigh in the same instant he stiffened behind me, drove himself to the root inside me, poured the warmth of own release into me. His arms went from restraining and directing me to binding me tight to his chest, shifting only long enough to slide the red velvet mask from my sweaty face. His full lips sucked at my earlobe and jaw and the sensitive line of my neck, his cheek leaving thick, rich streaks of face paint I could feel slick against my skin.

"Donovan," I gasped, as my orgasm flared with a particularly forceful tremor along my inner muscles. "Donovan," I moaned as the quavering subsided. His hips...his cock... still pumped me lightly as I sagged in his embrace, spent and sighing. "Donovan."

And I had to wonder, distantly, in a fog of emotional exhaustion, if I'd ever be able to say this man's name again without feeling the threat of climax in response.

6

THOM DROPPED THE revenue reports on the crate where I was leaning. For a moment, he looked as though he planned to keep walking, without looking at me, without speaking. Then he hesitated, shuffled, and folded his arms over the navy blue sweater stretched snug along his swimmer's body. He leaned back on the crate with me as I stood watching Naomi and Olivia huddled together giggling where they sat on the center dais on the warehouse floor. Both women wore form-fitting yoga clothes that allowed them the maximum range of movement for rehearsal. The outfits highlighted how a tall, muscular gymnast and a slight, lean ballerina type could be equally beautiful.

"You still haven't responded to any of the command performance offers on Olivia," Thom observed blandly, his disapproval evident in the tightness of his voice.

Things were getting bad when even my mild admin manager was being terse with me. But, then again, everyone was on edge right now, with that incident involving the reporter and now suspicious-looking new tenants in one of the long-abandoned warehouses up near the front of the industrial park. It didn't ease our concerns much that we only saw activity there during the day. We'd still had a break-in—one of the back rooms, with minor bits and bobs stolen. More concerning, Olivia's California driver's license and Piper's passport had gone missing about the same time.

When I didn't respond to his statement, Thom repositioned himself in front of me, blocking my view of Olivia. "Shall we go over the top three proposals?" he offered, his tone a good deal less helpful than the actual words implied. "They're all just into the *five figures* now, Donovan. That would go a long way to cover the cost we've incurred taking the warehouse for another week and outfitting Olivia in nothing but custom-designed costumes. Swarovski crystal and Russian sable aren't cheap, sir."

"True, but the increased ticket sales justify the expense. We don't need to book her for private performances yet; she's too raw. And I don't think it's unreasonable to give her more than two weeks of training before we expose her to that kind of attention."

"That kind of attention, sir? You mean amorous suitors? Men who might expect to strap her to a cross, whip her, *and then fuck her*?"

Through my clenched teeth, I grumbled low, "You don't have to keep reminding me, Thom. It's quite obvious you don't approve of what happened between Olivia and me. What you don't seem to comprehend is that I disapprove as strongly as you do."

"Clearly, as you tossed her out immediately afterward."

The back of my neck tightened and flushed cold. "The next morning, actually."

"Oh, right, completely different, that."

"You'd have had me insist she keep up her training by continuing to act as my submissive offstage as well as in center ring? After I'd had to tell her what a mistake it had been to…to become involved as we had?" I snorted. "You're a callous bastard, Thom."

"Is that ridiculous justification effective? Really? Because that's an ethical contortion that puts our best acrobats to shame."

"Watch your tone with me, Thom." I was hugging my arms tighter across my chest to avoid taking the front of his sweater in my fist. "Whatever you think of my slip with Olivia, I'm still your boss and the Ringmaster of this show."

"Oh, I know," he assured me with a nod. "You might want to remind Olivia of that, though. That brat routine she did last night when she kept defying you during the performance…it was so convincing that I think the crowd thought she might *actually* have been disobeying you. Imagine that. But it was a great hit, wasn't it? That ovation and the repeated calls for an encore. The roses and the private notes don't seem to impress her much these last few nights. But, of course, the diamond-studded collar delivered on behalf of that chap Finley and Gwynne brought with them last Sunday—she liked that, didn't she? And all the little trinkets from the fellow who's always wearing that wolf mask. She likes him just fine. Let that keep on and we might have another Evi on our hands."

"Thom," I growled, my jaw twitching, "walk away from me right now."

When he did, I found myself glaring at Olivia and Naomi, with my assistant glaring right back. For the last week and a half, ever since I'd let my frustration and attraction to the little kitten get away from me, I'd been on the receiving end of looks so glacial that they made my skin prickle at the chill. No, I shouldn't have taken the liberties I had with Olivia, shouldn't have broken the cardinal rules that I'd lived by for more than five years, since I'd founded the Cirque de Plaisir. It would have been better had I simply resorted to my usual contacts, found a fuckable blonde, gotten it out of my system without involving Olivia. But I hadn't. She had every right to freeze me out, refuse to speak to me unless we were in rehearsal, hide herself away with Naomi and Piper. It was the grandstanding and disobedience on stage that rankled me, the not-so-subtle transformation from breathless innocent to adoration whore. That and…

That and the passive-aggressive attempts to make me jealous with that gaggle of admirers at every after party. The worst was the fellow in the wolf mask. His numerous requests to book Olivia for a private performance, bank details included, identified him as a Mr. Stephen Unwin, a particularly posh businessman with a variety of investment properties. The only greater irritation than hearing her pointedly cooing about him to Naomi or Gwynne whenever I was around was the concern that some of her crowing was sincere. That she was letting herself become attached to a client, letting herself believe the fantasy we were supposed to be spinning purely for their benefit. That she was making herself vulnerable to a stranger in a wolf mask even after the debacle with that reporter. It smarted that I had myself to blame at least in part for that, whether Kitten was trying to make me jealous or merely seeking solace after my rejection.

Either way, I was the motivation for her careless behavior.

A flurry of giggles from Naomi and Olivia and the distinct mention of the name Stephen further darkened my mood, and I came up from my reclining pose against the equipment crate. "Right then, ladies, it sounds like you've had enough of a break to recover. I expect another hour of work *at least* on that floor routine before dinner and prep for tonight's performance. Up. I want that front tuck with a round off flawless enough that I can believe Olivia can do it in heels without breaking an ankle."

Kitten cast a sidelong glance at Naomi as they stretched and clamored to their feet. Her mutter was audible enough for me to catch her grouse, "After doing it for two straight hours this morning, it's as perfect as it can get."

"Then I'll expect nothing less than perfect every time for the next *two* hours, Kitten."

The hard line of her lips displayed her displeasure at my endearment, an address I had taken to so quickly and naturally and which had proven a difficult habit to break. Especially when I fell back into the usage to goad her from time to time. I could be passive aggressive, too, but I could tell I still had the greatest effect on Olivia when I was plain old aggressive.

Olivia executed a dozen flawless dance-like tumbles with Naomi right beside my assistant to monitor her form and generally nod encouragingly and approvingly with praise that Kitten, frankly, didn't need. I motioned the tall acrobat out of the way and put myself in the mix to see how my submissive would improvise. Her choice was to whirl out of my reach and turn her chin and her little round bum up at me in challenge. And *that* was all of *that* I was having.

"Excuse us, Naomi," I said as I lunged at Olivia and

hefted my stunned assistant over one shoulder. "Enough," I bellowed and smacked her ass when she wriggled and swore at me.

When she couldn't get away from me, Kitten gripped my t-shirt, digging her claws into my back to steady herself. "What's your fucking problem?"

"Sir."

"What?"

I tried not to chuckle at the fact that Olivia was picking up a British accent. It showed more pronouncedly when she shot back one-word answers at me. "The correct address is what's your fucking problem, *sir.*"

"Fuck me if I'm going to say—" she started to protest, then winced at the unfortunate phrasing. I felt her stiffen. "Never mind that," she said in an under-breath grumble.

In the waning hours of the afternoon, too late for costume touch-ups and repairs and too early to dress for the evening performance, the costume room was all but abandoned. A scathing glare from me cleaned out the stragglers. Only once we were alone—a rarity these last few days—did I set my fuming assistant down on her feet.

"Time for a little talk, Olivia. The insubordination and the brat routine are going to stop right now. It's unprofessional and jeopardizes the mystique of this troupe."

Though I expected sass, what I got was calmly folded hands and a tightly controlled voice. "I don't agree with that assessment, sir."

Warily, I shifted to give her a half-step of space and put my hands on my hips. "You don't, eh?"

"The longest ovation we've received so far was for my brat routine, with the possible exception of the night I darted into the audience to pick out someone to come up onto the center stage to help you discipline me."

"Yes, a bit of improvisation that I believe I already indicated I did not appreciate." She'd fished Mr. Unwin out of the front row, of course, where he'd spared no expense to make himself quite a fixture.

"But is this about what you want or what the audience wants?"

"I worry about what the audience wants, Kitten. You worry about what I want. My circus. My troupe. My rules."

"Mine mine mine." The sass was edging up into her voice again, and that accent was all California. "Letting your ego make decisions is hardly good business. No improvising. No command performances with your assistant. And rules about rules about rules. No rehearsing with any other Doms, especially Rafe. No drinking at the after party. No sex between the Ringmaster and his slave."

Olivia gasped when my hand shot out to grip her arm and haul her up close to me. "No acting like an attention whore on stage or with the clients, either, but you can't seem to manage that one, can you?"

"So I'm only allowed to be a whore when you want to push me against a wall, is that it?"

"Right, I've had it." I dragged Olivia bodily with me to a low trunk where I threw her face down over my lap and laid about six hard smacks against her Lycra-covered ass with my open hand. She renewed her squirming with a fury, pushing and scratching at the arm I was using to hold her down. That only provoked me further. Without thinking about it, I jerked her yoga pants and silk panties down her thighs and resumed her spanking—bare-assed now.

All I could think about was that round, naked buttocks and the angry pink glow of blood rising to the surface of her smooth skin as her circulation responded to the quick smacks, delivered hard enough that my hand was stinging as badly as her ass, I was certain. Her writhing ground her against my knees, and within moments, I could see the glistening moisture building at the neatly trimmed lips of her sex. No matter how much she hated me, no matter how sincere my insistence that I was not going to molest my assistant again, neither of our bodies cooperated when we were alone together, when tempers flared and breath thickened and blood rushed to our heads and our groins.

I held Kitten more firmly to keep her still while I left off spanking her to trace one fingertip along the cleft of her pussy, to smooth the sheen of wetness along her engorged sex and over that so sensitive span of tender flesh leading to the tiny bud of her anus. I made no attempt to penetrate her either vaginally or anally, just toyed very lightly with her tensing, trembling passages. Just tortured myself with the thought of feeling her body sucking at my fingers or my tongue or my throbbing-hard cock. It took what I had left of my concentration to focus on what Olivia was saying, to make sure she wasn't telling me to stop. She never said it, even while I'd been spanking her. Cursed me, yes, but she had never asked me to stop.

When Olivia had finished struggling, had exhausted herself, and sagged there panting and glassy-eyed and red-faced, I made myself pull my hand away to caress her ass somewhat less suggestively. "That's a good girl, then."

"Page…," she started to gasp, then paused to swallow hard. I wanted my tongue in that warm mouth. "Page three."

"No vaginal or anal penetration of any kind. I kept my word this time, didn't I, Kitten? And I might have found a new way to discipline you. Mouth off at me in onstage again, and I'll spank you bare-assed in front of the crowd until they can all see how wet you get—then send you to bed without an orgasm."

"Asshole," she spat suddenly but predictably. I reached out, finding that the most immediate handhold was her ponytail, which I gripped to rein her in and control her renewed struggle. It took only a moment for me to recognize that a wild-eyed panic had gripped Olivia. She clawed at my hand. "Don't! Don't do that. Don't hold me like that." Her tone and volume rose with each word until her protest was a distressing squeal of true and obvious terror.

I let go instantly, and Kitten scrambled off my lap on hands and knees before twisting to face me while she crawled backward along the floor.

"Olivia," I said, holding my hands up in a motion to calm her. "Olivia, stop. It's all right. I've let you go." She kept scurrying away until I jumped up to lunge for her, to kneel in front of her and gather her up with my arms around her stiff shoulders. "What is it? Stop and tell me."

She let me help her tug her clothing back into place, but she didn't speak for the longest time, and then only to whisper, "Just don't. Don't ever pull me by the ponytail like that, okay?"

"Okay," I promised gently. "I won't do that again."

But she wasn't going to tell me why, that much was clear from her tight-lipped pout. It took ten minutes just to get her to unlock her arms and rest against my chest. I settled onto the floor and cradled her between my legs, wishing I knew what had happened to Kitten before she'd come to me and who exactly was responsible. Her reaction made it utterly clear that Olivia was here escaping something. How much worse that made my decision to violate her trust and take her that night. She needed the circus as a haven, it was apparent now, and she needed me as her protector.

Yet I couldn't resist… couldn't help rationalizing the urge to gently grasp her chin and tilt her face upward so I could lightly kiss her forehead, her eyelids, and finally her lips. No resistance. She endured my touch, then relaxed into it, and I opened her lips with mine and dipped my tongue into her mouth. So slowly, so tentatively and tenderly. We sucked the lush bows of one another's lips and gingerly entwined our tongues. And when she sighed and rested her head on my shoulder, I massaged her scalp with my fingertips until I realized she was actually dozing in my arms.

When she finally opened her eyes, the only thing Olivia said was, "I don't know what you want from me."

And I didn't know either.

I knew what my rules and boundaries were, and I knew why I had them. There had to be a firm wall between fantasy and reality, behind the tent canvas, behind the characters we all played. Without that sense of detachment, we could each have faltered and forgotten the people around us were real living beings with wants and needs that demanded respect. Not just personas. Not just pretty illusions there for our private entertainment.

Olivia was not really my kitten. The patrons offering thousands of pounds each for the prospect of a command performance with her, showering her with adoration and gifts, did not exist solely to rebuild her wounded self-esteem. I had to make her understand that without playing on her resentment of me or making her think I was saying she wasn't worthy of attention and praise. But at this rate, she was going to lose herself in the image she portrayed for them. And I wanted my awkward little American assistant back, doe-eyed and breathless and clinging to me.

I couldn't stand to watch her become the... the type of woman I had reason not to trust. The reason for page three.

And sometimes, when I was tired, I wondered if I was going to drag those hurts around behind me forever. They'd already toured every country in Europe and half of North America. I wore them like my own harness, too tight across the chest, cold metal rings gouging into me whenever I began to relax.

An apt metaphor. I wore it on center stage with me that night, as I directed Olivia through her first performance of the new kitten routine. I felt the constriction of old fears as she rubbed up again my leg and meowed for me and posed coquettishly to preen and lick her paws while the audience cooed and laughed. I nursed a familiar ache as I admitted silently to myself that I would have wanted Kitten as my real submissive, had the circumstances been different.

Had I not already built my life on the mystique of the cool, aloof Ringmaster of the Cirque de Plaisir... had I not cobbled together a sense of continuity and even security from the troupe of performers who followed me like beautiful vagabonds from country to country even while I maintained an emotional distance from them... had I not formed such a strong aversion to the kind of consciously coy and manipulative performer I was trying to prevent Olivia from becoming... she hadn't completely lost herself yet, hadn't begun to toy with people's affection without regard, hadn't broken my heart so far.

Two weeks after the fact, Thom's warning to me finally made sense.

After the show, I navigated the gauntlet of important clients and special guests half-heartedly. My mind was elsewhere, with Olivia, wishing I could take her back into my bed that night—just to sleep. Knowing I couldn't.

When Rafe brought a new guest to meet me, I couldn't quite grasp what he was saying the first time through and had to shake off my distraction and make the blond Dom repeat the introduction. "Mr. Barrymore," he repeated, presenting the gentleman again. From behind a silver mask, the man's grayish green eyes shone keen and metallic and perhaps a bit cold, a fair match for the cropped and stylishly ruffed gray hair that betrayed minor glints of what was once light brown or very dark blond. The practiced smile on his long, thin face suggested a cultured man who was not the least intimidated *or impressed* with what he saw around him. Ours was a brief exchange of pleasantries—with me only a little surprised to hear another American accent, East Coast this time it seemed—that stalled as he peered at me obviously and at length.

"Do forgive me, Monsieur Ringmaster. I have the distinct impression I've seen you before somewhere."

I bowed slightly and joked, "I have that kind of mask."

He pursed his lips as though he'd almost found that amusing. "It's in the eyes, I think." But then he took a deep breath and waved the whole matter away with a gesture of his manicured hand. "Makes no difference, of course, and it's surely bad form to try to guess my host's identity when we've all gone to such lengths to preserve our secrets. I'll let you see to your other guests while I enjoy the *unique* refreshments and the attractive scenery."

I felt a distinct relief the silver-masked Barrymore hadn't added his name to the long list of admirers requesting a private performance from my submissive. Odd duck. The arch of Rafe's brow as the two men turned from me said the Dom agreed with my impression.

Then I was left alone to pick up my thoughts on Olivia again, as I scanned the crowd for her. I'd already forbidden myself to act on my earlier musings, but I did want to make sure she was holding up, after the emotional encounter in the costume room. A few yards away, she was leaning close to listen to something amusing from a distinguished older Domme, Kitten's pink lips poised on the brink of a smile that looked ready and willing to bow with laughter. And I was glad someone had managed to bring back some semblance of ease to her manner.

When Thom brought a herd of Gucci suits over to meet Olivia, I frowned behind my crooked finger. How many offers would come of this group, I had to wonder. She must have been tired, I thought, because she greeted each of them graciously but with none of the obvious flirtation she'd been wielding so freely as of late.

Then Kitten's gaze came to rest on a tall, slick fellow with swept back black hair and one arm curled tight around Naomi's waist. If anyone in the immediate group saw the color begin to drain from Olivia's face as he chatted to her, they didn't show it. A passing tray replenished everyone's champagne, and jests flowed just as freely. Olivia smiled faintly and withdrew one slow, careful step. And when something witty Naomi said sent the men into a bout of raucous laughter, and Slick threw his head back with the loudest crow of all, my assistant ducked behind a passing couple for cover as she outright fled.

When I caught up to Olivia in the corridor beyond the after party, I found her shivering. "Come on," I said and drew her away to my room, giving her no opportunity to argue. Once alone with her, I told her flatly, "I want to know what that was about. What exactly did that man say or do to make you run out of the party?"

Head bowed and shaking, Olivia refused to look at me. "There's something I should have told you after the incident with that reporter. This was bound to happen. When my license went missing, I knew it was coming."

"Why are you dancing around the subject, Kitten? Just tell me."

"I was already afraid that you were going to fire me, and it wasn't like I was Ilsa or Jade. No one pays that much attention to *the entourage*. Goddammit. Why now?"

Was she going to talk around the matter forever? Probably. So I tugged her with me to the chair behind the writing desk and drew her into my lap again. After only a moment of fretting, Olivia relented and grew still, then relaxed against me muscle by muscle until I had her head on my shoulder again. She curled against me, like she was hiding from something, taking refuge under my wing. I tried not to dwell on the swell of pride I felt at that impression, knowing I hadn't earned it yet.

"Goddammit," she repeated in a deep sigh.

"Tell me."

I saw her roll her eyes when I glanced down at her freckled face. "The French accent gave him away. He can't tame that down to save his life."

"Who, the black-haired fellow attached to Naomi?" I pressed impatiently. Did I need to peel him off my acrobat as well?

"His name is Yves Vachon," she tsked in disgust, like the man's very name was an insult.

My mind caught on the familiarity of the surname. "Vachon… Vachon…"

"Actor."

"Ah, of course. The Olivier Martinez redux. He's been doing those sappy Hollywood romantic comedies every man prays his girlfriend won't pick for a movie date. I think Naomi can handle him."

"He should leave Naomi alone; he's married." A heavy pause in Olivia's voice indicated she'd left her statement unfinished. "To Jade Keane. The Hollywood actress. She gets all the hot psycho chick roles." I thought I caught Kitten muttering, "Which is not a stretch."

"And?"

"She's my cousin."

"Okay. Jade Keane. Olivia Keane. Makes sense."

Kitten straightened up to peer into my face. "Jade Keane…," she repeated, as though I should have understood something significant in that name. I rarely followed young American actresses, being an Audrey Hepburn man myself. Now the occasional Spanish actress, on the other hand… "Ilsa Keane… *Martin* Keane…"

"Ah, that name I recognize. Broadway actor, right? He walks on stage, and they throw an award at him. Takes himself quite seriously. The kind of man they honor every other week on *Inside The Actors Studio*. Isn't he supposed to be practically acting royalty in your country? All the way back to his great great somebody or other in silent films?"

Olivia rubbed her furrowed brow. "Maybe…maybe we're just not as famous here as I feared."

"So you're related to Martin Keane?"

"*Uncle* Martin," she huffed, seeming distressed at my ignorance. "He's been my guardian since I was two. After the car accident? Heartthrob Eric Keane and It Girl starlet wife Alanna Ford killed when their convertible wrapped it-

137

self around a tree two miles from the scene of James Dean's historic crash? Sound familiar at all?"

It did, heartbreakingly familiar. "Yeah," I admitted, finally beginning to grasp what Olivia was trying to say by not saying it. There were certain details of my own life I was just as hesitant to disclose. Yet now it seemed cruel to deny her even a mention of the similar background we shared, and how it was I remembered an obviously seminal event in her life.

"My mother was an entertainer when I was younger," I explained. "She kept up with all the celebrities in America and Europe, just as part of the life. I remember her sitting down in front of the television when the story hit the London news. She said she'd met Eric Keane, that he'd been very charming and introduced her around to everyone important at a film industry party where she first ran into…" I cleared my throat when I realized how that statement ended. "Where she met a lot of famous people." Then, moving on from the topic as quickly as I could, I tilted my head at Olivia and used my fingertips to gently nudge her crystal cat mask up off her face. Freckles on peaches and cream… I liked that her innocence marred her seductiveness at times like this, when she looked at me just so.

After a moment of staring silently back at me, Kitten pulled my mask away as well. It felt like the first time I'd been bare-faced with her in weeks. Recklessly exposed but also relieved, free if only for a few unguarded moments.

"So you're one of the famous Keane clan. I can see why you'd been concerned about the reporter—the embarrassment to your family if the tabloids broke the headline that Eric Keane's daughter was the star of an erotic BDSM revue."

Olivia sighed her breath out hard, blowing back stray

blond strands of hair writhed free from her carefully coiffed updo. She shook her head. "No, I just didn't want Martin to find me."

"Why?" I asked, but my suspicion was already building, as I thought back to the memory of Kitten scrambling away from me on all fours in panic.

"I told you. I'm his ward."

I cocked my brow. "You're twenty-four, Olivia. He doesn't own you."

"No, but he owns everything I own. He has control of my trust fund until I turn thirty-five, and he's been using that to keep me working for Jade since I was sixteen." When the clouded look in my eye conveyed that I didn't quite understand, Olivia continued, "He wouldn't actually allow me to take acting or voice or ballet lessons, but when Ilsa or Jade needed someone to help them rehearse… I ended up picking up knowledge just from being surrounded by movie and theater life all the time." Olivia's hands balled into fists atop her tensed thighs. "I wouldn't have minded being the personal assistant for Ilsa—she's my older cousin. But Martin wanted me working for her younger sister, probably because he knew I couldn't stand Jade. There's something about that man that… that revels in making me unhappy."

"And now Vachon—his son-in-law—shows up here as a guest," I observed thoughtfully. "You think your uncle sent him to look for you? But, really, what are the chances that in all of London, anyone would come to look for you here?"

"If my missing license ended up with that reporter, and he'd decided to follow up on just who I was, he might have contacted the family publicist. Yves even said he was in London on family business."

"So your uncle is obsessive about controlling you, but

you don't think he'd come himself?"

Olivia rolled her eyes. "Long story, but, no, Martin wouldn't travel to London if he could get someone else to go in his place."

"Okay, so what if Vachon figures out you're here? What can he do? Order you home? You've already defied your uncle with the full understanding that you were writing off your trust fund for the next ten years. They've got no leverage to make you do anything."

That idea made Olivia blink at me doubtfully.

I took hold of her chin, waiting patiently for her to meet my gaze. "Are you afraid that after all those years under his thumb, you'd feel you had to go back if he commanded it?"

"A little," she confessed in a heavy breath. "I'd have to know there was something else for me. Something here." Her gaze shifted shyly away from mine. "Someone."

I stopped Kitten as she focused those crystalline green eyes on my lips and started to lean toward me. I knew what she wanted, besides a kiss, and I knew I wasn't prepared to give it to her. Better I didn't. Better I remain her protector, the unassailable Ringmaster, than let myself become... something else. A suitor. A lover with the natural tendency to fuss over her and indulge her when what she required for her own good right then was guidance from a mentor.

Dejection shone in her eyes, deepening soft lines again, and I shook my head. "Don't, Olivia. Don't think about this, any of this, tonight. Go grab one of my t-shirts and get into my bed. I'll make sure nothing disturbs you while you get some sleep."

And she gave me the smallest of smiles, curling only one corner of her mouth. "Not going to join me?"

"No, Kitten." I wasn't going to pretend to myself that I

could lie down next to Olivia and feel her against me and not repeat my previous mistake. Just the thought made my head and chest and groin pound.

I was still nursing a headache and an erection by morning, after dozing uncomfortably all night in that chair, when I slipped quietly out of the room with a mind to collect breakfast for both Olivia and myself. By the time I realized I was still in costume, including face paint, I'd already made it downstairs and knew I was going to get queer looks for it. At the buffet, Thom handed me a folded tabloid instead of a plate.

"You'd better have a look," he told me, and I knew it was bad when I realized he was no longer giving me attitude. His gaze shifted to the other performers scattered throughout the room, gymnasts and acrobats and riggers all chatting and sharing their meal, and I got the distinct impression that they hadn't yet seen what he was showing me.

POSH SEX CIRCUS ENTERTAINS THE WHO'S WHO OF LONDON

As soon as I saw the headline, I flipped the fold on the rag back down. "Let's chat," I told Thom, and we retreated discreetly to his paper-strewn office. I took a few seconds now in private to scan the story, which seemed deliberately vague, promising to name names without actually doing so and providing no photos. Still, the description of the warehouse where the masked BDSM orgies with beautiful submissives from around the world took place was just detailed enough to cause us trouble.

"Distressing, isn't it?" Thom finally interjected, sitting on the single clear spot on his mess of a desk and leaving the folding chair for me. I settled wearily into the seat as he observed, "We're not nearly as debauched as the story claims. I feel we've somehow let ourselves down."

After I let that quip set in, I breathed out a chuckle, unable to do much else.

Having gotten the humor in the situation out of the way, he said, "I'd remind you we got through the problems with police harassment in Istanbul last year fairly unscathed, but the British media *are a whole other story*. We're screwed on the balance of the rent, you know. Either we cut our losses on London and get on our way to Leeds or we have to find a new venue for the balance of this week's shows. Problem is…"

"Yes?"

"We're already getting cancellations. I doubt we'll fill a third of the seats if we stay here, but cutting the London dates short means we have to pay out the guarantees to the vendors. That cuts into the operating capital to set up at the next location."

"That would be about the size of it," I agreed. A tangible silence formed between the admin manager and myself, and I rubbed my fingers over my bleary eyes. "Don't say it, Thom."

"I don't really have to, do I?"

"It's not the only way to dig ourselves out of this."

"True, I suppose." Thom grabbed a calculator and a notebook with the pages practically crawling with his busy handwriting. After he checked figures and jabbed at the calculator buttons in a purposeful flurry, he scribbled some numbers, then a few more. "If Naomi takes a couple of requests and I make a few calls to some clients who are quite fond of Rafe and Griffin, to see what I can book for them, we'll probably be able to make do."

"Probably," I repeated, knowing as well as Thom did, even without checking his math, that *probably* wasn't so much a *possibly* as much as a *hopefully*...a *doubtfully, but maybe*. "I can't believe I'm even considering... No."

"Donovan, don't you think Olivia should actually get to participate in making this decision?"

"She'd say so, but she's from a constitutional republic that thinks it's a democracy, and the Cirque de Plaisir is neither."

"She believes she's one of us now, sir. You want to tell her that's not true? That she doesn't have the same stake in the show that the rest of us do? One private performance, Donovan. *One*. It would make all the difference in this situation."

I directed a momentary glower at Thom and his damnable, sensible arguments. "The top offer is really worth that much?"

"It is."

It physically hurt to swallow the knot of pride and possessiveness lodged in my throat. "Only on the condition that I'm her escort and only I dominate her. The client can watch and make requests on the specific forms of discipline, but that's it."

Thom nodded. "He should be agreeable."

"Fine, yes, do it. Where are we going? Who's the client?"

The manager didn't need to check the details before telling me, "It's over in Lennox Gardens in Knightsbridge with a Mr. Stephen Unwin."

Fucking perfect. I was throwing my submissive to the wolves and delivering her myself.

7

MY HIGH-DRAMA MAGENTA stilettos tapped out a hard, relentless staccato as I strode hurriedly along the wet driveway with Donovan Haigh holding me drawn tight to his flank. The darkness of early evening and the raised hoods of our overcoats hid the fact that we were walking into a lavish three-story in Chandler's Cross with peacock-feathered carnival masks on our faces. Still pinning me to his side, which was fine with me, the Ringmaster sounded the buzzer and nodded his greeting to a silent butler. The man collected our coats without the slightest glimmer of surprise or even interest in his eyes at our appearance. Donovan wore a black formal suit with tails, only the mask and his black leather gloves suggesting he was doing anything more unusual than attending a concert or dinner party. I was another matter.

The brilliantly colored fuck-me heels, complete with

ribbons lacing up my calves, matched the "barely down to there" bondage dress. More magenta ribbon circled my wrists and crisscrossed up my arms to the just above my elbows. The term "fit to be tied" haunted me as I followed along behind my Master across the familiar marble flooring of Finley's posh garden estate. This was the private domain of the man himself, the owner of the most exclusive BDSM sex club in London, maybe all of Britain. And he liked few people well enough to extend the invitation. The last time I'd been here as Gwynne's guest, with a certain young blond lord eyeing me and describing all the things he wanted to do to me, I'd flushed fire red and hidden from him the rest of the night in Finley's library.

Now I was a submissive arriving for my first command performance. How a month had changed me. How meeting Donovan Haigh had changed… everything.

In the chic black and white parlor, the Ringmaster greeted Gwynne at her fashionista best and our slightly-built, balding host. Neither of them wore masks, but there stood Naomi and Rafe in full costume, having arrived shortly before Donovan and me in a separate car.

"I appreciate you being willing to provide playrooms for us, Fin," Haigh told the notoriously reticent and mild-mannered club owner. "For my submissive's first private performance, I just didn't feel comfortable taking her to a strange home I didn't know."

"Good call," Gwynne told him with a nod of approval, then winked at me. "You ready for this?" And all five of the people in the room turned to gauge my reaction.

I nodded. "Uh-huh." Eloquent response, Olivia. I was sure that had inspired boundless confidence, and I tried not to roll my eyes at myself too obviously. After all the talking it had taken to convince Donovan I could do this, I could help dig the circus out of the problems that were (to put it lightly) largely my fault, I didn't want to give him pause now.

Being back in this house, and for this reason, I was expecting the same paralyzing surge of anxiety that had assailed me every time I'd visited Finley's club in my month as a London tourist. Long minutes of chit-chat passed before it occurred to me that I'd endured far more vulnerable and erotic situations—in front of an eager audience, no less—since little Olivia had run away to the circus. For these purposes, I was the Ringmaster's slave, his kitten. The attention that had once unnerved me now sustained me, even when I didn't think I could withstand another night of excruciating desire for the Master who dominated me only for show, only for a paying crowd, never because he looked at me and couldn't help himself. At least I had these moments of protectiveness from him, as I suspected any of his performers would have. At least I could hope—fantasize—that there was some small ember of jealousy in the Ringmaster at having to share me, that a performance like this could set it alight.

The sound of the door buzzer cut through the angst-ridden feedback of my thoughts, and I held my breath and listened as two distinctive male voices exchanged pleasantries while drawing ever nearer. Yves Vachon, dressed in Italian designer wear that bore a hint of gigolo sleaze in the shiny materials and clashing mix of bronze and blue, practically fell upon Naomi like the hungry animal he was. Jade would have castrated him if she'd known. The leggy gymnast just shook her head subtly at Rafe to prevent his intercession while the French fop growled and groped at her. I shud-

146

dered, for her sake, to think what Yves anticipated getting from his command performance, but I trusted that the blond Dom could handle the amorous Frenchman.

When Vachon stepped aside, without warning, there stood Stephen Unwin in the doorway. The lone black wolf who watched and waited, as I thought of him. My client. My Master for the evening, even if the hand that would discipline me would not be his directly. With the two men in such close proximity, I had the chance to note Unwin was a little broader than Haigh and a little older, with coloring that didn't quite match the Ringmaster's but ran true enough that…that I could pretend on the nights I really needed to feel like it was Donovan there fawning over me, desiring me. Stephen wore that same black wolf mask that subtly contrasted with his wavy brown hair. "Kitten," he muttered warmly and smiled.

From the corner of my eye, I saw Donovan stiffen at the address, saw his cheeks go taut and hallow, and I blushed at the impetuous, even impertinent insult I'd done the Ring-master when Stephen had asked what he could call me and I'd given him permission to use Haigh's special endearment. It was an offense committed out of anger and rejection some days ago and put out of mind until now. But really, what would Donovan have had me do differently? Give a client my real name? All of the submissives had stage names, for their safety. Kitten was the only one Donovan had ever given me. I tried not to read anything into Haigh's reaction, too tired of false starts with the man, continual disappointment. No, it was basic possessiveness, I'd have guessed if I had to pinpoint the cause of his displeasure. Just the principle of the matter.

"Sir," Haigh greeted my admirer, and they shook hands

before regarding one another for a long breath, neither apparently inclined to exchanging further niceties.

It was Stephen who balked first at the awkward tension. "May we begin, Monsieur?"

There was a pause, lasting only a fraction of a heartbeat, before Donovan responded, "Of course."

In a surreal procession, Donovan led the way upstairs to a large bedroom with dark wood floors polished to a high sheen and a wide empty space suitable for large pieces of bondage equipment, if so desired. I followed close behind, with Stephen even closer on my heels. I caught my breath but said nothing when he reached out to brush his hand lightly down my spine, the first time he'd ever actually touched me. Inexplicable guilt mixed with the wave of excitement that crested in my stomach at the sensation.

"Please have a seat, sir," Haigh asked of our guest and motioned toward the oversized bed with its pristine white linens. "I must reiterate that you shall instruct me in the manner of discipline you wish me to impose upon my slave, but only I actually lay hands upon her. Are we clear on that point?"

Stephen's full mouth twitched at one corner in an uncomfortable smile at the Ringmaster's enunciation of "my slave," but he nodded. In an expensive mahogany brown suit, Unwin crossed his legs and folded his hands over one thigh, as though making a physical promise to behave. "We are, Monsieur."

"Very well. You mentioned a preference for hard restraint, if I am correct."

And I felt my breath thicken in the back of my throat. Hard restraint. Severe binding. Of course, I trusted Donovan to know what I could take, to understand my limits better than I did, to safeguard me from all physical harm. But there was the matter of coming fully into the moment now and only just realizing what it was going to feel like to have the man I so desired dominating and handling me according to the directions of the man who so ardently desired me.

Stephen nodded and then grew very still, his attention fixed on my face as he said, "Begin by removing her dress, if you would, please."

"You underst—"

He cut Haigh off. "Yes, her underwear will remain… this time. As agreed. I understand."

The contract had neglected no points of negotiation.

Donovan's touch was deft, efficient, and ungentle as he bared my body. Even with pink lace bra and panties, I blushed as furiously as if I were naked. The ardor of Stephen's gaze left me feeling as though there were no barriers between us, like he could touch me with his glance. Half of me wanted to turn and throw myself into Donovan's arms so he would cover me, shelter me. The other half refused to feel guilt or shame at enjoying the appreciation of a handsome, lustful man. And Stephen was just that. The proof of his desire was the blatant bulge pulling his suit pants taut over his groin.

My heartbeat began to thrum in my ears, then pound, then roar as my gaze drifted from my patron's straining erection to the soft-focus gleam of arousal in his grayish eyes. I heard Stephen telling Haigh to make me kneel, to bind my elbows together, to wind stiff strands of rope intricately around and across my flushed breasts to sensitize and tease and torment me. Then to crop me, along my upturned ass and the backs of my thighs, to catch my peaked nipples through the yielding silk of my bra with the leather tab at the end of the stiff rod. Then to pull my head back and make me arch, make me stick out my tongue to lick the leather tool as Donovan slid it back and forth over my lips.

After that, everything took place beyond a dull roll of pulse and panting breath that I hardly recognized as my own. When I was afraid I might sigh out Donovan's name, I began to concentrate on what I knew of Stephen, the confidences and little glimpses of himself he had entrusted to me over a half dozen nights flirting and bantering at the circus after parties.

He was almost forty but he seemed to wear it not in visible years but in the way he carried his experience, a heavy weight but one he bore without stumbling. A successful businessman who owned restaurants and nightclubs and an interest in several resorts. The sort of man with the means and inclination to keep and pamper a submissive. But a man with less flash than Haigh and more of a steady simmer. No running hot and cold, only and always just pleasantly warm.

Whenever I'd heard him chuckle, it was a rough but relaxed grumble vibrating from deep in his chest and the back of his throat. I had a hard time now imagining that sound with Donovan's voice in my ear, telling me to bend forward or spread my legs and display my silk-clad mons. My reaction was sluggish, dreamy, and I felt as woozy as if all the blood had rushed to my head. Blinking, I gazed down at the hands lightly slapping my rigid nipples and my trembling inner thighs and expected to see the square-cut manicure of Stephen's fingernails. I felt instead the light, enticing abrasiveness of Donovan's touch, his skin roughened by working alongside his troupe on rigging and sloughing the tent when it was time to move to the next stop on the Cirque de Plaisir's continual trek.

The fevered pressure of conflicting sensations—conflicting desires—pressed in on me like humid air before a storm, making it hard to catch a deep breath. For playing the perfect submissive, teasing and seducing my patron with my lustful obedience, I was hopeless tonight, too overcome by the experience of being at the mercy of both these men at once.

My head cleared little by little once Haigh stopped bending me this way and that, stopped tying me into positions that arched and opened me and made me want to beg to be fucked. As my pounding heartbeat tired of thumping violently against the inside of my head and slowly receded back into my chest, I became dimly aware that Stephen was speaking directly to me, coaxing me to talk dirty for him and plead for him, to beg to be his. And Donovan was forbidding me to respond, reminding the client that I remained the Ringmaster's slave alone, regardless of the arrangements of the performance.

By the time the orgasm threatening to tear brutally through my sex faded back at last to a dull quiver, resigned to a manageable distance, silence had replaced the heated tones of both men. Cool glares passed between them as Donovan untied me, helped me to my feet, carefully dressed me. Haigh was trying to hurry me from the room when Unwin shot up from the bed and caught me by the hand. Stephen's kiss along the back of my curled fingers demanded I repay the tenderness with a smile and the barest caress of one fingertip along his smooth-shaven, square jaw as I withdrew my hand slowly from his grasp.

"Our contract is concluded," Donovan stated flatly, gathering me by the arm again. I didn't think Haigh expected the subtle but amused smirk Stephen afforded him.

"A pleasure," Unwin insisted, unruffled by the air of competitiveness, "and worth every pound and pence."

In the car on the way back to the warehouse, where the rest of the troupe was busy packing the circus to move, I asked, "Do we have enough now to set us up in Leeds?"

"Quite comfortably," Donovan answered without diverting his gaze from the roadway. "You won't have to do anything like that again."

Staring blindly out the window of Haigh's black sedan, I wasn't sure the reassurance pleased me. Between my clamped thighs, my pussy still burned for penetration, for relentless and passionate use. By Donovan. Always Donovan, my first and greatest weakness. The archetypal lover and Master I couldn't help wanting. But also for Stephen, who would at least have me if I offered. Who caught his breath whenever he saw me. Whose eyes glinted with a passion that Donovan always kept shuttered from me, if he'd felt it at all since that first night.

As he had once threatened, though I didn't think it was conscious or intentional, Haigh sent me to bed without an orgasm. I wouldn't have minded if the sustained arousal had given me good dreams, but I slept fitfully instead and rose and dressed early to get out of the room before my restlessness disturbed Naomi and little ginger blond Piper.

In Thom's empty office, which had been stripped down to the bare essentials prior to our move today, I stared at the digital clock display that said it was five in the morning. That made it nine at night back in Los Angeles. For what that mattered. But it did matter, I realized as I found myself pulling out my international cell to dial one of the few numbers I had committed to memory. She answered on the third ring, in a refined voice much like the cashmere and pearls that were her trademark, in contrast to the alternating trill and shriek that characterized her sister's moods.

"Ilsa, it's Olivia."

After a rush of breath and declarations of relief, my cousin contained herself. "Where are you, Olivia? Are you all right?"

"Fine, Ilsa," I insisted over her theatrically grave tones. "I'm… I'm where I said I'd be, still in Europe."

"Were you really serious then when you emailed that you were working there? Aren't you coming home? Jade has been frantic."

I couldn't suppress a sudden snort. "Why, has her dog been puking on her bedroom carpet again?"

After a moment of quiet on the line, my eldest cousin blew out a slow breath, "Well, I can't say she doesn't deserve that, but this is about you, Olivia." A strange statement, I thought, even coming from Ilsa. Though it was Jade who treated me like Cinderella, Ilsa couldn't help framing my role in the family as an extra, a bit player at best. From this distance, I could finally see that. If we went to dinner to talk about promotional schedules or vacation plans, she never asked or wondered what I liked or where I wanted to go. Always assumed I had no plans, no one I might have been dating. Seldom introduced me to people we encountered in shops or restaurants, unless it was to offer to send me on an errand for someone else.

"I'm just calling to let you know I'm safe," I lied. Truthfully, I needed to hear that time-honored Keane dispassion under the cursory display of obligatory concern. I had concluded long ago that there hadn't been a sincere emotion shared between two Keanes since my grandparents passed away while I was still in grade school. These days I had more

153

meaningful conversations with Thom or Naomi or Rafe about what was for lunch than I could have had about life and death matters with Ilsa or Jade.

And then I got down to business. "How mad is Uncle Martin?"

"Not... not really mad," Ilsa insisted, proving she couldn't improvise any better than I could. She was always one to have me standing just outside the shot feeding her forgotten lines. "He's concerned you've let the wrong people influence you. I mean, people who know you have a trust fund."

Because money was the only thing that made me interesting. God, but this call really was just the thing I needed to help me reaffirm my conviction I'd done the right thing running away.

Running away to the circus and Donovan Haigh. Maybe he didn't want me the way I wanted him, but I knew he'd at least protect me and make me a part of something bigger, like someone who mattered. An equal. Which was an odd way to think about being the Ringmaster's slave. It was no less true for being a contradiction.

"Listen, I have to go now, Ilsa. Take care of yourself." *Don't say hi to Jade for me.*

"Wait, Olivia. If...if you're still anywhere near London, take down this number."

"Why?"

"It's my father's hotel. If you need him—"

"It's what?" I snapped, vaguely aware I'd barked loud enough to wake anyone sleeping in any of the adjacent rooms. "He's not... He's not in London." It wasn't a question or even a plea. I just wasn't going to have it. *Martin could not be here.* Before I'd finished declaring this to myself,

I'd already started hyperventilating and jabbed at the button to end the call with Ilsa.

With tears in my eyes, my heart skipping and pulsating wildly in my chest, I paced a short path back and forth out on the main warehouse floor. A couple of times I almost gave in to the urge to march up to Donovan's room and cry to him about Martin. Warn him there would be trouble. Beg him to make me feel like it was all going to be fine anyway. Demand that he hold me. But I refused to indulge either my dread or my impatience. I could wait for Donovan to come downstairs with everyone for the quick continental breakfast Thom had told me was traditional on the day of a move. Until then, I just had to keep a firm grip on myself.

Only that wasn't how it worked out when Donovan, clad in a plain chambray shirt and jeans for sloughing the show, came downstairs engrossed in conversation with Griffin. As soon as the American gymnast stepped away, Naomi needed to ask a dozen questions about the new Leeds location. And I couldn't interrupt, not after seeing the worry on the strawberry blonde's face, when Piper insisted she needed to talk to Haigh about that missing passport and how anxious the whole issue with the tabloids had made her and how she was thinking maybe it was time for her to take a few weeks of vacation to sort out how she was feeling about all this.

When it was just Donovan and Thom, I pressed forward to insert myself into their conversation. But before I could cut in, the admin manager—looking hangdog—slid a folded newspaper from the back pocket of his jeans and handed it to our boss. I faltered, open-mouthed and about ready to tell Donovan I had an important matter to address with him, when Haigh's brow creased with a stricken look that I just…wouldn't have expected from him. Peering over his arm to snoop, I saw the morning headline centered over a grainy long-range photograph of Donovan himself obviously taken when he'd been out and about in street clothes.

SEX CIRCUS MASTERMIND IS SON OF INFAMOUS BURLESQUE QUEEN BY IRISH ACTOR TEAGUE

Stunned, disbelieving, I skimmed the first few paragraphs thinking the headline must have been misleading, but it just got worse. The reporter named everyone from Donovan to his mother, Brigitte Rose, now Brigitte Rose Somerset—Lady Somerset, who was such a grand social fixture in Leeds that the papers often referred to the silver-haired beauty as the White Rose of Yorkshire. And, of course, the story quoted "trusted sources" with details of a liaison between the one-time dancer and actor Quillan Teague that had supposedly resulted in the birth of her only son and the eventual end of her marriage to long-time manager George Haigh.

What to say…? Donovan stared at the newsprint without appearing to breathe. Then he blinked hard and roused himself from whatever thoughts he held close and private, but I still saw the gleam of bewilderment and hesitancy in his forlorn blue eyes as he glanced my way.

Before I could decide how and even whether to comfort him—would that just be a personal trespass, with the discord there had been between us?—Haigh handed the paper off again to Thom but focused on me. "I need your help, Olivia. Things are a mess with the move, and that story is going to throw some of the people around here into a panic. I need to take Thom with me to make some pointed inquires about these stories, and I need you to keep everything and everyone on track here."

It almost surprised me to be able to say, "I can do that, gladly," and really mean it. I'd managed Jade Keane and her multiple households, so I knew I could do as Donovan asked. And even more importantly, it gave me a way to help him through this, put to rest one of his many concerns, contribute something to the troupe after I'd set this whole mess in motion with one thoughtless decision my very first night with the circus. "You don't have to worry about anything going on here, sir. Go do what you need to do."

And yet watching Donovan go, as he strode off in a rush with Thom, made my chest hurt. I hurt for him. I hurt to be with him. I hurt that we didn't have the kind of relationship that would have made me the person he kept by his side, the person comforting him when no one else could see. I consoled myself that I had my part to play, my supporting role, and it needed my attention. After all, by now I was professional-grade support staff, designed that way by both fate and family. This time, at least, I was willing.

The primary order of business was packing up the lorries and cars and getting everyone on the road before they started to dwell on the possible consequences of a media scandal. But neither business nor personal crises would wait for us to make the four- or five-hour drive north to Leeds. Word of the newest tabloid headline seeped into the bustle of activity, sowing doubt and concern and slowing the work as people mulled to whisper and wonder with each other. The business mobile Thom had entrusted to me rang constantly, usually with clients asking to speak directly to Donovan, and sometimes with vendors notifying us that they would have to cancel their agreement to partner with the Cirque de Plaisir for the next round of shows. Piper repeatedly tried to interject, insisting she needed to speak to me, but I had to keep waving her off to deal with one more vendor, one more client.

When the heavily muscled Griffin came to stand by me where I was gesturing wildly to an imaginary image of the person arguing with me on the phone, I just wanted a little bit of good news. Finally snapping the damn phone closed, I sighed, "Please tell me we're all loaded and ready to pull out."

He nodded somberly. "We are."

"Thank God."

"But Piper's gone."

I perked one brow at him, unable...unwilling to comprehend. "Gone?"

"She just quit. The stolen passport, and the security breaches, and new scandals breaking in the papers day by day..." Griffin shrugged. "Having Donovan disappear on us right now was more than she could take."

"Donovan did *not* just take off," I protested, throwing up my hands. "Shit, I should have talked to her when she needed me. Everything I do here just makes matters worse. God, I'm sorry, Griffin. I can't apologize enough. Your partner..."

With his long brown hair gathered back with a band at the nape of his neck, I could see Griffin's broad, friendly face take on an edge of sympathy...for me. "No, no, Olivia. Don't do that to yourself. This has been coming on with Piper for more than a couple of weeks. She's tired of the constant travel and always hiding behind masks and stage names. Yeah, that means I have to find a new partner—

hopefully one who is more excited to be here with us. It's not like Piper and I were, you know…" He shrugged again.

Which answered an unasked question. Just as the damn business mobile rang again. What now? Another spooked client looking for the personal reassurance of the Ringmaster himself? One more vendor backing out on us? Or was it too much to hope it might have been Donovan checking in on our progress, maybe with an update of his own?

"Stephen Unwin calling for Thom."

I choked at the sound that gruff voice, so comforting to hear just then but so unexpected. With my tone calm and flat, I didn't think Stephen would recognize he was speaking to me. "Thom is unavailable at this time, Mr. Unwin. Could I take a message for him?"

"Please, yes. He arranged for a command performance on my behalf last evening, and I'd like to inquire about another with the same young lady as soon as conveniently possible."

My stomach spun and bobbed inside me at the mention of our meeting last night. The thought of the intimate and vulnerable and dirty position I'd been in at his request and direction and delight made me lightheaded with… I couldn't decide. Nausea? Embarrassment? Eagerness? God, but it wasn't the time for this.

Beginning to gather up my overnight bag and duffle, the only personal items I had that I still needed to pack into one of the vehicles, I caught myself shaking my head as though Stephen could see it. "I'm sorry, Mr. Unwin, but that won't be possible. Our stay in London has concluded. We leave today."

"What? Wait. No," he rushed to argue, and the distress in his voice took me by surprise. "I need to see her again.

Surely that's not so difficult. Where's the next stop? I'll come there."

"I… I'm sorry, sir, I'm not at liberty to disclose the new location," I told him, then put my hand over my mouth so he wouldn't hear my quickening breath, and so no one here would see the look on my face—this confusing mixture of affection after hearing how desperate Stephen was to see me, the sickening guilt of wondering if I'd let things get too serious with him, and the dejection of seeing in someone else the same unanswered longing I felt every minute that Donovan Haigh was on my mind.

I had to wonder what Stephen heard in my voice, because he paused and then asked, "Kitten, is this you?"

The panic of being recognized made me stumble for a response. "Stephen, I… We're leaving. It's almost time to go."

"Don't. Come on, don't just… tell me you're leaving and hang up. I want to see you. And I would like to think you want to see me."

"There's no time."

"There is," he insisted, and he engaged all the powers of that low voice and the years he'd been honing his persuasive skills. "I'll play by the rules. A command performance. And I will pay."

"Stephen, our lorries are literally pulling out of the lot right now as I'm watching them. There's no way…"

"Half again the payment for last night. You bring whoever you feel you need to as the Dom or bodyguard or chaperone, whatever."

Half *again* the largest payment ever offered for a private performance?

And yet…Donovan had said the financial situation

was in hand now; we didn't need me to take another appointment. Assuming he'd been completely honest with me, hadn't glossed over the details. But *half again…*?

"Now, Kitten," Stephen insisted, his timbre taking on the smooth, calm command of a man comfortable with employing his dominant tendencies. When I hesitated, he told me to hold the line, and the business cell beeped with an incoming notification. "Check that," he said. "It will be the confirmation of the fund transfer. Paid in full. The Lennox Gardens address, Kitten. I'll expect you within the hour."

Feeling distinctly lost, I stood in the doorway of the warehouse, at the very same loading gate I'd used the day Gwynne had introduced me to the Cirque de Plaisir. Before I'd learned, or even imagined, how infatuated *or obsessed* I could become with a man like the Ringmaster, and how quickly. Before I'd realized the utterly improbable experience of becoming the submissive darling of the underground London BDSM scene. Before I'd become subtly but increasingly dependent on the adoration of one man—or many—to nurse me through the rejection I suffered from another.

I shook my head to get myself focused. What were the facts at hand? Donovan trusted me to get the troupe out of this media glare and on its way to Leeds, while Stephen was expecting… "Stupid idea," I swore to myself even as I glanced down twice, quickly, at the intimidating string of numbers depicted in the transfer confirmation. "Stupid to even consider…" Even if the money undoubtedly would have come in handy for us all right now. "Donovan would throttle me."

"You? Never." It was Rafe's voice. The blond Dom walked around from behind me, his enormous travel pack balanced on his shoulder like it weighed nothing. I had to admire that about Rafe and Griffin, and to a lesser extent even Donovan and Thom despite their less demanding duties. No one was going to find a more toned, pumped, sculpted group of men anywhere. "Looks like we're the last ones out, love. You ready to go?"

I started to nod, then gripped the mobile a little tighter in my hand. Still unable to will myself to start walking toward the cars, and gnawing my lip, I stared down at the little cell screen. At a loss to make this decision on my own, I held up the phone for Rafe to see.

His eyes widened. "Oh, for fuck sake. For that, Donovan can throttle me. Let's do this."

8

THE LEEDS LOCATION was just outside the city in an abandoned school with a large gymnasium. That didn't provide quite the same cachet that a spruced-up warehouse did, especially when anything even vaguely steampunk increased the chic quotient exponentially these days. At this kind of notice, though, I'd take what I could get.

By the time Thom and I drove into the school compound after a sixteen-hour day of personal visits to every London contact I had of any influence, nightfall had already set in. No way to assess if the new venue was going to take more trouble in clean-up than it was worth in cost, convenience, and privacy until we could get right up to it and look around. But I did like the old brick facades and all the additional buildings, potentially offering more privacy than our usual accommodations would.

I could still remember the first year of the circus, when I was a Ringmaster presiding over just ten of the wildest, most innovative performance artists working the small nightclub scene. When we slept five to a one-bed camper with pieces of costumes hanging everywhere. And when the fee for a command performance was a pint at the local pub.

If anyone had told me then that, in five years' time, I was going to have to deal with vendor guarantees, tabloid reporters, contracts on thousand-seat venues, and the details of my parentage reduced to lurid headlines… I might have thought it sounded fun. Because twenty-five-year-old men with virtually no one counting on them and only a couple of hundred quid to lose can afford to be idiots.

"Enough," Thom insisted from the driver's seat and reached over to stop me tapping this morning's folded up newspaper against my thigh.

"Sorry, hadn't realized. Long day, you know?"

"Yeah," he agreed blandly, "I think I do."

"Anxious to see how much set-up they got done without us." Anxious to see what kind of damage the tabloid scandal was doing to morale, especially among my people with family members who didn't know anything about the Cirque de Plaisir or their loved one's involvement in it.

"I'm sure Olivia has her eye on things."

"Uh-huh," I agreed, though even I thought it came off grudging and brusque, not because I doubted her but because… maybe I was still irritated with that damn command performance she'd taken with the wolfish suitor who'd kissed her hand. She'd looked pretty damn giddy when he'd done that. Like she did when I touched her. But, of course, I already knew my little kitten was an adoration whore. The more applause, the more flattery, the more gifts, the more

164

flirtation, the better.

For starting out so quiet and uncertain, Olivia certainly had blossomed into a seductress who got what she wanted. Except for me. Assuming I could really say she wanted me, not just another admirer, *any other admirer*.

Indeed, she was a girl just like my dear sweet Mum, and that was saying something I'd rather not have. Brigitte had dragged me around the world like one of her props, usually hurrying us on to the next big show before I could get to know any of the people surrounding us and sometimes as I was only just beginning to connect with someone—a mentor or even a girlfriend.

When we parked along a fractured concrete path, tall grass fringing the pavement, I felt a suggestion of guilt for my thoughts, as Olivia greeted us straight away with extra torchlights.

"Ah, bless, love," Thom told her as he grabbed one of the flashlights. "I'd rather not break an ankle tripping over rusty playground equipment in the dark."

"Well, honestly, yeah, there's not much light out here," she admitted as we three strode toward the hulking blackness that was the enormous athletic hall. "We'll have to go heavy on the usual string lights and maybe add a few battery-powered lanterns, but I think you'll find it's worth the trouble. Several of us were even batting around ideas for attractions to put in some of the other, smaller buildings. The optimism level is actually kind of high right now."

I sighed out an entire day's worth of frustration. "I'm not bothered hearing some good news for a change today."

But then her step faltered. "Not all good. About half the Leeds vendors have pulled out. Ticket sales are at half capacity—and Piper quit."

Until Olivia had added that last part, a string of curses had been building in my throat. Afterward, well, I guessed I didn't really have anything to say to that. Tumbling across four continents over her three years with the Cirque de Plaisir… two years with Griffin as her partner for some exquisitely erotic Chinese pole routines that no one would ever forget or repeat… then one month of bad luck in London, and the little Scottish sprite was on her way back to her mother's cottage outside Edinburgh, if I knew Piper. Given the amount of whiskey the old woman kept under the kitchen sink, I thought the trip sounded like a good idea myself.

Thom and I put our rucksacks down just inside the long empty hall, ringed three-fourths of the way around with a balcony that did add a nice visual impact and offer new possibilities for simultaneous acts. It needed a scrubbing and a couple of layers of paint scraped away, but we had the manpower. As with our first night anywhere, crates and duffle bags acted as the only furniture and cushions, all draped in sweaty clothes and tired bodies.

While the admin manager went to find us dinner, I caught repeated glimpses of my assistant hovering just within my peripheral vision. She wanted something. Attention, maybe. With all her London admirers left behind, Kitten would have to rebuild her adoring audience. Sad to say, I had every faith she would.

I stopped rummaging through the outer pockets of the pack, where I was sure I'd secreted a flask of Talisker whisky, and turned to face the little blonde. "Olivia? You want something?"

"I do." Her hands nervously twisted the tail of the thin white pullover that brought out the color in her cheeks and further brightened her green eyes, not that I noticed, oh no. Olivia sighed and stepped closer. I instantly wished she hadn't. Raspberry vanilla cotton candy. A smack in the face after this day. She still smelled of…of surprisingly promising auditions, sable-trimmed bustiers, and innocence. And we'd left all that back in London, under a spirit-crushing flurry of tabloid bullshit. "I need to say I'm sorry," she said.

"Pardon? What are you talking about?" Then I squeezed my eyes shut and rubbed them hard. "Christ, not about that headline this morning, please. I'd like to pretend no one I know is going to stare at me and squint and look for the Teague resemblance. Or tell me how sad they are to read my mother was an erotic dancer who ended up in bed with the wrong drunken Irishman. I'm not torn up about it, not even a little. It certainly wasn't a boring life learning to drink shots at fourteen with the band in the oldest private bur-lesque club in New Orleans, or losing my virginity to two gorgeous Spanish dancers in a Madrid dressing room. And the baccarat games between me and the French countess who threw the most decadent parties in Paris to introduce my mother to the intellectual elite were *fucking legendary.* So…."

When I finally pried my eyes open again, Olivia was blinking at me like I'd just waved a strobe light in her face.

"I meant Piper. I want to say I'm sorry for Piper leaving. If I'd been able to keep things together a little better this morning…."

The bitter chuckle that knotted up my throat tore at my voice from the inside. "No," I managed to mutter after sus-tained effort. "No, that wasn't you, Olivia. Everything that drove Piper away—safety issues, security, press—all went back to me not having the situation in hand."

"You're going to take the responsibility for me letting

that Walker fellow get our scent, then?" she asked blandly. It was a pleasant surprise she seemed reluctant to accept my reasoning. I knew plenty of women who, in her place, would have told me not to be so hard on myself even while letting the blame rest with me. Both my mother and Evi came to mind.

Behind the defense of my folded arms, I nodded. "By extension, I was responsible. I should have kept a closer eye on you. I am the Ringmaster of the Cirque de Plaisir. It's my job to be a controlling bastard who knows what all my people are doing and tells them when and how to do it."

From behind Kitten, Thom grumbled, "Speaking of…" He was staring at the business mobile we'd left with Olivia, with his nose scrunched in a sign that he didn't understand whatever he was looking at.

My assistant snatched the phone from the startled manager. "Not tonight, Thom," she insisted with a fair amount of irritation sharpening her tone and her reflexes. "You two have been out all day. Get something to eat and find someplace you want to set up your bedroll. You and I can sit down together tomorrow, Thom, specifically so we can talk about how I handled things today."

"Smashing idea," I agreed. "Leave me out of it."

With no care for dinner, unless I could find that whiskey flask, I dragged my rucksack behind a set of folding wooden bleachers on the far side of the gym. On my way, I passed Naomi and Rafe where they sat cross-legged on a sleeping bag. From their gestures, I'd have guessed they were discussing floor routines. From the overly unconcerned expression the Dom adopted, along with the telltale stiffening of Naomi's shoulders, I suspected that wasn't their only topic of conversation. In the morning, after some sleep, I'd decide if I cared to look into whatever they were hiding from me.

I had spread out a sleeping bag, not bothering to unzip or climb into it, and pulled off my shirt to settle down in just my jeans. That was when I spied Kitten again as she leaned around the bleachers. Wondering if she'd just go away and leave me to my mood, I didn't acknowledge her as I stretched out, turned away from her onto my side, struggled to get comfortable, rolled back. She was still there, so I sat up. "Another apology?"

Olivia took that as an invitation—which it wasn't—to slip around the wooden barrier and sit on the floor beside my bedroll. "It was busy today," she told me, as her gaze explored the many snaps and zippers of my pack and its overflowing contents, instead of focusing on me. Which meant she was making her way toward a subject she didn't want to bring up straight away.

I wanted her to get to the point before I gave in to the reckless impulse to jerk her into my lap and make out with her. Not just kiss her but run my hands up under that sweater to knead the yielding curves of her breasts while she trembled for me, to suck the lobe of her ear and rub the inseam of her tight jeans, ideally while she let her fingers roam along my bare shoulders and the bulge of my pecs before grabbing my ass through my pants. All the things a boss didn't do to his assistant, a gentleman didn't inflict on a woman under his protection. Things I couldn't do if I were serious about all those rules of mine and remembering what it meant to be the Ringmaster with everything under control, the way it had been before I'd become infatuated with an innocent who was so unlike….

Wow. A lot of memories came attached to those feelings when I finally hauled them up out of the subconscious murk.

An innocent so unlike the pretty Spanish dancing girls and jet-set countesses, cabaret singers and artists' models, who were all there one day and gone the next, always following the spotlight and the party. None of whom I had thought much about in the five years I'd been building the Cirque de Plaisir, forging a reputation, bringing in the best performers, and making a lasting whole out of all those parts. Christ, how goddamn psychologically acute of me, psychoanalyzing myself now. I'd have rather had the whiskey to put myself to sleep.

"Busy today?" I repeated, struggling not to laugh at how tired I was after spending all day trying to determine who among my most trusted associates was selling me and my troupe out to the fucking press. Who I had misjudged. Who I had brought into my inner circle at the peril of the people who depended on me not to be wrong about that kind of thing.

Part of me said I shouldn't have been surprised—look how wrong I'd been about Kitten. And part of me said I wasn't wrong at all about her. I thought that was probably the part that still wanted to fuck Olivia, feel her cling to me, hear my name on her lips like it meant something to her.

"Busy, but you handled what you needed to, it seems," I told her.

Surely a modicum of praise wouldn't have done any harm, so long as I watched my gut instinct to cloister and coddling her. To put her on a pedestal only to have the next bloke come along and help her down at my expense.

Olivia's eyes lingered over a slow study of my face, particularly my mouth, making it so painfully tempting to lick my lips that I had to turn my head and chuckle be-

170

hind a fake cough and, yes, run my tongue quickly around my mouth. I had to wonder if my expressions sometimes hinted at the thoughts behind them. She seemed guarded as she said, "Obviously, there was a lot to do to get the move going and then start the set-up here with you and Thom occupied." She avoided direct eye contact until she added, "But it's something I think I can pick up as you need me to. So..." She shrugged. "So you know there's someone who'll look after this kind of stuff when you can't be here."

Unprepared for her again, I thought as I realized what Kitten was saying, only slowly and cautiously grasping that she was trying to tell me she'd help me keep this all together when I needed someone to be where I couldn't. Even on days like this. Even behind the scenes. Even when there would be no spotlight and no admirers and no opening night bouquets involved.

In true Kitten style, Olivia had me feeling like an arse again.

"Hey," I whispered, putting on a small grin for her, the best I could manage under the circumstances, "enough care-taking for one night, okay? Go get some rest so I can put you to work in the morning." And this finally got a nod and a smile before she left me to myself, walled off in my corner.

"Damn," I said aloud once I was alone. Emotionally disarmed by a freckled blond California girl, a kitten who tiptoed around topics and brushed up against them and mewed until she got her point across in a way I couldn't defend myself against because I couldn't see it coming. Then, next thing I knew, she had me sitting here believing she might actually have been invested in this endeavor and what it meant to me, for what she could put into it as much as what she might get out of it.

It posed an interesting set of questions—like what she'd do if I wanted her to step away from performing because I planned on taking her as my actual submissive. It was a theoretical consideration, practically a rhetorical exercise, as I'd never done so with anyone before. Never even imagined what it would be like. Was that fair, though, to a woman who loved the spotlight?

No, that wasn't even the right question to ask. I uncurled my body to lie back on the sleeping bag, hands tucked behind my head, and looked hard at the real issue. Was it fair to pull a woman—Olivia—out of the spotlight when it was the sun that made her blossom?

Back in London, Kitten had learned to trust in her ability to read an audience. She'd learned she had a right to her sexuality, to enjoy wielding the influence of lust and fantasy. She'd even learned that she could upstage her Ringmaster, didn't have to play supporting actress to anyone unless she wanted to. All between arguments with me, of course.

In hindsight, I had to wonder if the power struggles between us had been necessary. Useful? Counterproductive? The stronger my insistence that Olivia remain my unproven innocent, the more jaded she became. Would she have fled my direction if I hadn't chased her at every deviation?

Something I'd have to think about, I decided. Something to digest, maybe a little at a time. A little every day. Every day. Analyzing everything that went wrong in London while we rebuilt in the Yorkshire countryside. Until it was time to raise the striped tent again, to paint our faces and assume our roles, and to ask what to do differently in a different city.

So in Leeds, I stepped back to watch Olivia charm a new audience. And damn if she wasn't so much more deliberate about it when I wasn't yanking back on her chain all the time. She was a brat when I wanted a brat and a kitten when I wanted a pet, and the soft edge returned that I had feared no experienced submissive could regain once lost.

One week passed without contending with my assistant. Two weeks with no new headlines about the sex circus mastermind. Three weeks of such strong ticket sales that it *almost* made up for London and had me seriously considering whether I wanted to move us on to Amsterdam or try something we'd never done before—giving ourselves two or three months to play with the particular design of a venue, enjoy the area, maybe even eat at the same restaurant twice.

The calm was poised to last forever, which was when it didn't.

Following a perfectly good performance, amid an after party abuzz with color and light and every possible degree of seduction lavishly displayed along the gymnasium balcony, a black wolf stalked into my view.

Through the crush of beautiful people in fantastical costumes, I kept my gaze steady on the familiar face, familiar mask, as the back of my neck tightened. Out of an abundance of both caution and potential temper, I gingerly deposited my champagne glass on the next glinting silver serving tray that passed within my reach. "Thom."

My manager was standing almost back-to-back with me. He leaned toward me when I beckoned, but he resisted having to turn from charming a certain footballer who'd been in the audience and the after party five straight nights in a row. A little obvious, that, but Thom liked the easy catches. "Only, if it's important, sir, please. No recreational cockblocking."

"How did Stephen Unwin get an invitation to a Leeds

performance?"

A groaning sigh sounded from behind me, followed by a polite request that he be excused for just a few minutes, before Thom stepped up beside me. He was glaring in the same direction.

"I have no fucking idea how he found us or got in tonight, sir," Thom answered with a level of disgust in his voice that I rarely heard from him in regard to anything and that, frankly, confused me coming from my numbers man.

"So you didn't invite him from London in hopes he'd make some more obscenely large offers for command performances by my submissive?"

"Actually, sir, after the last few sums he proposed to get her back to London, I thought it might be better to preserve the distance between the man in the wolf mask and your kitten. I have my doubts about his…"

I raised my brow. "Liquidity?"

Thom huffed in offence. "Mental stability." And it was so true that I had always appreciated Thom as a keen judge of character, providing as there was no personal sexual attraction involved.

"Ah, I believe the gentleman in the wolf mask has seen us and would like to say hello."

I consciously loosened the curl of my fingers as my hands hung at my sides, to prevent myself from greeting the man with clenched fist. For once I was glad Olivia had disappeared behind a wall of flirtatious followers, not to surface for an hour or two, usually. Unwin's purposeful stride through the crowd's otherwise unhurried mingle and mull suggested I might have been gearing up to get the fight I'd been anticipating since that night I'd had to tell him I took issue with him demanding vows of love and ownership from

Kitten during a standard private performance. I wouldn't court a violent outburst here, I decided quickly. Better our confrontation not happen in the middle of an after party, no matter the personal satisfaction it might have provided me.

In light of the man's behavior the night of the private performance, I would have forbidden any more bookings for dear Stephen had we not left London the next day, making it a moot point. Of course, the vast majority of our patrons received invitations only when we were in residence in their area, so it *shouldn't* have been an issue while we were staying in Leeds. And if nothing else it was an invaluable exercise in setting and maintaining professional boundaries—and weeding out those individuals who couldn't abide them.

"Monsieur." Stephen's address was directed toward me while his gaze ranged everywhere but. Looking for Olivia? When he had frequented the London performances just a few weeks before, I hadn't recalled him having such an anxious demeanor, tugging on his suit cuffs and shifting his shoulders as though uncomfortable with the fit of his jacket. It was hard to decide with a man whose build tended to fill out more in the stomach and chest as he matured, something like the physique of an American footballer, but I might have said Unwin's clothing fit a tad loose, as though he'd had a sudden recent weight loss.

"Sir," I responded, still watching him carefully. "I am surprised to run into you so far from home. How is it you find yourself in Leeds? As the guest of a local patron, perhaps?" One I wanted stricken off our client list. After that business with the tabloids, trust was a touchstone issue with me. Even the most established clients had to clear their guests at least three days before attending a performance now.

Unwin's smile was weary and brief, as he shrugged and tried to deflect the inquiry with a chuckle. "Hardly matters, does it?"

"Quite a bit, actually," Thom corrected him. If I was studying Unwin, my manager was dissecting him, noting every detail of behavior, appearance, and inflection while returning no feedback at all. "Who invited you?"

Waving his hand, which shook so slightly that it was hardly noticeable, our after party crasher ignored the question again. "I do have a matter of some importance I wanted to discuss with you, Monsieur Ringmaster," Stephen insisted as his tone spiked with controlled irritation. "You don't seem to be receiving my correspondence about a command performance I have been looking forward to arranging for some weeks now."

"We have received your requests, sir," I assured him politely, "but we cannot accommodate you."

Several seconds after this response, the gentleman was still staring at me blankly, as though he hadn't understood me or perhaps simply could not believe me. And at this point, I found his manner so erratic and anxious that the possessive, competitive rancor I bore toward him over his past behavior toward Olivia faded from a desire to beat this obsession out him to hoping I could have him escorted gently out before he came apart at the twitchy, teary seams.

I waved Rafe over. "I believe the gentleman is not feeling himself. Please see to it he gets back to his car safely."

This brought a reaction from our guest at last, Unwin's gray eyes blinking rapidly at me from behind the wolf mask. "Don't be ridiculous. I'm fine. I only wish to make a perfectly reasonable business agreement with you. Stop being difficult about this."

"Sir—" Rafe began lightly and reached for the man's sleeve.

Unwin jerked away and stared incredulously at the blond Dom and then at me. "Are you…? Are you keeping her from me? She *wants* to see me, and you know it."

I was feeling less sympathetic as Stephen grew more agitated. Nothing dampened a party faster than rising tempers, including my own. In that spirit, I maintained a level tone and restrained myself from advancing on the man, but I also wanted to be done with him. "I'm afraid not, sir. She doesn't speak of you. It was a single private appearance that you paid for and she performed. It was business, and that business has been concluded."

This got a snort from the wolfish stalker, as I was starting to think of him. The urge to punch him was coming back hard and fast.

"One time?" he spat back at me. "You think it was only one time? She didn't tell you she came to me without you, then. That's very interesting, don't you think, Monsieur?"

I'd have discounted this wild assertion off-hand had Rafe not seized Unwin so abruptly and practically frothed, "Shut your fucking mouth," into the man's reddening face.

"Rafe?" I asked.

When the blond acrobat finally looked at me, it was sidelong and guarded, his jaw clenched. And he was still holding Stephen tight by the jacket.

"Tell him," Unwin said. He was looking at and talking to Rafe. "You know. You were there. Why don't you tell your Monsieur Ringmaster she was with me?" Then his gleaming eyes shifted my direction again. "Lennox Gardens. She came with your man here. And she didn't tell you. She didn't want you to ruin her time with me."

When I started forward, with leisurely steps, Thom cursed lightly. I heard him call for Griffin, and I assumed that the cautioning hand I felt laid gently on my shoulder from behind a second later belonged to the muscular American gymnast. I leaned toward Unwin, not much, not right up into his face. That would have been difficult with Rafe still manhandling him.

"You're close to her then, are you, Mr. Unwin?" I muttered, my polite smile anything but friendly. He nodded, of course. I just couldn't decide if he was *completely* delusional. "You and *my* submissive?" He snorted derisively and lifted his chin in challenge. "Then you know, don't you? Just like I do?" I watched his mouth wrinkle into a frown as he tried to understand what I was talking about. "Prove you're telling me the truth, sir. *Say her name.*"

Just a moment earlier, the black wolf was tensed and anxious, as he jostled Rafe. Now I watched his shoulders relax as a thoughtful look passed over his face. Then they sagged as realization drained his bravado.

"You don't know it," I said, each word clear, smooth, perfect, irrefutable. There it was. The inevitable end of Mr. Unwin's trip to the circus.

And yet… And yet there was still a hard, bitter line to Stephen's mouth that said he *believed*. Rafe's hold on him had loosened enough that the man mirrored my gesture and leaned just an inch closer to me.

He whispered, "Left breast, below and left of the nipple. A strawberry birthmark the size of perfect pound coin."

I knew Rafe had heard this and that it meant something to him when he let go of Unwin and simply shoved the man away in an unspoken command that the uninvited guest leave now, just *be gone*. With an inexplicably satisfied grin, Unwin shuffled back, still watching my face, waiting. Griffin stepped around me, hands displayed as he urged Stephen to turn, to keep going. I remained there with Rafe and Thom, certain that last exchange did not mean what Unwin wanted me to think it did. But Rafe wouldn't look at me. When I glanced toward Thom to see if he found the blond Dom's behavior as peculiar as I did…Thom wouldn't hold my gaze, either.

9

THE AFTER PARTY was winding down like the flush of a fine glass of wine that relaxed me but never got me drunk— no sudden hangover. The crowd thinned little by little as people who had sipped good champagne and nibbled good food and laughed in good company wandered arm in arm into the night with their fill of memories. Naomi and Rafe and Griffin were all spending those last few minutes wishing goodnight to favored patrons. And I was just making a final circuit of the balcony to smile and nod to regular guests as they gathered their coats.

This was one of my favorite moments of any perfor-mance day, the minutes between the after party and... a good night's sleep, or pizza and beer with Naomi and Rafe, or a coffee and bullshit session with Thom. When I was very lucky, Thom would make some extravagant snack from completely improbable ingredients I would have bet he picked at random from the pantry. When I was very *very* lucky, I ended up alone with Donovan.

Tonight, I took my time making my way down the balcony stairs, with the heavy train of my red satin couture dress fanned dramatically behind me. In the front, the hem didn't quite hit mid-thigh, baring just about all the leg I had. When I walked, even Donovan paused to appreciate the red stockings with the ornate lace appliqué.

Haigh was ushering the last guest out the double-door entryway of our repurposed gymnasium as I stepped up not quite next to him and waited. It was hard to keep my eyes—and dirty mind—off him in the new costume, an elegant black suit with a vaguely Victorian cut but with a white linen shirt left open to reveal his chest. Arcane symbols painted in gold scrolled under his collarbone and between his pecs right down to the waistband of his pants and the base of that delectable V of muscles along his groin. The new mask was red, like mine, and matched the single red feather mixed into the band around his top hat.

This pause, right before it was down to just us two, was always electrical and anxious for me. Especially with the way things had changed between the Ringmaster and his assistant over our weeks in Leeds. It was because I'd finally shown him I was part of this troupe, I thought to myself with a subtle nod. I had worked longer hours than anyone but Thom and Donovan himself getting us back on our feet here. He had to realize now that I was in this for the long haul.

Whether that meant anything more to Donovan...I couldn't have said just yet. We didn't have the huge rows anymore during rehearsal. He didn't have to pull me out of the after parties anymore to scold me. But it also wasn't like he'd torn up page three and taken to ravishing me every night or made me his real-life submissive. I still hoped, of course, but the fact that I was just holding that hope instead of clinging to it helped balance me, helped me separate fantasy and reality, and relieved me of the need to immerse myself in the false warmth of adoration and praise and lavish gifts. Usually.

My thoughts stilled instantly when Haigh turned from the now-locked doors and stood just in front of me. I held my breath. And there it was, that perfect moment of stillness as we lingered close, not saying anything, just kind of being there together. I loved it best when it lasted a really long time, when we occupied ourselves with casual conversation and not much of anything else, or when we stood at the large windows upstairs and looked out at the starry night. Mindless chit-chat and trivial busy work had never made me feel so peaceful. It mattered most that I was just within his orbit, that space around him that filled with his presence and let me feel him without touching him.

Tonight, though, Donovan broke routine. There was something about his smile, vague and a little mysterious, as he said, "I've been meaning to have a chat with you, young lady. Into the Headmaster's Office." Which was really just the administrative office off the main gymnasium floor, now serving as his private quarters. It was one of those mostly wood rooms, and Donovan had polished quite a bit of it just because he could, when he wanted to wind down in peace. So it looked almost like a bedroom should, despite the futon mattress still being on the floor and the "dresser" against one wall being an imposing wooden teacher's desk.

Once he had closed the door behind us, Donovan tugged

me by the hand across the room and took me by the waist to deposit me abruptly on top of the desk. Then he stood in front of me, to one side of my crossed legs, still wearing that soft but incomprehensible smile. The demon prince persona he'd been playing with for some new routines—which had necessitated this high-fashion costume change for me—didn't include as much stage makeup as some of the previous Ringmaster incarnations. When he pulled off his red velvet mask, there was just a trace of dreamy black eyeliner around his eyes for the sexy fallen angel look. That and a bit of color to his lips, accentuated with a gold-sheen balm I wished I could feel smeared against my skin. And, yeah, I'd have bargained my soul away to him, no question.

My gaze traced the slow, deliberate, *improbable* motion of his hand when Donovan caressed the inside of my knee, as he asked, "So what do you think of how things have been going since we left London?" My mouth had fallen slightly open as I stared, as a charged tingle shot along the inside of my leg and inside *me*. Haigh's fingers curled along my stocking-clad flesh, and his thumb rubbed back and forth…back and forth…along the curve of my now-trembling knee. The other hand pushed off my mask and set it aside. "Olivia?" Still silent, I continued to gape down at his hand a moment more, before finally looking up into his face. "So what do you think? Do you like Leeds?"

I nodded languidly, admiring those blue eyes, then realized how I must have looked and made myself blink a few times and take a breath. "Yes, it's been great here. Everything we've been able to do with so much more space! And it being so peaceful and private in this area. I can't imagine a better place for us." I tried to suppress the awkward giggle that threatened to erupt at my choice of phrase, innocent enough but not what came to my mind. "For the troupe."

"You don't miss the excitement and bustle of London?"

Though I shook my head no and started to explain, I could only choke out a couple of words as Donovan's hand climbed a little higher on my leg. Outside of the context of the show, in rehearsal or performance, he hadn't touched me like this—intimately—since that day in the costume room when he'd started out spanking me and ended up cradling me on the floor while he kissed me. I'd never really understood how much of his distance from me I could attribute to his rules and belief that becoming sexually involved with his performers conflicted with his responsibility to protect them… and how much was just a lack of interest in me. After all, he'd only ever acted on our attraction when he was angry with me or when I was in terrible distress, usually related to something about my family. That was, when anger loosened his control of his cock or when that protective urge demanded he comfort me. But just now he didn't seem angry, and I wasn't upset.

"London was fine," I answered softly, but it was awkward to say. It hurt—ached to think about how cold Donovan had been with me sometimes and how desperate and lonely I had been, still scared I wouldn't be able to complete my escape from my family. The city was beautiful and exciting, and I loved having Gwynne so near, but I was relieved to leave behind the drama of the tabloids and the possibility of Martin tracking me down. I glanced shyly again into Donovan's eyes, gleaming blue and so brooding and intense with that smudgy black liner, and I wished I could tell him what I was thinking—that he'd actually care to know.

"You don't miss all the gifts and admirers?" he pressed, only to distract me from my response again by pushing my knees apart and stepping between my spread legs.

Anxiously, I moved my hands from my lap to the desk, palms flat in the grainy wood to both steady and center me as I felt my rising desire go straight to my head. "I have admirers here," I protested teasingly.

"You do?" He was playing surprised, tilting his head, fingertips skimming the outsides of my tensing thighs.

"Just not as many," I said, nodding, "and not as demanding. That leaves me more energy to play the submissive to you." God, I'd been so afraid to push my attraction with Donovan lately, I couldn't even make that *sound* flirtatious. But was it rational to worry I'd offend Haigh by flirting with him after he'd brought me to his room, put me up on a desk, and spread my legs so he could stand between them rubbing my thighs? I couldn't take this. "Donovan, why are you doing that?"

He didn't fully look at me, only glanced up very briefly and very coyly from under his lashes and the waves of black hair that had fallen over his forehead. "Don't like it?"

"Of course, I like it," I sighed, letting my frustration out in an irritated tone. "I liked it first time, before you pushed me away. Now I'm just confused." A gentle squeeze from Donovan's hands along my thighs made me squirm. "Confused and horny," I muttered under my breath.

"You want me to stop?"

"No, but in London, you said—"

"We aren't in London anymore, Kitten." And with that declaration, Donovan abruptly stepped back, grabbed me by the knees, and pushed my legs upward, straightening them out above me while I gasped and fell back to my elbows on the desk.

I should have made him tell me what he was doing—

185

what he meant by this. But his gaze was fixed my red silk panties, and one finger had begun to trace the cleft of my sex through the warm, and now instantly damp, material.

Already shivering and breathless, I gasped, "Donovan, please don't tease me."

His thumb pressed into my panties to toy with my clitoris, making my hips tense and shake just a little, just enough to make it clear how great my need was already. Always. Whenever I thought of Haigh like this. "No teasing tonight, Kitten. I'm tired of rules and contract pages and wondering what you taste like. Unless you tell me otherwise right now, I'm going to spend the night taking you in all the ways I've been refusing to let myself want." Another upward glance of those naughty blue eyes. "Objections?"

I shook my head, swallowing my instinct to ask why. What had changed? Why tonight?

"We're in costume, Olivia."

It took me a couple of seconds to wrestle down the nervous surge of disbelief that had me breathless and unable to speak. "No objections, Ringmaster."

Then I bit my lip at how dirty and needy that had sounded, escaping me in a low rasp of a moan. My head still told me this made no sense, this shouldn't be happening yet, even with the rapport Donovan and I had begun to forge between us since we'd arrived in Leeds. But my body was trembling and wet for him, and my chest ached so badly at the thought of being held by this man that I couldn't bear to turn this moment away… even if he changed his mind again afterward, and a moment was all I'd have.

Donovan's fingers dug along my hips to find the waistband of my silk thong. Then he pushed my knees a little harder back with his shoulder so he could pull the panties out from under me and slide them smoothly up my legs and over my heels. "In that case," he said in a soft-edged murmur, "I believe it's time I got to see how my submissive reacts when her Master's tongue is in her pussy."

The groan elicited by this dirty talk from that slow and deliberate British accent was still vibrating through me, from solar plexus to throat to lips, when Donovan urged another out of me. Two gentle, teasing fingertips opened me as he blatantly stared at the engorged pink flesh of my sex. The look on his face, one corner of his bottom lip caught by his upper teeth, the other corner crooked enough to hint at a wicked grin, said he liked what he saw: the proof of how much I wanted him. How ready I was for my Master.

Bending low over my pussy, his face sensual with the glint of lust in his eyes and in the way he licked his lips, Donovan pushed my legs back yet harder, almost flush with my chest. The anticipation was already making it hard to breathe, and now this position made it worse. The grin he gave me made me believe it was intentional, like the manipulation of breath in the yoga positions Griffin had started teaching me.

Then Donovan slid his warm, wet tongue into my sex, and it was all I could do not to slam my head back into the desk. He didn't begin with a tentative flick but a deep, probing lick that said he wanted to taste *and feel* me. My passage tightened and fluttered at his attention, as he pressed that handsome face hard down into my softness and explored as much as he could of me. And moaned against me. And began to fuck me with his mouth.

Now I did roll my head against the wood beneath me, and flailed out to catch and hold the edge of the desk. "Ring-master," was all I could think to say, and Donovan rewarded me by playing one rough fingertip along the small eager bud of my clitoris. "Oh, yes, please," I whispered. "Please do that for me, sir."

My eyes were squeezed shut, wetness seeping from the outer corners, when I heard him gruffly promise, "I'll do more than that for you, Kitten." Two fingers took the place of his tongue to slide in and out of me with a maddening twist, and his mouth moved over my clitoris. The first few kisses were soft and lazy, his tongue swirling around and around the tender pearl, like winding up a spring at the base of my spine. Then, when I was panting openly, he added the teasing flicks and careful scrapes from his teeth. And by the time he'd started sucking my clitoris with constant, increasing pressure and appreciative hunger, my orgasm was already tickling and fluttering its way along the walls of my sex.

No man had ever done this for me. A bit of oral sex, yes, but never ravished me with his mouth and obviously relished doing it. Never made me feel like it was me he wanted more than sex. Wishful thinking or not, the look on Donovan's face, the greedy moans from the back of his throat, the hands that held and probed and caressed and seemed to want to really feel every part of me… all said this was about taking *me*.

When my legs started to shake obviously against his shoulder, Donovan lifted his face and slowly straightened up over me. My eyes shot open when I realized he was withdrawing, denying me my climax, and I couldn't suppress a whine keening up from the very bottom of my stomach. I wanted to cry and curse at being teased, but the look on his face… his full lips were wet from me, and a subtle gleam highlighted the lower angles of his cheeks and chin. I wanted precisely what he was thinking then, as he spread my legs again and pulled me up into a kiss. Tasting myself on Haigh's mouth made me so lightheaded with giddy disbelief that I reached out desperately for handholds in the material of his jacket. His skin smelled of musk and sex and spicy fruit, and I wanted to devour him as well.

I broke the kiss to begin nudging him back so I could slide off the desk, asking permission with my eyes.

"Yes," Donovan rasped, and he whipped his jacket and the white shirt beneath it back from his chest and down his arms to be done with them while I settled on my high heels between his hard, tensed thighs. Once I'd released him from his pants and could now hold and stroke and lick his erect cock, I knew my memory hadn't been playing tricks on me—and that I wasn't getting much of Donovan Haigh into my mouth.

That didn't seem to concern him. With his hands in my hair, he pushed my face against his smooth-shaven groin and went glassy-eyed with pleasure from the feeling of me just nuzzling and licking and squeezing his thick member and full, swollen balls. "Kitten," he breathed, then more haltingly, "Olivia." That look... I would have given anything to make him look like this every night, to know that he'd spent all day imagining all the ways I'd give myself to him when we were alone.

When Donovan's abs started to flex and strain with his breathing and a pearly drop of moisture formed on the broad head of his cock, he let go of me and pivoted to lean on the edge of the desk. He nodded toward his shiny black boots. "Get this off of me," he ordered, and I stripped this rest of his clothing from him as quickly as I could. Not quickly enough—he brushed and rubbed and squirmed against me, helping and hindering and making me rush all the more. And then he leaned there against the desk, the sexiest man I'd ever seen, from the curve of his calves to the bulkier muscles of his thighs, from the gently carved abs to his broad pecs, and with that black hair rakishly curling down over one eye as he regarded me with a distinctly moody intensity. With the gleam in his eyes and along the gold symbols painted down his chest, and from the light catching the curves of his athletic body just so, he looked every bit the fallen angel he intended.

When I'd finished sweeping his clothes out of the way, Haigh snatched me by the wrist and spun me around before hugging me tight back against his naked body. Despite the switch from the usual circumstance—the Dom naked and exposed instead of his submissive—he was still the Master, my Ringmaster. And my every thought was still for his pleasure. I knew, with Donovan, I didn't have to worry about mine.

When I laid my small hands over his larger ones, as he massaged my breast firmly through my gown with one and possessively cupped my naked mons with the other, it was because I wanted him to know I adored his every touch, wherever and whenever, as hard or as soft as he saw fit.

The light prickle of whiskers around Donovan's mouth scraped the crook of my shoulder, and he rasped into my ear, "There are not enough admirers and flatterers and gifts in the world to replace a submissive's true Master, Kitten."

I reached back to thread my hand through his hair, so thick and soft. "I know, sir."

"You know," he said, breathing heavily, pausing to suck my earlobe and tug at it with his teeth until shivers shot down the opposite side of my body. "But do you understand?"

190

"Make me understand."

His large, rough hand slid from my flushed breast to my chin, and he angled my face just right to kiss and lick and nip his way along my jaw. "Make you understand?" he repeated, hot breath sending chills over wet skin. "That no one adores you like the Master who safeguards you?" I nodded, writhing against him, wishing I could feel more of his body through the frustratingly thick layers of satin and lace and lining. "But the Master who punishes you... Do you understand he loves you, too?"

"I do. I understand," I sighed, my head lolling heavily against Donovan's warm, firm shoulder as I relaxed into his touch. It was all I could do to restrain myself from making a foolish declaration, one that was true but also new and fragile and too easily bruised. I needed more time to grow into it before I could voice it to the man it belonged to, the man I would belong to if he'd have me.

"We'll see."

It was a strange thing for Donovan to say, and in an ominously low, ragged voice. There was an emotion there I couldn't name, but it sounded like it was swelling inside him, just behind the words. I was too afraid to let myself hope—too much—that it was the same emotion I was feeling for him.

"Be still," he whispered then, as he dragged down the zipper of my dress tooth by tooth, so slowly that the only sound associated with the action was the release of my breath. He peeled my dress from me silently, then unhooked and tossed away the strapless bustier that had been beneath it, all while he buried his face in my hair like he didn't ever want to pull away. Even when I stood there in only heels and red lace stockings, he lingered, fingers trailing along my shoulders and down my arms and back again. I thought I could almost feel him shaking, and I wondered if he'd let me turn and hold him, or if that would unsettle the tenuous control he had on whatever was going on inside him.

"I'm going to fuck you, Kitten," he said then, words breathed thick and rough and hot against my scalp. But it wasn't seduction edging his voice, like he was just talking dirty to work up his needy little submissive. He sounded like he did when he was training me, instructing me. But also like he was warning me, and I was afraid there was something going on here I didn't understand, something important I could miss, and then…. What would happen?

I pressed back naked against Donovan, against the demand of his rigid cock and the tensed, flexing muscles I felt along his pelvis and stomach and arms. "Sir."

"Shh," he whispered when anxious little mews began to rise in my aching throat. "No point in fretting now, baby. We're here, and it's just time for this to happen. I'm not going to be gentle, but you don't need that anyway, do you?"

"No, sir," I answered, promised, pleaded. I'd started rubbing my bare ass against his groin, bucking just a bit, but he took me by the shoulders and pushed me away from him.

"Go to the bed, Kitten. Lay down for me."

Though I wanted to take Donovan's hand and pull him with me, I simply obeyed. And when I had, when I had stretched myself out on the pillows of Haigh's bed, I watched him come to me so slowly, almost sadly, and not looking at me. Those blue eyes were unfocused, half-closed, as he quickly knelt between my thighs and laid his thick, erect cock along the lips of my sex without attempting to enter me. He moved in for a sudden kiss that he pressed to my mouth roughly, deeply, until he were both pulling at each other's hair.

Then, when we had to break the kiss to breathe, he muttered against my lips, "There's never been anyone else who's done this to me, Kitten."

And I could have said it to him then, this declaration I kept secreted in my aching chest. With the way he was looking at me, his gaze so soft, I could have told him how I felt about him. An inexperienced little wallflower who'd been allowed to play the beautiful submissive for the man of her dreams; it was inevitable I'd fall for him. But it was too soon. He wouldn't have believed it, wouldn't have taken it seriously.

Donovan raised himself up to his knees then, hips angled forward and rampant member taunting my ready sex. My hands lay idly against my chest, and he took me by the wrists to put my arms above my head. There was a moment when he was staring down at my breasts, and I realized he'd never seen the little birthmark just under my left nipple. But he made no comment on it, just shifted his gaze to meet mine and watched my expression as he drove himself into me, almost half his length in one thrust.

I keened out something between a curse and his name as sudden pain flared inside me with the rough invasion. Just like the first time, it was a torment that could only be soothed by taking me deeper and harder. I knew, of course, about endorphins and hormones, but there was more to this need. It was about being taken to the hilt, right down to the core. Nothing spared, nothing denied.

Donovan angled down over me and used his weight to keep my hands pinned to the bed as I bucked and squirmed to take more of him, as he drew back only an inch before thrusting forward again. No more penetrating stares and husky promises delivered with the dark, possessive edge of a true Dom's voice. Just his body lording over and driving… slamming into mine. And me curling my legs around him not only for leverage but because I had to, because I couldn't help arching and coiling and squirming and tensing. The more I writhed, the harder and deeper Donovan pierced me, demanding with actions instead of words that I be still and spread myself and take the force of his need and possession.

No sighs and kisses, just panting and the low grunt of effort at the end of each thrust. The light slapping sound of sweat-slicked bodies forced to fit one another over and over… the throbbing and tightening of my sheath as it seemed like Donovan's cock swelled larger and harder… the feverish heat rising off our skin… until it all felt like a delirious dream of inhumanly beautiful but fragmented images and waves of overwhelming sensation shifting and blurring one into the next.

My orgasm did not have a clear moment it began or ended. My whole body shook violently beneath Haigh's, my muscles burning from being tensed too long and with the struggle of my effort to fuck Donovan as much as he was fucking me. There was just that distant recognition that I felt a sharp pleasure couched in that constant hard quaver vibrating my insides.

I couldn't have said I knew when Donovan came. He never paused, never lessened the force he used to piston in and out of me with that almost feral pace that only overcame us when our conscious minds receded. But as my body numbed from burning ache to a heavy tingle and it became too hard to struggle, I lay still beneath Haigh and recognized the thick warmth pooling inside me. He kept thrusting and grinding his hips until the heaviness finally pushed him down over me, where he collapsed with me in a tangle of sore limbs.

Neither of us moved for I didn't know how long. We ended up with Donovan resting with his elbows and forearms on either side of my head, his face buried in the crook of my neck. My legs curled over his hips and my arms up under his so I could grip his shoulders from behind. His cock was still inside me, the persistent quaver of my pussy making it feel as though he'd never softened.

When I felt Donovan's face burrow deeper against my neck, it just came out of me, this feeling I couldn't contain. "I love you." And the moment turned slow, drawn out, surreal, as Donovan lifted his head, not to look me in the eye but to lay soft, nuzzling kisses over my face. His hair tickling my cheek. His breath filling my mouth through my parted lips.

Hovering over me as though to kiss me, Donovan murmured, "Did you say that to Stephen, too?"

It was a question that didn't fit my dream, a hard sideways jerk to my languorous mood. "What?" I asked, hearing my own voice still slurred with the afterglow of frenzied sex.

"When you went to him without me and let him have you, did you tell him you loved him, too?"

And I finally made myself focus and study the look on Donovan's face, as the haze of lust evaporated slowly from his expression in favor of a set jaw and a hard glint in his eyes. When I shifted my hands from his shoulders to his chest, to push at him, he rolled away. Onto his back. Not looking at me.

"I don't know who told you about that, but I never let Stephen Unwin have me. Yes, I took one more performance request from him, when you were not there to advise me, but I took Rafe with me. He could tell you—"

"Yes, so he said," Donovan responded flatly, his voice growing cooler and more disinterested with every word he said. "Rafe swears you were never alone with Stephen, never undressed, and never fucked the man. Whatever it is about you, Kitten, you have one of my best friends lying for you. Two—Thom didn't tell me about the payment when he saw it, because you asked him to keep it from me."

I sat up and turned from Donovan, curling down around my bent knees and hugging my legs to my chest. "You have this all wrong, Donovan. And I don't know why you think I'd... yes, I mean, I did keep it from you, but I only went because we'd just been in so much financial trouble. That was so much money. Then I got scared you would think... exactly what you do."

Behind me, Donovan's breath hissed out of him briefly in what sounded like a bitter chuckle. "So you betrayed me and gave yourself to another man for the sake of the troupe."

"I didn't," I started to protest again, but I had to put my hand over my mouth instead, to keep from crying aloud. I felt like I'd been turned inside out, just like this whole last hour with Haigh. We'd gone from him murmuring to me about a Master who loved me—and me confessing I was in love with Donovan—to Haigh coldly insisting I'd betrayed him by having sex with Stephen Unwin and getting Rafe and Thom to cover for me.

"Why?" I demanded then, and I didn't care about the rise or the sniffles in my voice. "If you think that of me, why did we just do this?"

Only a pronounced pause answered me at first, before he finally said, "Because there was no reason anymore to deny I wanted this... now that you're leaving."

"You're firing me?" Of course. This was the way it would end, just as I'd really started to believe I'd found a place and people I could build a life around, and my exile would be my own fault. One stupid mistake based on wanting to prove myself too much, wanting to help so badly that I'd do something I hadn't even wanted to do, all to earn Donovan's trust and his love. No matter how much I did for anyone else, no matter how much I sacrificed myself....

"It's for the best," he said.

I was sure it was, for him. For me, purely aside from the emotional damage, it was a disaster. No job and no visa. Haigh might as well have packaged me up with a bow before shipping me back to L.A. None of which was his concern, was it?

As I darted up from the bed and started to squirm back into my dress for the humiliating walk back to my room, I thought of the day I auditioned for Haigh and how awkward it had felt to dress afterward with a whole room watching. Funny but fitting that this would be so much worse, with only one man in the room who wasn't bothered enough now to watch me dress.

No farewell or false sympathies. Haigh said nothing else to me before I fled his room. So the last words ever between us would be that trite bullshit consolation that this was for the best.

Back in my room, I fell into a heap on my bedroll and waited for Donovan to come comfort me, then realized he wasn't coming, that he was probably already asleep. I packed one bag with tears streaming down my face, pleading in my own head for this to turn out to be just a very bad dream. It was late enough at night that the whole experience had that horrific nonsensical quality of not looking or feeling quite right or entirely real. By the second bag, I was pissed, ranting to myself about Haigh's stubborn ingratitude for everything I'd done.

As I stood in the cold and the dark by the side of the road and waited for my taxi, I relented and let myself consider the terrible possibility that being the submissive of Donovan Haigh hadn't been so different than being the ward of Martin Keane. They employed different techniques, certainly, but hadn't both of them made it their special purpose in their relationship with me to make me understand I was flawed, couldn't be trusted to make the important decisions about my own life, and needed to be made to understand that obedience was my only true virtue?

Fuck you, Ringmaster, sir, I thought as the black cab drove me away. I hoped the guests and the troupe pestered him about where I'd gone and that everything I'd done back there at the school slowly undid itself, from the new filing system to the way I'd organized Donovan's costumes. I hoped Thom and Naomi and Rafe and Griffin missed me and hated the new assistant. Then I cried at the thought of being replaced, of Donovan touching anyone else and calling her his submissive.

10

SHE'D BEEN GONE two days, coinciding with the break in our weekly performances, but we were back at it tonight—and the Ringmaster with no submissive. The assistant was not an essential position, I told myself. I could have used any of the female performers to act as my slave for the exhibition of the Ringmaster's domination skills. What bothered me more, as I folded or hung bits of my costume that I'd just had laundered, was that I was still organizing everything the way Olivia had arranged it.

And after standing there thinking about how she'd touched everything and ordered everything, how my every belonging sat where she had put it… after realizing I could still imagine her smell perfectly, and that it made my mouth water… after picturing her doing the same bloody thing for Unwin now… I pulled every scrap of clothing from every rack, drawer, and trunk and threw them in all directions.

That's how Thom found me, panting and with clothes covering the floor, when he tapped on the door of my quarters and stepped inside. He slipped sideways in through the doorway, gingerly avoiding the layers of colorful debris, and surveyed the room without commenting.

"Thom?"

"Was it really worth all this to punish her for making you jealous?"

"Excuse me?" I kicked a path through the piles of clothing to confront my admin manager. I had both height and weight on Thom, but it didn't drive him back even a step. He regarded me with a deliberately droll expression and didn't bother to raise his face to look up at me. "Weren't you the one warning me off of her back in London?"

"Circumstances change, Donovan. Christ, keep up. Once she'd gotten over you jilting her by indulging that little brat phase and worked through the customary wild girl period from suddenly having hundreds of men willing to pay thousands of pounds to see her on her knees in front of them, she'd settled right down. You can't pay someone to care for you the way she did."

I kicked another pile of clothes, in lieu of hitting something. "Oh, is that what she was doing with Unwin? That's why she had to lie about it?"

Thom shrugged. "Rafe said nothing happened between them. He has no reason to lie."

"Except that everyone feels the need to protect her."

"Right, that was why you tossed her out of your room that first time after you fucked her, to protect her feelings. And somehow you actually managed to get her to buy that tripe."

"You know I don't act like that with my assistants," I growled at Thom, clenching my fists.

"Until you did, and losing that control scared the piss out of you. Fine, all right, understandable, none of us like realizing we've been topped from the bottom, but she didn't deserve to get used again and dismissed after that. And don't tell me you didn't fuck her before you fired her. I saw you bring her back here that night once the after party was over."

"Yeah, I did," I said, huffing out the admission like a challenge. "She's been trying to get me to fuck her since she became my assistant."

This finally got something besides a cool, snide reaction from Thom. He glared at me and shook his head. "I think you need to come with me, sir."

And he led me down the dim hallway and through the striped canvas curtains we'd hung from the walls instead of erecting an indoor tent, to the main floor of the gym. Thom pointed to the custom mobile bar, outfitted with a greatly expanded selection of rare and expensive spirits that had padded our bottom line quite nicely in this new city. "Olivia on her knees while Rafe belted her—that's how we paid for that. *She* paid for that."

Then he motioned to the long drapes of red and white canvas that had replaced the indoor tent, allow us to preserve the use of the balcony for the performances as well as the after parties. "Olivia again."

He pointed to updated equipment and upgraded décor and shook his head in disgust. "Olivia," he said, after every new item he brought to my attention.

"You and I discussed this," I railed at my manager, my ire rising higher and higher the longer he talked. "That first performance for Unwin was enough to get us set up here."

"And it was," Thom barked, the first time I could ever say the man had actually raised his voice to me. "But the rest of it? All the upgrades? Come on, Donovan. You wanted to believe one performance was all it took to get that, so you did." Then he got up in my face, like the little street scrapper he'd been when I found him years ago. "Did you know that Olivia didn't even take her cut of that second performance? No, because even after you found out about it, you didn't ask. You didn't want to know. How do you feel now about fucking her and showing her the door?"

It was all I could do not to let the nausea churning in my stomach surge up through my chest. All I could do not to grab Thom and throw him. In a low, simmering mutter, I asked, "Anything else you want to say to me?"

Thom whipped a folded newspaper from his back pocket and threw it against my chest as he turned to stride away.

"Ah, fuck," I groaned as I let it fall to the floor. We'd gone weeks without the headlines following us, without the media sniffing out our new location. But now everything was going sour at once—Olivia gone, Rafe and Thom hardly speaking to me, and now this.

As though to add insult to injury, as I bent to pick up the newspaper, Thom called over his shoulder, "And your mother's here to see you."

Absurd. "What?" I shouted, but he was gone.

When a feminine voice cleared her throat, I looked up toward the balcony, where the unmistakable Brigitte Rose Somerset stood at the rail and nodded to me.

"Fuck me," I whispered under my breath, knowing I had to go up and speak to her. On the way, I glanced down at the front page of the paper.

GAY SON OF LEATHERBY CAPITAL TRUSTS DIRECTOR A BOY TOY FOR SEX CIRCUS CELEBRITY CLIENTS

"Oh, Christ, Thom, I'm sorry," I muttered to myself as I skimmed the smear job that not only outed the youngest son of the Leatherby investment fortune as gay, but suggested he was a paid escort for high-profile clients who were still in the closet, mostly footballers. The article went on to say that Thom's family was applying heavy pressure on authorities to locate and shut down the international prostitution ring.

I thought for a minute about finding Thom, asking if it was as bad for him as it sounded, what kind of fallout there would be with his family, but with the tension between us over Olivia…. Plus, there was the matter of a certain Lady Somerset waiting to speak to me.

At the upper landing, I tossed the tabloid into a bin.

"If you're trying to shield me, Donovan, I've already seen it. That was last evening's edition."

I finally turned and looked square at her, the White Rose of Yorkshire, and still a beauty. Brigitte was in her late thirties when I came along. Thirty some odd years later, in her late sixties, she'd traded in the long chestnut hair for a striking silver shoulder-length bob that set off her blue eyes, the same she gave me. She still had the body and the mouth of a burlesque queen, and the wits of a woman who'd all but managed herself for twenty-five years. Dad was a personable guy, but never had the edge Mum did. I'd always thought he was better off after the divorce, when he'd settled into a little cottage in Gloucestershire and let Mum continue her adventures without him, toddler in tow.

Better off… just what I'd said to Olivia. Though firing her had not been the same as Mum's divorce after her indiscretion with Quillan Teague. Brigitte said some people just weren't suited to the life of travel and constant performance, it was bound to break their hearts, and they were better off if we just let them go. But I'd thought she was a bitch for making my dad go away, until I was old enough to understand everything that had happened.

And now Thom and Rafe and Naomi and probably even Griffin thought I was a bastard for dismissing Olivia.

"Do I get a hug?" Brigitte asked after I'd stood there lost in my thoughts for far too long.

"Of course, Mother." She still gave warm, firm hugs, like her handshake.

"I'm glad you're still calling me that, when you call me at all."

I was Ringmaster of the Cirque de Plaisir, and a silver-haired woman could still make me hang my head. "I know I should have called you right after the paper broke the story naming both of us, but…."

"But that would have involved explaining why you hadn't told me what you've been doing all these years." In her pale blue silk blouse and matching slacks, her expensive kitten heels and real pearls, she looked like the last person who'd gesture at the circus décor around her and beam such a smile. "I never really pegged you for being an entertainment director for a tour company. A terrible lie, that one. This…"

"Doesn't embarrass Lady Somerset?"

Brigitte burst out in a vibrant, unladylike laugh that reminded me how easily she charmed people. Every town was her town, everybody she met her kind of people, no matter the social stratum. "Darling, an investment banker would have embarrassed me. The mastermind of a secret bondage circus… I'm jealous I hadn't thought of it at your age."

Despite myself, I laughed. I hated it—*hated it*—when Brigitte made me laugh, made me like her. Not that I didn't love her. She was my mother. But she was also a supremely self-centered woman.

"It's not as bad as the papers make out. There's no prostitution ring," I insisted as I walked her to the smaller balcony bar and poured her a gin and tonic, one of her favored afternoon drinks. She winked and nodded, and I made myself another, knowing she didn't like to drink alone.

"Oh, I knew that," she told me, waving away the thought with a delicate hand adorned in diamond rings and skin that was getting paler and thinner by the year. Not that I'd seen Brigitte in several. "I raised you with more respect for performers than that. The tabloids must have their scandals, though, and that means as much illicit sex as possible."

"Is this causing problems for Adam?"

"Please," she huffed again between sips of her drink. "If Lord Somerset was scared of a little muckraking, he'd have never married a burlesque star, and divorcée with a son besides."

I took a deep draught from my own gin, light on the tonic, and sighed. "Then you're not here to scold me for sullying the family name."

"To the devil with that," she swore and set down her empty glass with a resounding clink. "Once the evening edition said you were somewhere near Leeds, I thought it was a good time to see what you were up to—since you obviously weren't inclined to come visit your mum—and if you'd accept a little help."

I eyed her cautiously. My mother wasn't the helpful type. "What did you have in mind?"

She took a moment to search through her expensive handbag, the kind most women couldn't afford. I was sure Brigitte didn't even have to endure the waiting list. After a moment, she produced an unmarked envelope.

"And this is?" I asked.

"You obviously have someone feeding information to the press, or maybe a reporter has gotten access to performances. Adam heard you were making inquiries along those lines with mutual friends in London, but he has media connections you don't. Those papers include copies of a certain tabloid editor's notes regarding a freelance team working to break a major entertainment story. You can see if any of the names or addresses leads you to your leak."

I took the envelope from her and, without opening it, tapped it lightly on the bar. "This is very helpful of you, Brigitte."

"And very unlike me, you want to say." Which made me smile and stare sheepishly into my glass. "I know what kind of woman I am, Donny, or at least the kind of woman I was when I was dragging you from city to city right up until the time you hit sixteen and decided you were staying on with that club in Berlin."

"That job only lasted a few months."

"I would have guessed, with the way you and the owner's daughter were looking at each other. But I also knew you were angry with me for dragging you away from everyone you ever started to get on with. It was hard to have friends, let alone a girlfriend." When I didn't comment, filling my mouth with gin instead, Brigitte shook her head and motioned with the wave of her hand to the balcony, the circus.

"I was surprised at the idea that you'd have put together a travelling show, with as much as you hated the constant change back when you were younger. Then I actually got to see it…and hear that little argument—"

"Ah, yeah, sorry about that," I sighed into my glass. Sorry she'd had to witness it. Sorry it had happened at all. Fine time for my mother to come see me, when everything was falling down around me and I was powerless to protect… to protect those I loved. I just hadn't seen any of this coming, from the reporters to the tabloids to letting one little blond submissive get to me so badly.

"Don't be sorry," Brigitte insisted. "You don't argue like that with someone unless they're family. So, really, you have the best of both worlds here, don't you? You get to travel and indulge the wanderlust that is all you've ever known, but you do it with a troupe of people you care about, so you have that sense of security you never had when it was just us and I was so busy in the spotlight."

"I didn't mind." No point, fifteen or twenty years later, making an issue of past hurts.

"Oh, dear boy, it's harder than that to lie to your mother, especially when we're so alike."

I choked on that last swallow of gin, feeling it burning the inside of my nose. "So alike?"

"You don't apologize, either, not in plain words," she said, as she glanced at the envelope resting on the bar.

An apology in not so many words… that was what my mother had brought me in the plain little envelope I held in one hand as I walked her out to her car. I wouldn't have pegged my mother for the kind of insight she'd shown into our relationship while we'd shared those drinks, never would have guessed she ever suspected how I'd felt about all the traveling, about never having friends, always having to leave girlfriends right after I'd just gotten to like them.

Back inside, in Thom's office, I rapped on the frame of the open door and regarded him with the sort of wary calm that blokes usually display right after an argument with one of their closest mates. I handed the envelope to my admin wizard. "Will you help me?"

11

A SIMPLE WHITE blouse and loose black slacks with conservative black heels, my hair in a high, neat ponytail and makeup in mostly nude shades. I fussed in the mirror that hung on the back of the closet door in Gwynne's guest room, and changed belts and jewelry a couple of times.

From the doorway, Gwynne said, "You know, if absolutely necessary, I could get you a job at Finley's."

I leaned in close to the mirror to examine my eyes. Was it obvious I'd been crying for two days straight? "I know," I told her.

"But it's not really an option, is it?"

"No," I agreed and shook my head. "Not after everything with the Cirque de Plaisir." Not after Donovan Haigh. How I'd lost my mind around that man, thinking I could be some kind of cult starlet in a glamorous erotic revue. I'd just made a fool of myself and gotten my heart broken in the process. Part of me felt like it was time to admit I was meant to be the lesser Keane following along in the shadow of her famous family, where I lived a life lacking in excitement but also heartbreak. A life lacking fulfillment—that was the sticking point and the reason I was letting another part of me make one last attempt at securing a different future.

"It's past four, Gwynne; get out of here," I cautioned my friend, knowing Finley expected her at work tonight. "I've got someone to drop in on about a job, maybe. I'll call you later to let you know how it went."

I didn't tell the spitfire redhead what a long shot this was, going to see Stephen Unwin for a job at one of his clubs or resorts. The whole matter of the way we'd met and the attraction we'd shared made this a messy situation and a delicate prospect. Could I get Stephen to take me seriously, to offer me a job without expecting services more in line with a submissive than a manager?

Time to find out. I'd been calling Stephen all day, getting no answer. So I took the chance he'd see me showing up at his townhouse in Lennox Gardens as initiative rather than desperation. It was just after five in the afternoon when I climbed the clean white steps of the brown Georgian three-story and rang the bell. No one home. Unsurprising, I told myself. A man who owned multiple restaurants and clubs probably wasn't a standard nine-to-fiver—too much to do. So, in lieu of a better option, there I sat on his front stoop like a stray hoping for a home and trying not to look too pathetic shivering in the cold.

It was after seven when a dark sedan pulled up to the curb and Unwin stepped out. I squinted, unsure it was him. He looked too tired, too anxious to be Stephen. Then I realized what the matter really was. No mask. I wouldn't have guessed he'd look so different without just that much of his upper face concealed, but as he drew near, peering just as hard at me… Yes, those were his gray eyes, his full mouth and wide jaw.

Standing at the bottom of the steps, the breeze ruffling his dark suit, Stephen tilted his head at me, "O-Olivia?"

"Yes, Olivia," I said, coming to my feet and descending the steps to hold out my hand. "Stephen. I wasn't sure you'd recognize me."

He took several long moments studying me, a smile growing little by little on his broad face. "It's the hair," he muttered as he took my hand, "and the lips. Rose petal lips."

I blushed furiously, my stomach lurching at the flirtatious appreciation in his voice. This was going to be a problem, I feared, trying not to dwell on the sense that he just didn't look…right. Without the mask, he resembled Donovan even less.

"I hope you will forgive the presumption of me showing up like this," I told him as we shook hands and I pointedly kept a respectful distance. When he seemed to want to lean in for a hug, I stepped aside as though I assumed he wished to proceed up the steps to his door, which he did slowly. "I've been trying to call you."

Realization lightened his oddly anxious face, smoothing worry lines from his brow and eyes. "Ah, yes, I apologize for that, Olivia. I've been so busy today that I wasn't taking calls from numbers I didn't recognize."

"I understand completely. You've got to be a busy man with all your business holdings. That's…" Deep breath, Olivia. "That's actually the reason I've come to speak to you."

"And sat out here too long, by the look of you," he interjected. "Come inside and let me get you a coffee, lass."

Now I really did feel like a stray, enough that I almost turned crying and ran back to Gwynne's, feeling I'd have been better off if I'd just taken my original flight back to Los Angeles. This—everything since I'd missed that flight—was uncomfortable and frightening and *hard*.

"Thank you," I told Stephen in a soul-deep sigh that reconciled me to the bleakness of my situation. "I'd really appreciate that."

Inside, the townhouse was much as I'd remembered it from that second command performance, the night the circus had left London. The place was all polished wood floors and cream-colored modern furniture, a bit like a vacation home or an executive rental, with no family photographs, no personal clutter.

I could stand in the living room and look around the corner of the open dining area to the kitchen and watch Stephen making coffee, past the granite breakfast bar. He'd removed his suit jacket, and the looseness of his white dress shirt made me wonder if he'd been working too hard, like he'd lost weight and hadn't had his shirts replaced or tailored yet.

"I'm not with the Cirque de Plaisir anymore," I called to him as we carried on a room to room conversation.

"No?" Stephen asked as he came back around the corner with a coffee cup for each of us. We perched on the sofa to drink it, and I shifted to settle myself, hoping I wasn't making it too obvious I was trying to put a few more inches between us. "What are you doing now?" he pressed.

I tried not to read too much into the way his gaze lingered at the neck of my blouse, over the top button. It wasn't, after all, the all-out leer I had dreaded. "That's why

I've come to see you, Stephen. If—if you don't mind me still calling you by your first name." Oh, to hell with it, I thought. "We did meet under such unusual circumstances, and I'm not sure how to approach this," I confessed, and Unwin breathed out a warm chuckle.

"I understand, Olivia. Yes, please, call me Stephen."

There it was again, I thought, the warm graciousness that had drawn me to Stephen at the after parties, when I'd been left so lonely by Donovan's careful distance. It was awful of me to find it creepy now, just because we had no masks to hide ourselves and he didn't look like the man who had just used me and tossed me into the street.

"Thank you," I said and forged on, so far outside my comfort zone now that it didn't even matter anymore. "I'm here because I remember we talked about what you did for a living—the clubs and resorts. You know I have experience with a very large troupe—the Cirque de Plaisir has over a hundred performers and support staff—but I also have extensive experience with personal management of A-list entertainers. I'm hoping you might have a use for those skills in one of your venues."

Stephen put his coffee cup down on the glass table between the couch and the huge white Georgian-style hearth and turned those gray eyes on me with an unmistakably sensual focus. "I'd prefer to put your skills to use much closer to home, Olivia, if you'd let me."

Trying not to giggle self-consciously, I put my coffee cup down as well and folded my hands in my lap, scooting a little further away on the sofa, trying to make it seem I was only angling myself toward him a little more to look him face to face. "I really… I really feel like that wouldn't be the best idea or the best use of my skills. It's important to me

213

that you know I came here to you with wholly professional intentions. I want you to be able to trust that I am an expert organizer and manager."

"I know that, Olivia," he said softly, reassuringly, as he reached out to smooth a stray hair behind my ear. I flushed hot when he did that, knowing our conversation was headed in the wrong direction. His fingertips grazing the curl of my ear sent a shiver of vertigo through me, like the room was turning sideways. It wasn't unlike the panic I'd felt for years whenever Uncle Martin had reached for me. I'd always felt dirty afterward, even when there had been no overt sexual behavior, just like I felt now.

Stephen's fingers caressed the line of my jaw, then spread down my neck, and I clumsily shirked off his touch.

"Stephen, please, this isn't why I'm here. I didn't want to give you the impression… the impression that the way we first met would… would… I'm sorry," I mumbled hurriedly. "Could I use your bathroom? I'm feeling sick."

"It's okay, Olivia. You're not sick, darling. Don't worry. Now that you're here with me, I can take care of everything."

As the room tipped in the other direction, and I reached out one hand to grab at the sofa back, the other to push Stephen away as he moved closer, the strangest thought occurred to me. "How… how did you know my name was Olivia?"

I wasn't sure I was awake, in a bedroom I didn't recognize and with no memory of how I'd gotten there. One lamp, beside the bed, shone in the dim, unfamiliar room, and I was alone. I stared at the polished wooden floor for several minutes before it occurred to me: it looked like the floor of Stephen's Lennox Gardens townhouse. Only then did snippets of the conversation over coffee on his couch rise to the surface of my memory in disjointed sound bites. But why was I in a bedroom now, still clothed but with no sign of my shoes? What would have made me feel so suddenly ill and caused me to pass out? There was no reason I'd....

Unless Stephen had put something in my coffee.

That last moment came back to me. How had he known my name was Olivia? No one at the circus would have told him that. Was he another reporter? Was he working for Martin? Each question shot through me with a chill but also with a sting of sadness—at what a fool I was. I had pinned my hopes upon Stephen, first to soothe my pain over Donovan's disinterest, then to save me from having to return to Los Angeles. And he'd been playing me all along. Donovan even thought I'd betrayed him over Stephen. What an idiot Haigh would have thought me now. I was sure he was glad to be rid of me, if I was this naïve, so desperate for affection and approval that I was just looking for someone to lie to me.

Unsure what I was going to do or find, and still feeling lightheaded, I slipped from the bed and went to the bedroom door, which stood partially open. Through the gap, I saw the upper landing and the stairs down to the living room... but no sign of Stephen. No movement at all. I listened. If there were any sounds, I couldn't make them out over the rasp of my nervous breathing and the pounding of my heart as it beat in distress in my head and all my extremities.

Unsteady on my feet, I took my time tiptoeing out of the bedroom. I was certain I'd be discovered at any moment, chased and caught and... then what? Held prisoner? Beaten? Raped? Murdered? At the top of the stairs and again at the bottom, I paused to listen for activity in the house. Again, nothing. In front of me, beside the couch, sat several suitcases, a man's coat slung over one. To my right, on the other side of the living room, stood the front door, just there, nothing standing between the exit and me.

Wobbling a little, I rushed for the door, realizing too late that I was passing an open doorway to my right. From the corner of my eye, I caught the shape of a man turning toward me.

"Olivia, no!"

Stephen's voice called after me as I lunged for the door and jerked it open. Cold night air hit me in the face and sobered me enough that when a hand locked around my elbow, I responded my throwing my weight behind it and striking Unwin in the gut. Though he bent double, winded, he never let go of me. When I started for the door again, he dragged me backward.

"Stop, Olivia. I'm trying to help you, love," Stephen huffed, still struggling to regain his breath. "He'll find you if you don't come with me, Kitten. We can run away if you'll just stop fighting me."

"Run away from who?" I demanded, even as I was twisting to break his grasp on my arm. "Let me go." The last thing I needed was another man trying to save me. From what, the last one who wanted to be my protector? I'd had enough of all of them.

I squirmed too much, too violently for him to hold me after I'd caught him so solidly with an elbow to the stomach. As soon as I felt his grip slip off my arm, I spun back toward the door... and the four men who were even then filing in through the open doorway.

And first among them… silver hair and oddly flat, metallic green eyes. A long face with eyes that didn't crinkle or brighten when he smiled. "I believe the deluded Mr. Ullock is referring to me."

Uncle Martin.

12

NOT THE RINGMASTER'S best performance, I had to admit as we took a final bow and the lights went up to help the crowd sift down from the bleachers and out into the night. I was distracted—yes, that was one word for it. Also guilty and... regretful. And dreading the three-hour after party.

At the foot of the stairs up to the balcony, however, Thom stopped me by slapping that unmarked envelope my mother had provided against my chest. "You need to see this, sir."

Nodding to special guests as they ascended the stairs, and stepping to one side for a moment of privacy, I fished a single piece of paper out of the envelope. Thom held a small torchlight over the sheet so I could see the highlighted notation on the photocopy of the editor's day planner.

Meeting Walker's partner Ullock at 7pm, Knightsbridge.

Then it gave an address in Lennox Gardens. Thom pointed at the scrawled street number. "That's Unwin's address, but it doesn't belong to him. You remember that client from Paris who asked for several London invitations? The title comes back to him—and he vouched for both Vachon and a fellow named Barrymore."

"So Unwin, who somehow found out we were in Leeds right before that last headline broke, is using an address for a house owned by a man who vouched for Martin Keane's son-in-law and is associated with the partner of the reporter I tossed out of the warehouse in London? Do I have that right?"

Thom nodded grimly.

"Olivia was afraid her family was trying to find her to make her go back to the States with them. Do you think Unwin… or maybe his name is Ullock… is in contact with Keane? I mean, how much of this has been about flushing Olivia out of hiding?"

In the contained glow of the torch, Thom was peering hard at me.

"What?" I asked.

"After the way you blew up about her taking that command performance without your permission, wouldn't it have been just as easy to assume she was feeling information to Walker and Ullock?"

"Is that what you think?" I asked indignantly.

Thom shook his head very slowly. "No, and neither do you."

I wasn't sure if Thom's comment angered or wounded me, but there was a distinct burning in my chest that wouldn't let me swallow it down or breathe it out. Your decision, Haigh, I told myself. Move the circus again as we'd discussed this afternoon after my mother's visit, head back to the lower-profile venues in Eastern Europe, or go find out what was going on at the Knightsbridge address, even if I didn't like what awaited me. The only thing I could imagine worse than finding out Olivia had been betraying us—me—all along to a couple of reporters was realizing I'd been tricked into tossing her out like… like an unwanted kitten to be picked up alongside the road by anyone who cared to stop. Anyone who had been waiting for the chance.

Despite the bitter aftertaste of pride, I folded up the copy again and stuffed it into my pants pocket. "You and the boys can handle the after party?"

"We can," Thom assured me, "but wouldn't you rather take Rafe or Griffin with you?"

"For what?" I asked as we stalked through the gym, upstream through the colorful crowd, to the curtain that concealed the hallway and my quarters. "This isn't going to be an American-style shootout or a high-speed London car chase. Unwin or Ullock or Walker *or whoever* will be there or he won't. And Olivia."

"You'd almost rather believe she betrayed you, wouldn't you?" Thom asked as we paused at my door.

Inside, without responding to his question, I stripped off my hat, mask, and jacket and put a black coat on over the white shirt and black trousers of my costume.

At the sink in the nearby bathroom, Thom dampened a rag and brought it to me. "The grease paint might look a little peculiar if you got pulled over."

"Fair enough," I conceded as I scrubbed at my face on the way out to the parking lot. And there I was, pulling away in one of the plain black cars we kept for troupe use, while

Thom watched. Half past eleven at night, and I was on my way to London, most likely on a wild goose chase. But if it wasn't… if this was where I needed to go to find out how to stop these wild headlines from driving my troupe away… if Olivia had ended up someplace she shouldn't have been because I'd promised to protect her, then hadn't… Thom's warning about grease paint and getting pulled over made more sense as I found myself racing down the motorway at half again the speed limit.

I arrived in Lennox Gardens, Knightsbridge, at about two in the morning, expecting to find… I didn't know what. The cynic in me predicted an empty townhouse or worse, a romantic scene in the living room, down on the floor in front of the hearth, Olivia in Unwin's arms. Or maybe just a reporter using the address as a cover, a thank-you note on his counter from Martin Keane, expressing appreciation for locating Olivia.

The neat row of Georgian townhouses, all lined up to enclose a manicured central park, was quiet and dark except for one. I checked the address on the paper in my pocket and, disbelieving, checked it again. That was the address, the only house on the block with lights still on. Nothing good ever came of whatever went on with the lights on in the wee hours of the morning. Those were the argument hours, the Daddy's moving out hours, the life won't be the same after this hours.

Those were the hours when you heard a woman cry out in distress, and I did, just as I was making my way cautiously up the walk toward the front steps.

"Don't, please."

The muffled cry didn't sound particularly like Olivia, but the circumstances made the likelihood too great to ig-

221

nore. I rushed up the steps without the caution the situation deserved and was reaching for the knob to the front door when two rather large gentlemen, one with a baseball bat, stepped up behind me.

"Right, mate, this is a private party, but seeing as you've got this far, go on in."

"Maybe I have the wrong address," I suggested.

"Let's see." The ginger wall of muscle to my right pushed the front door open, then nudged me forward into the up-scale cream-and-wood townhouse. "Anyone recognize the bloke we found prowling around the front?"

My gaze shifted from Vachon, where he stood in a bright blue Italian suit and a rather surreal grin as he popped the cork on a bottle of wine, to a thin gray-haired fellow in a tasteful gray overcoat who sat cross-legged and composed in an overstuffed chair… with Olivia perched still and pale and unblinking on the arm. On the couch, Unwin sat curled with his arms over his stomach like he was nursing a punch, his face red and wet with sweat.

"Definitely the wrong address," I muttered, thinking back to that moment when I'd told Thom I didn't need to bring Rafe or Griffin with me. Another grand miscalculation.

"Don't be ridiculous, Monsieur Ringmaster," the seat-ed man—Martin Keane, I assumed—urged me. "You are just in time for a glass of wine. Please have a seat." When I hesitated, surveying the room for more hired muscle, exits, makeshift weapons, he sighed. "Nigel, if you would."

The ginger thug clamped one hand down on my shoul-der and guided me to a seat on the couch beside Unwin. Though I felt the muscles along my back tense with the need to whirl on him, flip him over one arm and down onto the glass coffee table, I wasn't fool enough—not since I was twenty-two—to think I could take on a whole room of men by myself. Still, being shown a seat like a naughty boy before the headmaster, right in front of Olivia, didn't do much for my disposition.

"Ullock, I presume?" I asked when Stephen glanced at me.

"Very good, Mr. Haigh," Keane said with a nod, his steel-gray hair perfectly combed and unmoving, just like the mean, glassy orbs that passed for eyes in the man. "You have better information than I thought you would."

I nodded in return. "But they weren't always working for you, were they, Walker and Ullock here?"

"No, when they first managed to secure fraudulent invitations to your Cirque de Plaisir, they were just a couple of freelancers trying to sniff out a sex scandal to make their entrée to one of the bigger tabloids when Ullock figured out your assistant wasn't just the average carnival whore. He contacted me through our publicist to ask if I knew where my niece was, and how much I'd be willing to pay to keep him from plastering her photos all over the London tabloids as Keane daughter turned burlesque harlot."

As he referenced Olivia, Keane traced his hand up her back, as though in a gesture of comfort. The shiver that rattled her shoulders was distinct enough for me to catch it from two meters away. Then his pale, manicured hand gripped the end of her ponytail and jerked hard, until she squealed and arched back, using her hands to grip the over-stuffed chair arm behind her for balance.

"I swear, Olivia, I'd have never turned you over to him," Unwin or Ullock—Stephen—blurted out, but no one reacted to his declaration.

"Olivia has been a bit of a gadfly lately," Martin explained, pulling her hair harder.

"Don't do that," I growled and started up from the couch, despite the hand on each shoulder, one from each of the goons. "She doesn't like it."

Very slowly, Martin eased the pressure on Olivia's hair, and let her straighten. She kept her gaze trained downward, not looking at me. Refusing to look at me after what I'd done to her. I tried, for her sake, not to stare at her as the weight of guilt solidified into a stone in the base of my gut. For so long, nothing had seemed worse than the weakness I felt at the scent of raspberry and vanilla, at the feeling of warm peaches-and-cream skin pressed against me or turning pink at the end of my lash. But watching the way her uncle handled her, while I sat on the couch under the watch of Martin's bodyguards, was the ultimate expression of my weakness, a weakness which had made me turn aside a woman who said she loved me, who *did* love me.

"And you would know what my niece does and doesn't like, wouldn't you, Mr. Haigh?" Martin taunted me. With an unconcerned gesture, he had Vachon pour glasses of wine all around, then sipped his with an utterly relaxed demeanor. "You Teague men have a way with women." I cocked one brow but didn't respond further. "I knew when we met at your little after party that I'd seen those eyes before. Your father is a drunken Irish bastard who apparently puts his dick in anything that stays still long enough."

I shrugged, then leaned forward to take up the wineglass provided for me from where it sat on the coffee table. "I wouldn't know. And really, I'd say I got my eyes from my mother."

"No? Daddy didn't claim his bastard son by his little burlesque slut?"

To which I laughed and had to put my hand over my mouth to keep from spurting wine everywhere. "My apologies," I insisted once I'd swallowed. Starting to get a feel for the crowd, hitting my stride, I crossed one ankle over the other knee and threw an arm over the back of the couch. "It's just I wouldn't expect to hear that kind of language coming from an actor of your caliber, Mr. Keane. It doesn't seem quite natural."

This brought a snicker to Martin's perfectly bland, straight face. Then he smiled. Then he actually laughed. "You have your father's bravado, Haigh. Neither of you are believable actors, but you do put on a good show. Tell me, did it gall you at all, that you didn't get the Teague name? The fame? The legitimacy?" He snorted as he sipped his wine again. "What there was of it. Is that little circus of yours your little way of following in his footsteps?"

I believed I had Keane's number now, and I made a show of lowering my wineglass to regard him at length. "You aren't serious, are you, Keane? I know it can't be easy for you knowing he's so much bigger a star in Europe than you are, but it verges on psychopathic, this fixation on the man. You're going to try to torment the son he's never even met with all this pseudo-psychological bullshit?"

That smile faded from Martin's overlong face, and he went back to pulling on Olivia's ponytail. "You're as charming as your father, Mr. Haigh. He is charming, don't you think, Olivia?" She just gritted her teeth and squeezed her eyes shut.

Just hold on a little longer, Kitten, I was praying in the back of my head. I knew it looked like she was back under her uncle's control, without a protector. I'd tossed her out, and Unwin had turned out to be Keane's man. But I wasn't leaving without her. Whatever happened after that, whatever she wanted to call me, however she wanted to curse me, I deserved—for protecting myself while professing to protect her.

"Martin, we can work this out," Ullock was insisting then, pitched forward on the couch. Vachon, who had that ruddiness and languor about him that said that glass of wine wasn't his first of the night, lunged forward to shove the reporter back with one foot. "Martin!" Stephen pleaded. "Let me take her. You won't hear from her again, and the trust is all yours."

I watched Olivia's eyelids flutter very lightly, very briefly, as Ullock bargained for her.

Martin's brow knit in almost grotesque incredulity as he regarded Stephen. "What is it about my niece that has men making the most absurd bids for her? All that money I gave you to arrange those command performances, to gain the trust of Olivia and our Mr. Haigh, and you just used it to get off on having her whipped half-naked in front of you. Then, as if that wasn't enough to justify me having you thrown off London fucking Bridge, I find you packing and planning on fleeing to God knows where with her. Have you lost your mind, man?"

Vachon responded with a drunken hyena laugh, starting out loud and high and just getting worse. "Of course he has. Look at him. Ever since the circus left London and he lost track of her, he didn't eat, he didn't sleep, he didn't call. Bastard thinks he's in love with her."

And now Martin balanced his chin on his hand, regarding Ullock. "Which is a problem. All that money gone, and then you try to run off like this. Nigel?"

I was sure it was all show when Martin had the red-haired thug lay into Stephen with the bat. One, two, three blows on the shoulders and arms. But it went on even after the reporter curled into a ball, his arms thrown over his head for protection. After the first blow, which made Olivia jump, she sank to the floor at Martin's feet and stared wide-eyed, horrified but unable to turn away.

The sight of blood splattering along the white upholstery seemed to excite Vachon, who pumped his fist, sloshing wine and cheering on the beating. Martin called Nigel off only after Ullock stopped yelping… or moving. When I peered very closely, I could at least see the man still breathing.

The calm I felt told me I knew, deep down, that this situation was getting out of hand—was only going to get further out of hand. And I had to get Olivia out, even if it meant making me the center of attention to do it. It wouldn't be the first beating I'd taken, certainly, not after living hand to mouth on the streets of Eastern Europe once I'd broken with my mother. Just how bad this was going to be, I couldn't have said. Looking at those wide green eyes trained on the bloody mess on the couch beside me… it just wasn't a matter of whether or not the risk was worth it. She was.

I stiffened when I saw Martin lean down over Olivia, when her wide eyes shifted slowly upward to meet his. "You see what kind of trouble you've caused, Olivia," he muttered to her, and I bristled like someone had run a knife-edge along my back when she nodded. "What is it about you?" he wondered aloud. "Just like you father and your mother. Pretty but hollow. Not worth the time it takes to tell you what to do, but people still can't help thinking there's more to you than there is."

Glancing up, Martin caught me watching carefully. "You taught her a few new tricks, didn't you, Mr. Haigh?

I'd tried to teach Olivia self-restraint. God knows neither of her parents had it, or they wouldn't have ended up wrapped around a tree, right?"

Olivia's jaw stiffened when her uncle so callously referenced the accident that had taken her parents and made her his ward. She was playing his game, but Kitten was still in there somewhere. I had to wonder how detached she had to be to withstand her uncle's treatment and whether she'd have the presence of mind to run when the time came. *Just a little longer, baby*, I prayed silently.

Martin had her by the ponytail again, made her rise up on her knees, then jerked her around to face him. This was no good. I hadn't had time to work myself closer to Martin, to work my way under his skin like a thorn that kept prodding until it had to be dealt with.

"Your dead parents made you my ward, Olivia," Martin said clearly and coldly into her face. "You're all I have left of how much I hated your father and that empty-headed B-grade scream queen he married. If our grandfather and parents before him hadn't been stars, if I hadn't won my first Tony before he was even out of high school, your father would have been just another pretty boy working at a job with a name on his shirt. But he *was* pretty, and that made all the difference."

When I couldn't stand Keane hovering over Olivia like that anymore, I took my chance. Making a point of picking up my wineglass again, as though I wasn't sitting beside a beaten and bloodied man who was now groaning softly in distress, I snickered loudly. "And I thought Olivia was the drama queen. I see it runs in the family."

That steely gaze flickered toward me, exactly where I wanted it. "Hm, what was that, Mr. Haigh?"

"You turn your household into a modern-day reenactment of Cinderella for what? Because you're jealous of your dead brother? That's not Shakespearean; that's Brothers Grimm."

For a moment, one corner of Martin's pale lips twitched, and even Vachon, pacing and drinking and drinking and pacing, finally stood still and stared back and forth between us. "Cute sense of humor, Haigh," Keane muttered, nonplussed. "You have quite the way with words and quite the way with women. Shall we see what you taught my niece while she was in your care?" Then his gaze was on her again, the last place I wanted it. "Take your clothes off, Olivia."

"No," she and I said at the same time. Her voice was a whisper, mine a warning.

Martin smiled again. "Nigel."

I caught the bat with the side of my arm as the ginger bastard brought it down at my head. The crack against my forearm vibrated violently and painfully, but I had enough adrenaline flowing through my body by then to cushion the shock. I grabbed the other end of the bat and slammed it into Nigel's chin, but I didn't have the time to react to the second guard grabbing me by the shoulders from behind to slam me back into my seat on the couch. Then the redhead caught me twice in the gut and doubled me over.

"I'm doing it," I heard Olivia whimper, before she cried out louder. "Don't hurt him. I'm doing it."

Everyone turned to see the little blonde pulling her white blouse over her head without bothering with the buttons. The slacks were next, leaving her in a pair of lacy white underwear. Thankfully, Martin seemed satisfied with that. My worry was the leer on Vachon's face. And the bodyguards looked far too engaged in this exchange between Martin and his niece. Don't hurt him, she'd said as she had bared herself to the man she most feared and hated. Thom's voice intruded in my head, reminding me again that I couldn't have paid someone to care for me like that.

Now the Keane patriarch glared down at Olivia, half-naked, trembling before him. For a second, the sickening suspicion that there was a sexual aspect to his abuse darkened my thoughts and made me consider leaping at the man, no matter how futile. But then he shook his head, his lips curling back from his teeth in disgust. "I still don't see it. I don't understand what makes these men risk everything for you." Then a gleam lit his eyes, and that was more worrying than the cold, dull sheen of hatred. "Maybe it's just the pure love of beating you. I never really tried that. What do you say, Mr. Haigh. You've given my niece a good whipping or two. Is that the allure? That she takes a beating well?"

"Don't," I muttered low, a greater anger than I thought I could control simmering just beneath the thin veneer of self-control. "That is my prerogative, Mr. Keane, and mine alone."

Which gained me a perked gray brow. "What's that? More of your BDSM etiquette and hierarchy? As entertaining as it is, I think I shall have to break protocol to satisfy my curiosity in this matter. Vachon."

And the Frenchman set aside his glass and whipped his black hair back as he started toward Olivia.

"Not if you want to leave this room on your feet," I warned the bloody frog as I came up off the sofa.

But while Vachon was grinning me down and Keane's bodyguards were holding me back, Martin grabbed Olivia by the ponytail and made her bend over the coffee table. "Vachon," he barked again. "Do it!"

It wasn't enough to hold me down. Nigel had to use that bat between my shoulder blades and right to my kidneys more than once to keep me face down on the hardwood while the Frenchman drew his belt from his pants and lashed Olivia, my Olivia, so hard she yelped with each strike.

While I swore profusely, cursing both Vachon and Martin as he sat back with his wineglass and smiled, Stephen had roused himself to protest meekly. The reporter was conscious enough now to see the object of his obsession being tormented, and he struggled to sit upright, to reach out for Vachon, to form words with his split and bloodied lips.

Only when Olivia lay limp and quiet against the glass of the table, no longer struggling or crying out, did Martin stay Vachon's hand. "Enough," was his quiet command, then louder when the Frenchman did not immediately relent. There was by then a peculiar glint in Martin's eye that suggested to me he was even more excited by the violence than his son-in-law was. "It's late and we have an early flight back to Los Angeles. Get yourself together, Yves."

The Frenchman nodded, panting with arousal, erect from belting an unwilling woman into submission. In the circles I travelled, a man who did that found himself naked and beaten within an inch of his life in a ditch twenty kilometers from nowhere.

"What do you want us to do about these two?" Nigel asked, motioning with the end of the bloody bat to Stephen and me.

"Get rid of them," Martin snapped, struggling obviously to control the ragged edge to his breathing. "Make it look like they killed each other."

For a moment, the men just mulled over us, until Vachon stepped back. "You're not serious," he told Martin.

Clearly the younger man did not recognize the bloodlust boiling quietly in the elder.

"We have a problem, Vachon?" Martin asked, his voice still husky.

"Yes, beating is one thing. Killing is another."

"Do as I say, Vachon."

"There is no need, Martin."

"*Do as I say.*"

"This one," Vachon said, slapping a semi-conscious Ullock on the side of the head and eliciting a groan. "He's not going to be saying much of anything for a few weeks. Looks like your man Nigel broke his jaw. And that one," the Frenchman went on, motioning to me where the second bodyguard still had his knee in the middle of my back.

Before Vachon could finish his argument, Martin rose smoothly, gripped the wine bottle by the neck, and smashed it into the back of his son-in-law's head in a spray of wine, glass, and blood.

The next few moments were a jumble of confused curses, as Vachon fell and Martin's bodyguards stumbled toward him in disbelief. As Olivia, half-dazed, half-panicked, grabbed the corkscrew from beside her on the table and jabbed it into her uncle's side. As I lunged for her while the guards lurched for Martin. Keane was spurting as much profanity as blood and waving at his guards to stop us. He went silent as Stephen rose up from the couch, quite steady on his feet for a man half dead, and yanked the corkscrew from Martin's side to plunge it into Keane's neck.

Later, I would only truly remember reaching out for Olivia's hand, feeling it slide into mine. The familiar scent of caramel and cotton candy, vanilla and raspberry, filling me with such overwhelming melancholy that I could have fallen to my knees… Kitten's soft body against mine as I scooped her up and rushed her out the door to my car… wrapping my coat around her and holding her hand as tightly as I could as I drove with her straight to the nearest police station.

13

GWYNNE STEPPED OUT onto the deck of my rented beach house and into the late afternoon, late summer sun where I was lounging over a book. She dropped a small pastel envelope into my lap, and I laid my novel aside to study the exotic postage adorning one corner.

The redhead settled next to me in her own deck chair. "How many is that, Livy? One a week for... five months? Six?"

I tapped the envelope lightly against my palm. "They didn't start until a couple of months after Uncle Martin took the plea agreement. Now that the tabloids have moved on to other stories... a little more frequently."

Gwynne glanced at me sidelong from under the floppy beach hat protecting her pale skin from the Malibu sun. "You ever going to answer him?"

My usual list of excuses had run thin now. Martin's trial was over, the media hounds had all but lost interest in me, and the trust was now mine to manage. I was no longer concerned that going to Donovan would lead the public eye back to him, back to Thom and Naomi and all the people I'd grown close to at the Cirque de Plaisir. My fear was now entirely for myself. Yes, I knew Donovan Haigh needed my absolution, or at least felt he did. And it wasn't entirely fair of me to let him stew.

He had hurt me. If Donovan hadn't set things off between us that first night he'd taken me…

But… but if I hadn't let Philip Walker get so close… if I hadn't thrown myself into the role of the diva submissive and courted Stephen's attention… if Donovan hadn't run so hot and cold, unable to decide if he wanted me enough to break his rules or not… if I hadn't taken that command performance knowing he wouldn't have approved… if he hadn't assumed I'd betrayed him… and if he hadn't come to my rescue in the townhouse that night….

And now nothing was the same. Stephen and Yves Vachon were dead, and *the* Martin Keane was serving a prison sentence. I was mistress of my own trust and my own fate now. And the Cirque de Plaisir had been driven so far underground that most people didn't believe it existed anymore, except for people in the know, and me. I had a shoebox of unopened letters, from Buenos Aires and Sao Paulo, from Melbourne and Auckland, from Vienna and Berlin. The one in my hand bore a Czech postmark.

I waited until I was alone that night to pry open the frail paper of the latest envelope.

Kitten,

*I know you won't read this. Or if you do, you
won't answer. I have to send it just the same.
No one has taken your place and no one will.
I'm not afraid anymore to tell you that.
If the impossible had happened, and you are
reading this, we're outside Prague...*

In an abandoned railroad yard. It was the first time I'd
ever seen a real striped circus tent, pennants waving in the
breeze, as the taxi driver dropped me off at the rusted-out,
disused ticket station and drove away rolling his eyes like I
was crazy. It *could* have had something to do with my poor
usage of the English-to-Czech dictionary. If he hadn't known
some English, I wasn't sure where I would have ended up.

The theme was rather gypsy-like, I thought as I shoul-
dered my pack and crossed track after track, passing freight
cars that had been converted to sleeping quarters and concession stands and even a small bar. I was nearly to the tent,
huge and bright and dreamlike in the twilight, when Naomi
and Griffin dropped out of a nearby rail car onto the grav-
elly dirt and stopped to gape in my direction. The tiger girl
nearly threw herself at me, sweeping me into a hug that
pulled me off my feet and made my light sundress fan out
around me. Then she passed me to Griffin, who only put me
down when Rafe demanded his turn. They were all dressed
in scarves and vests and full gypsy skirts—considerably
shorter than usual—or snug riding pants and spit-polished
boots. No one said they were sorry or asked how I'd been or
acknowledged in any way that I'd ever left the troupe.

Thom was the last to hug me. "You found us okay?"
I nodded. "M-hm."

Then the sandy blond nodded over his shoulder to a rail car set back from the others, where a familiar figure stood at the sliding door, waiting. "He's been expecting you for… well, yeah, a few months. Go on, then, love."

The walk to that rail car, knowing Donovan Haigh was watching each step, seemed to take an hour, and my stomach was sick by the time I got there. But I couldn't resist looking at him forever, not after I'd flown halfway around the world to see him, with him crouched at the door of the car with his palm held out to me.

I slid my hand into Donovan's just as I raised my gaze to his… and caught my breath. Haigh lifted me into the car, pulling me so briefly against his body to steady me. I needed it. I'd forgotten how weak those blue eyes made me. He had let the scruff around his mouth and chin grow out a bit more, lending him a wilder look, but it suited the gypsy theme… and him. The Ringmaster was still the most handsome man I'd ever laid eyes on.

He gave me a moment to look around, at the familiar futon with its thick layer of pillows pushed against one wall of the metal car. His costume trunks were the chairs and tables, and a layer of worn but clean quilts made a carpet to ward against cold metal underfoot in the morning.

When I smiled, Donovan chuckled and shook his head. "Glad you approve," he muttered, the first words he'd managed to say to me. Then, after a breath, he added, "Are you hungry? Or thirsty?"

"Thirsty," I agreed, and he found a bottle of champagne, which he served in metal cups. I raised a brow at him. "Veuve Clicquot in an abandoned rail yard?"

"Only the best for special guests."

We sat side by side on two cushions on the floor drinking quietly for some time, and looking out at the Czech countryside. It could have been a different century, beautiful and green and so much less complicated. And yet it was unbearable, sitting this close to Donovan Haigh and not really saying anything.

I finally broke the silence, knowing it was awkward, not caring after traveling so far. "Why did you ask me to come?"

"Why did you agree?" was his response, in that careful British accent.

I laughed, but I was thinking, *Goddamn you, Haigh.* "What is it you need from me, Donovan? You've apologized, at the courthouse the day we were both testifying. I told you then you had nothing to be sorry for, or we both had too much to be sorry for to worry about it, either way."

"Not absolution, if that's what you're thinking," he murmured where we sat leaning so close, almost touching. Almost... "There are things no one can forgive a man for but himself."

"And have you... forgiven yourself?"

The soft hiss of his breath as he chuckled made me wish I could feel that warmth on my skin, on my neck. Made me wonder what the hell I was doing here torturing myself. "No," he admitted, "not for most things. One thing most of all."

I lingered over a deep swallow of the champagne, hoping it would take the edge off this odd, bittersweet reunion. "And what's that?"

"Firing the best assistant I ever had."

Ouch. "And that would be me?"

Haigh turned those eyes on me, and I felt it even though I'd been avoiding looking at his face. He was wearing tight black pants above shiny black boots, and the black and gold satin vest was too small by… by a lot. Enough to show off his biceps and pecs and the suggestion of the shape of his abs. I wasn't sure it was better, avoiding his eyes by staring at that body.

"Yeah, definitely you," he agreed.

"It was an interesting experience," I admitted, unable to keep the wistfulness from my voice. "I'm glad I did it even if…."

"Even if…" he coaxed.

"I could never do it again." What I'd felt in the ring, what I'd offered Haigh, that kind of vulnerability shouldn't ever have been for show. I knew I'd never give myself to another man the way I'd given myself to Donovan, and I knew I'd never want to do it in front of another audience. He was peering at me as I said this, and I'd have sworn there was a suggestion of a smile in the corner of his full, entirely too kissable mouth.

"And if I didn't want you to?" Donovan asked, which made me rear back an inch to read his expression. "Well, that is, if I still wanted my submissive… my Kitten… but I didn't want it to be for show… If I wanted it offstage only, for real…."

"What are you getting at, Donovan?" I finally asked, too tired after… after everything… to wonder anymore.

The Ringmaster took my cup and set it aside with his, then leaned in to sigh warmly against my ear and the side of my neck. "I wanted to know what you thought…." He paused to take a deep breath, then groaned lightly at what he smelled. "Of a courtship in Prague." The full pads of his velvety lips sucked at my earlobe as my eyes sank closed involuntarily. I really hadn't come all this way just to let Donovan Haigh seduce me. Really. "Of a wedding in Lyon."

Which opened my eyes again even as it stole my breath. "And maybe a baby in Rome."

"Christ, Haigh, what are you saying?" I rasped, the knot of emotion in my throat ready to strangle me.

He pulled me into his lap, straddling him, wrapped his arms around my waist, and buried his face in my long loose hair. "I'm asking you to let me have some time to treat you the way I should have treated you all along. I never should have hired you as my assistant. From the very first moment I saw you, I should have known the connection we had was never for show. I'm asking you to marry me—not today, I know I have to give you time—and make a family with me, the kind I didn't have growing up. The kind you didn't have."

And I began to tremble, just a little at first, then harder, shuddering in Donovan's arms. He held me tighter and tighter against his body, his palms warm on my skin through the thin material of my dress. His mouth found mine, searching inch by inch along my neck to my jaw, until we met in a whisper of a kiss, lips hardly brushing. Then again, firmer, longer. Then his tongue, tasting of cool champagne, slipped between my lips to taste me, to explore every inch of the inside of my mouth, to tease the back of my teeth and toy with my tongue. His large, rough hands slid under my dress to massage and grip my trembling thighs.

We spent a long time like that, locked in a tight embrace, before my fingers wandered to his belt and the fastening of his pants. Before he drew the silky material of my panties to one side, to bare the wetness of my sex to the probing head of his hot cock. Before his lips found my hardened nipples through my dress and my bra and made me arch my back. Before his hand tangled in the hair at the back of my head to tug so gently as he urged me down on his rigid member. Before he bucked up under me and called me Kitten and commanded me to come for my master.

My Ringmaster.

Who courted me through Prague…

And married me in Lyon…

And called a three-month hiatus in Rome so we could welcome our son.

The End

Thank you for reading The Ringmaster: Cirque de Plaisir. If you enjoyed this book, please consider leaving a review in support of this author and her work. You can also sign up for the Erika Masten e-Newsletter at http://eepurl.com/pTLx1. Subscribers receive updates on new releases and exclusive promotions.

Also by Erika Masten

DOMINATION ROMANCE BY ERIKA MASTEN
At His Whim: His #1
In His Service: His #2
At His Mercy: His #3
Under His Sway: His #4
In His Grip: His #5
In His Wake: His #6
For His Sake: His #7
In His World: His #8

SHORT DOMINATION EROTICA BY ERIKA MASTEN
Priority Access: Uptown Sluts #3
Taken: Dominated #1
Tough Love: Dominated #2

Room Service: Dominated #3
A Firm Hand: Dominated #4
Dominated: The Collection
Dominated By Brothers: Hot Hard Ménage #1
Bad Boys' Submissive: Hot Hard Ménage #2
My Two Doms: Hot Hard Ménage #3
Rough Sex, Rough Love: Hot Hard Ménage #4
Hot Hard Ménage: The Collection
Claimed In Secret: Master Vampire #1
Claimed In Hunger: Master Vampire #2
Claimed In Passion: Master Vampire #3
Domination Sex: Conditioned Response
Military Maledom: An Officer And A Dom
Valentine's Dom
Backup: Ménage A Cop
His Submissive: Body Worship
Body Worship 2: Breeding Julia
Body Worship 3: Satisfying Julia
Body Worship: The Collection
Bridled: Bitter Creek Doms #1
Broken: Bitter Creek Doms #2
Public Display of Submission: The Dom Next Door #1
Sweet Resistance: The Dom Next Door #2
Weekend Submissive

For a full list of Erika Masten titles, see her website at
http://erikamasten.com.

About The Author

I'm the girl next door with an unexpectedly wicked mind (and an addiction to sexy high heels). There's nothing quite like the thrill of turning forbidden desires and secret fantasies into erotic tales with literary flare and a dirty mouth. Let me tell you a naughty story…

E-mail: erikamasten@gmail.com
Website: http://erikamasten.com/
Blog: http://erikamasten.blogspot.com/
Newsletter Sign-up: http://eepurl.com/pTLx1

Printed in Great Britain
by Amazon